Captor

Anita Waller

Print ISBN 978-1-912175-95-6

For the Huddersfield-based side of our family:
Matt, Richelle, Katie, Melissa
and our first great-grandchild, Lily Grace.
You light up our lives.

Yes, yours, my love, is the right human face.
I in my mind had waited for this long,
Seeing the false and searching for the true,
Then found you as a traveller finds a place
Of welcome suddenly amid the wrong
Valleys and rocks and twisting roads. But you,
What shall I call you? A fountain in a waste,
A well of water in a country dry,
Or anything that's honest and good, an eye
That makes the whole world bright. Your open heart,
Simple with giving, gives the primal deed,
The first good world, the blossom, the blowing seed,
The hearth, the steadfast land, the wandering sea,
Not beautiful or rare in every part,
But like yourself, as they were meant to be.

THE CONFIRMATION by Edwin Muir
15 May 1887 – 3 January 1959

Prologue

7 September 2014

The Coffee and Cream Café was quiet; two customers were seated at a table at the far side of the room, and they appeared to be deep in conversation, oblivious to anything happening around them. They were certainly unaware of Phil Latimer and Liz Chambers, holding hands across their table, enjoying the moment.

The waitress arrived, bearing a pot of tea and two cups and saucers with the tiniest jug of milk, all emblazoned with the name Coffee and Cream.

The couple released hands and Liz smiled at Phil. 'Maybe we'll have to go and milk a cow to get any more.'

He responded with a smile of his own, although he suspected he wouldn't be smiling for long. For the first time, the atmosphere between them felt… strained.

'You said we needed to talk?'

She hesitated, and bit her bottom lip. It was the glance down towards the table that told him this really wasn't going to be good. Her blonde hair fell forward, hiding her eyes.

'We do. I'm so sorry, Phil, but I can't see you anymore. So, so sorry…'

He put his fingers underneath her chin and lifted her head. Gently he pushed back the blonde hair he loved so much. Keeping his eyes on her face, he saw that her blue eyes were brimming with tears.

'But it's only a week since we sat at this same table and spoke of our love,' he said softly. 'That can't have changed – at least, with me it hasn't.'

She reached across the table and clutched his hand. 'And it hasn't changed for me, either. But there's a complication.'

'Gareth is coming home.' Phil could hear the flatness in his voice as he spoke the words. Her husband had been away for six weeks in Ireland and they had enjoyed the freedom of being able to meet without having to invent excuses for being away from their respective partners. In his case, he doubted that Rosie would be bothered anyway, but he knew that prior to their meeting and falling in love, Gareth had been the centre of Liz's life, along with Daniel, their fifteen-year-old son.

'That's not the complication. The complication is that I am five weeks pregnant.'

There was silence between them, while he allowed what she had said to take root in his brain.

'You're sure?'

She nodded, not trusting herself to speak.

'And if you're five weeks…'

She had to speak. 'It's yours.'

He put down the cup he had been holding almost as a comforter, and leaned back in his chair.

'And we can't be together? You're telling me that I not only lose you, the absolute love of my life, but another man is going to be bringing up my child?'

'Phil, please try and understand. I can't hurt Gareth and Dan, I really can't. But you know it's mainly Dan. If there were only Gareth, you and I would probably already be together. I know I don't talk much about Gareth, but the situation between us is a little how you've described yours with Rosie. And then there's my job. I've worked too hard to get where I am at Banton and Hardwick to give it up. I'll have the baby, and I'll be going back to work after my maternity leave. But, what is of more importance is that I would lose my job. You're my client, Phil, my client, for God's sake!' And then she did cry.

He stood and moved his chair so that he was by her side. He pulled her close, and let the tears flow.

'We were stupid?' he said eventually.

She wiped her eyes and looked at him. 'Stupid?'

'We're old enough to know how to prevent conception, aren't we?'

'You know I'm on the pill, but I took antibiotics for that damned ear infection. I'm so sorry, Phil, it's all my fault. We weren't stupid, I was.'

He sighed. 'I don't want to be without you. This has been the best six months of my life, knowing you were part of it. Please don't stop that, Liz, I'm begging you.'

'I have no choice. I'm going. Your case at work is almost completed, we have the final settlement figure, so there's no reason for us to be in contact. I love you, Phil, always will, but we can't be together. You know we can't. Maybe if there had been no baby, in five years things would have been different, but…'

He stood, as she turned to walk away, aware that the other two customers were now watching their every move.

'I'll respect that,' he said softly, 'even though I don't agree with it. But remember this always, Liz; if ever the situation at home changes, or your job is no longer an issue – in fact, any damn thing – ring me using our phones. I'll come and get you, no questions asked, and with exactly the same amount of love in my heart.'

She turned as she reached the door, mouthed *I love you* and walked out of his life, knowing exactly what she was giving up.

1

It comes at too high a price, having a baby, Liz decided. How do you hide the tears from fellow travellers as you remember his little face, now turned to his new, first day child-minder, happily smiling with no intentions of missing you at all?

She was aching for him, this unplanned child. It hadn't seemed so bad when she had taken him to meet Sadie Fremantle, to see if they bonded; Liz was only doing a bit of forward planning. Sadie was a single mum of thirty-nine with a twenty-year-old son, Christian, at Solent University, and she had taken the decision to become a registered childminder to bring in extra funding to supplement the money she earned auditing books from home.

Liz still had three months of maternity leave left; she was simply making tentative enquiries. Those enquiries had morphed into an afternoon every week while baby Jacob learned to know the woman who would be his surrogate parent. Liz had also taken Gareth to meet Sadie a couple of times, to get his views on the woman who would have such a massive influence on their baby son's early years, and Gareth had agreed with her choice.

And then reality hit, the tentative enquiries were well in the past, and she was to return to work.

Banton and Hardwick, solicitors in Sheffield's city centre, valued her. She wished they didn't. She didn't want to leave Jake with Sadie, she wanted to be there when he took his first step, got his first tooth, (which, at nine months and with no sign of a small white nub in his gums, was beginning to feel unlikely), spoke his first word; hence the tears as the tram took her ever further into the heart of the city on that cold January morning.

A couple of people spoke to her and asked if she was okay; she dabbed away the tears with a screwed-up piece of tissue and said she was fine.

Liz exited the tram outside the cathedral and crossed Fargate to nip into Boots for more tissues. She thought she might need them.

She headed down through Paradise Square and came to the imposing steps leading up to her place of work.

Liz felt wobbly. She had last walked down those steps only two weeks away from giving birth, with Gareth waiting in the car, hazards flashing as he was parked illegally. She had been carrying armfuls of presents. The practice employed many people, and although the two partners to whom she was attached had bought her the pram, every other member of staff had bought her an individual gift.

She took a deep breath and pushed thoughts of the last nine months to the back of her mind. She straightened her shoulders and climbed the steps.

No tears, Liz, she warned herself. *Be professional. Jake is in good hands, you don't need to worry. You're a forty-year-old woman, successful career, full of confidence, life sorted. Be brave.*

She didn't know the receptionist, and the receptionist didn't know her. *Good start, Liz,* she thought.

She introduced herself and Karen welcomed her with a smile.

'It's good to meet you, Mrs Chambers. I'm Karen Lee. Mr Banton said you would be returning this week. This is your ID tag,' and she handed over Liz's lanyard, complete with the new picture she had emailed to HR the week before.

'Thank you, Karen, it's good to meet you, too. How long have you been here?'

'Three months. I came as a temp, but I've been taken on now.'

'You like it?'

'Very much so. And it's a lot more secure than working for an agency.'

'I'm sure,' Liz said with a smile. 'I worked for agencies at one point in my life…' she shuddered. 'Are Mr Banton and Mr Hardwick in?'

'They are. I'll let them know you've arrived.' She pressed the intercom button and then whispered to Liz, 'I think they're excited to have you back.'

Liz laughed and headed for the door to the executive offices. She waited until she heard the gentle click as Karen released the lock, then walked down the corridor to her room. It was an old building, and Tom Banton and Oliver Hardwick had kept it as separate offices, rather than knocking walls down to make it open-plan, filled with small dividing partitions.

She walked into her office, the room that connected directly with both Tom and Oliver's rooms, and wanted to cry yet again.

Carefully positioned on her desk was a huge bouquet of yellow roses, and a pile of envelopes clearly containing cards. She put down her bag, took off her coat, and carried both to her small wardrobe; quickly ran a comb through her dark blonde hair, checked the miniscule amount of make-up she wore hadn't disappeared altogether under the force of her tears, renewed her lipstick, and closed the wardrobe door.

Her first job every morning had always been to put on the percolator and to keep it running throughout the day. It had been replaced with a coffee machine of some magnificence. She hoped it came with an instruction manual.

Her desk phone buzzed once, and she moved to answer it. At least that hadn't changed.

'Tom,' she said, and waited.

'You're early.'

'Of course.'

'I thought we agreed to your starting at ten instead of nine, to help with getting Jake to his childminder?'

'We did.'

'So…?'

'I took that as "be here by ten".'

'You like the flowers?'

'I love the flowers. Your idea?'

Tom Banton laughed. 'No, Chloe's idea. That's what wives are for, isn't it?'

'I should have guessed.'

'You should.'

'So, did you want something?'

'Black, no sugar, please.'

'Wow! Are you under instructions?'

Tom sighed audibly. 'I am. Chloe has given me an ultimatum. If I don't lose weight on my own, she's going to register me for a gym. And I think Oliver probably needs a coffee as well. We've missed you, Liz. We've had to make our own drinks.'

She laughed. 'Two coffees it is, then.'

She heard him return the laughter as he put down the phone.

She found the instruction manual for the coffee machine hidden behind it, so she worked out how to use it, then carried the drinks through to her employers.

'Waitress service,' she said as she entered Tom's room. He lifted his head, watching her. His ginger hair fell forward across his forehead, and he brushed it back, almost without realising he was doing it. 'About damn time. Promise me you won't have another baby.'

'Depends who's offering to be the daddy,' she responded. 'Tom Hardy, Rob Lowe, Benedict whatever his name is… I could be persuaded.'

He laughed. 'Erm… before we get Oliver in here, there's something you should know, so that you don't inadvertently put your foot in it. Oliver and Julia have split up. I don't know all the details, don't know why, just that the divorce is in the offing. He's not talked much about it… not to me, anyway. I don't know whether he'll tell you or not, but you needed to know. It doesn't affect anything here, Julia's always distanced herself from the business.'

Liz's face showed her shock. She'd known Julia since school days, and had recognised her the first day she had started to work at Banton and Hardwick, in the photograph that always stood on Oliver's desk. Oliver had confirmed that his wife was called Julia Froggatt in an earlier life, and he had passed on Liz's best wishes to Julia that same evening. They had met up many times since, sharing a coffee and, in Julia's case, marital woes.

Liz nodded at Tom. 'Okay, message understood.' She thought back to their last phone conversation when she had, somewhat abruptly, told Julia to either put up with Oliver's control issues, or walk away. She had obviously walked away, and Liz prayed that Oliver didn't know of her part in the marital split. She made a mental note to ring Julia – they hadn't been in touch for at least four or five months.

Tom leaned forward to press his intercom. 'Oliver, we have coffee made by a fair maid. You coming in here, or shall I send the wench into you?'

'Ten seconds.'

Oliver Hardwick was a handsome man, fairly small in stature at 5'6" and of slim build, but with an imposing presence; always quiet and ultra-professional within the office environment. He and Tom were almost the same age, with birthdays three days apart. At forty-three, Oliver looked slightly the younger of the two men. She remembered the feeling of amusement that all the significant men in her life, Gareth, Phil, Tom and Oliver, had been born within six months of each other, and all in the same year. A good year for the supply of handsome men.

Oliver's deep brown eyes searched out Liz as he walked through the connecting door and stepped inside Tom's office. He picked up the mug of coffee, walked around the desk towards Liz and said, 'You're early.' He leaned forward and kissed her cheek – she could smell the Creed that surrounded him – and smiled. He truly was quite delicious. She shook her head, dismissing her thoughts.

'I know. As you've both mentioned it, is that going to be a problem? You see, I think it's better than being late.'

The two men turned to each other, and spoke at the same time. 'She's back.'

2

Liz opened all the cards and stood them on her window sill, deciding not to take them home but to keep them at work on display for a week, before putting them away. Three were from people she didn't know, and she felt a pang as she realised how much she had missed during her nine months absence.

She sorted out her desk. It soon became clear, in anticipation of her return, Tom and Oliver had been filling her drawer with files requiring her attention.

She took them out to prioritise. All seven cases were new to her, and she spent the best part of her first day back reading through paperwork. She fired emails off as and when they were required, and she stayed at her desk through her lunch break, grateful for the sandwich Karen brought in.

She only rang Sadie twice. The first time was to discover Jake was happy, playing with his toys and crawling everywhere, and the second time she was told he was asleep, worn out by the excitement of the morning.

She felt momentarily disgruntled. He could, at least, have made a pretence of missing her, playing up, and testing his childminder. Did he have to be at his most pleasant best?

She was surprised to see that it was almost five, and she closed her computer and locked away the paper files. She was saying good night to Karen when she heard her phone ringing in the distance.

'You didn't put that through to me?' she asked. 'Stupid question, wasn't it? I'm standing here.'

Karen shook her head. 'No, I didn't. It'll be an internal call. Go home, Mrs Chambers. Whoever it was, they'll try again tomorrow.'

'Thank you, Karen, good night.'

Liz had forgotten how steep the climb back up to the tram stop was, and she sank gratefully into a seat for the long journey home. She exited the tram one stop further than her home one, walked across the road and up a hill to collect Jake.

Sadie smiled as she let Liz into her home.

'He's been absolutely fine, and he's all ready to go.' She picked him up from the play pen, and fastened him into his pushchair.

'Yours now,' she said with a laugh. 'Two stinky nappy changes, today, so you're welcome to the little monkey. I'll see you in the morning.'

'Thanks, Sadie. You've made this return to work really easy for me, but I'm glad I'm only doing three days a week until Jake's in school.'

Sadie helped Liz lift the pushchair out of the door, and Liz felt once more at peace. Jake was back with her, and all was right again in her world. So far, she hadn't been able to fault Sadie. On the days that she cared for Jake, she didn't have other children, and Liz appreciated this fact. It meant that Jake benefited from one-to-one care all the time.

Liz laughed as Sadie pushed back her purple hair. 'What colour will it be next week?' she asked.

'I'm fancying bright red,' Sadie answered, 'but we'll see, we'll see.'

Liz walked down the hill, and reached her own front door five minutes later. She unlocked it and instantly heard Daniel's music playing in his bedroom.

'I'm home,' she called, and she heard a muffled '*hi, Mum*' as she bent over to release the pushchair straps holding Jake prisoner.

Gareth followed her half an hour later. She was sitting on the sofa, Jake bathed, dressed in his sleepsuit and sleeping with his head on her shoulder.

'I wanted five minutes,' she said. 'I'll take him up now.'

Gareth leaned across and kissed his son on his head, bypassing his wife.

'Everything okay?' he asked.

She nodded. 'It's been fine. Give me a couple of minutes to put him in his cot, and we'll talk.'

Gareth walked into the kitchen to see Daniel taking a lasagne out of the oven. 'Smells delicious, Dan.' Gareth ruffled his son's hair as he went past.

'Of course.'

'With chips?'

'Sorry, it's salad. Mum's banned chips.'

'What?'

'Your fault, Dad. She says you're putting on far too much weight, so we're all having to suffer.'

Gareth's face spoke of misery. 'Has she included wine in this ban, or can I have a glass?'

'"When you've lost a stone" were her precise words.'

'Water it is then.' The misery had extended to his voice.

He set the table, and Liz joined them a couple of minutes later. 'Son number two asleep. Let's hope he stays that way.'

She sat down, and waited for Gareth and Dan to join her. 'Looks lovely, Dan.'

Dan placed the lasagne in the centre of the table and took out the salad bowl from the fridge. He added a dish of coleslaw, a jug of lemon water, and they all sat down. 'Vin de citron,' he announced, and his father glared at him.

'Not even vaguely funny, Dan.'

'Dad, eat your salad.'

Liz and Dan looked at each other and tried to hide the laughter.

'The quicker you lose that stone, the better,' Dan said, finally giving in and grinning at his dad.

'But it's winter. Nobody eats salad in winter.'

'You are,' Liz said.

'You're cruel,' Gareth grumbled, heaping another pile of coleslaw onto his salad to try and give it some taste. 'What's wrong with meat and potato pie?'

'Nothing. You want that tomorrow?' Dan asked. 'We've got enough meat in the freezer.'

Dan had taken on the role of head chef in the household. He intended going to catering college after leaving school, and Gareth and Liz were only too happy to let him feed them; he had taken over the day-to-day shopping in the early weeks following Jake's birth – and the cooking, much to their delight.

'So,' Gareth said to his wife, 'how was today?'

'Yes, good,' she said. 'There's at least three new employees I don't know yet, I've had lots of welcome back cards, and Tom and Oliver bought me a huge bouquet of roses. And a coffee machine. They also filled up my drawer with files all requiring urgent attention.'

'And did they get urgent attention?'

'Of course. All filed back into their proper places, I've emailed Tom and Oliver and told them what I've done, and I'll bet my drawer has another half a dozen tomorrow. I think they've missed me. They've asked me not to have any more babies,' she added with a smile.

'I echo that,' Gareth said drily. Liz said nothing; over the past three or four years there had been a gulf between them, one that seemed to be permanent since Jake's birth. Deep down, she knew she was keeping the family together for the stability this offered to Dan at a crucial exam-ridden stage of his life.

They finished off their meal with fat-free yoghurts poured over banana slices as a concession to the new regime imposed on Gareth, and Dan switched on the coffee machine while he loaded the dishwasher.

'It's good to have a slave, isn't it?' Gareth remarked thoughtfully, and Liz nodded in agreement.

Dan shook his head, and switched on the dishwasher. 'I am not,' he said slowly and carefully, 'emptying it. Do it before you go to bed, please. Right, I'm done. Coffee's ready whenever you want it, and I'm going up on the computer. Behave yourselves, no arguing, and no more babies.'

Gareth and Liz burst out laughing.

'Thank you, sweetheart. The meal was delicious, and I'll do breakfast,' Liz said with a smile.

'Mom. We eat cornflakes.'

'I'll get the box out. And the dishes.'

He shook his head and walked out of the kitchen. *Parents,* he thought. *Why do we have to have them?*

He switched on his computer, checked all three screens were functioning as per his instructions, and settled down to work on the game he was creating.

3

Dropping Jake off had seemed a little easier. Day two, and already the routine was starting to become... routine. Even the tram journey hadn't been quite so stressful, the first day nerves had disappeared, and she allowed her mind to roam through some of the issues raised by the files she had worked on the previous day.

She took coffees through to Tom and Oliver, then nursed her own cup as she pulled out the file that was troubling her. She was on her second read through when her desk phone rang.

'Mrs Chambers? It's Kelly from accounts.'

'Hello, Kelly from Accounts. What can I help you with?'

'First, welcome back. I rang last night, but you must have gone home. We've got an issue that we've never had before. Somebody hasn't cashed a cheque.'

'And?'

'It's one of your cases.'

'We sent a cheque to somebody? Why didn't we do a bank transfer?'

'They asked for a cheque.'

'Okay.' She hesitated. 'Is it Mr Banton's case, or Mr Hardwick's?'

'Yours.'

'But I haven't been at work for nearly ten months.'

'I know. It's the Latimer case.'

The air stilled around her. The Latimer case. Three little words. She shook her head, mentally clearing her thoughts but not clearing the flush that stained her cheeks pink.

'But that's closed. They won, we waited ages for the pay-out, and we paid them before I went on my mat leave.' Liz felt sick.

'Exactly. And they haven't cashed the cheque. I'm proposing we cancel it, because it's obviously gone astray. I'm a bit puzzled why they haven't rung us asking for payment. Will you sort it, please?'

Liz pulled a notepad towards her. It was for show only. She remembered the case with a deep clarity. 'Give me the details.'

'Cheque payable to Philip and Rosemary Latimer, dated 1 May 2015, amount £98,923. Our file number 0112/238LAT.'

She scribbled it down, covering for any future queries, and then thanked Kelly, saying she would get back to her, but to cancel the cheque because it was out of date.

Liz stared at the hastily jotted down notes, then moved across to her filing cabinet. She knelt and slowly pulled open the bottom drawer. A few more days in work and most of the old files in this drawer would have been archived.

She removed the Latimer file, closed the drawer, and for a few moments remained kneeling.

Her thoughts slammed back to that day in court when Rosie couldn't attend because of a hospital appointment for Melissa. Phil had been there, and after the court part was over, he had asked her to go for a coffee with him. She, quite simply, had fallen in love. He, quite simply, had also fallen in love. Right time, right moment, right love. They hadn't asked for it, they hadn't searched for it, it simply happened.

The double buzz on her desk brought her mind back, and she stood. One buzz for Tom, two for Oliver. She picked up her phone.

'Liz, do you have the Marlow file?'

'No, but I can get it. I can't believe it's still ongoing.'

'Then you'll be delighted to hear it's ending. I want to check some disbursements before finishing off the final invoice.'

'Give me two minutes.'

She put down the phone and moved into the small room attached to her office where long-term files that required multiple folders were stored. She found the file, carried it through to her office, then on to Oliver's office, after checking that everything seemed to be in it.

He smiled at her. 'Everything okay?'

'It's fine. Stop worrying about me. I can cope with being away from Jake for a couple of days.'

'Three days. Every week. Every Tuesday, Wednesday and Thursday. Today is only Wednesday and it's your first week. Are you sure you're fine?'

'I'm good.'

'Whatever you say. So… Latimer.'

She jumped at the mention of the name.

'Accounts say they haven't cashed the cheque. You chasing it up?'

'I am. It seems strange. Nearly £100,000 and they don't want it? I'll see what I can do. I've asked Kelly to cancel the original cheque and issue a second one, so at least it will be in date. I'll send it off tonight, recorded delivery.'

'Would it be better to hand deliver it? Then we would know it had got to them.'

No! she screamed silently.

'Yes,' Oliver said thoughtfully. 'Maybe that would be the best idea. Take a taxi, go about two-ish, then go straight home afterwards. Do it either today or tomorrow, your call. Pick Jake up a bit early. You're okay with that, aren't you?' His look as he turned his face towards her was intense.

She nodded. 'Okay. Anything else you need?'

'No, that's it, thanks.'

She went back into her own office and sat down with a thud.

She was being forced to see him again. This man she had spent eighteen months trying to wipe from her memory was possibly going to be at home with Rosie, when she called to give them the new cheque.

Had this been his intention all along? Was this why the cheque hadn't been cashed? Had he realised that eventually she would have to contact them? And was he still with Rosie and Melissa?

The questions raced around in her brain until finally Liz picked up her phone and asked Kelly to make sure the cheque was ready for the following day, as she would be taking it. On Oliver's direct instructions.

She picked up her handbag, unzipped the deep pocket on the lining, and took out the small Nokia that she hadn't used for eighteen long months. She sat and stared at it for several minutes, then texted.

Bringing new cheque to your house tomorrow. 2.30. Please don't be there. I had a son, Jake.

She was putting the phone back into the pocket when she heard it ping. For a second she froze. She had deliberately phrased the text so that no questions were asked, and therefore she wouldn't need a reply.

She took the phone back out and looked at the screen.

Okay. I love you.

It was as ambiguous as it was possible to be. Okay. What did that mean? Okay, come to my house. Okay, bring a new cheque. Okay, 2.30 is okay. Okay, I won't be there. Okay, we have a son. She knew what 'I love you' meant.

Once again, she put the phone away, her hands trembling. Roll on the weekend when all this would be out of the way, Phil and Rosie would be £98,000 better off, and she could get back to the life she had chosen.

Unwillingly.

She ran her hands through her hair and sighed. Ignore that word. She hadn't taken that decision unwillingly. Gareth and Dan came first, her needs and desires second.

Desire.

This time she banged her fist down on to the desk and moaned. She had to stop thinking. Had to stop coming up with stupid words that were turning her into somebody she didn't recognise.

Phil Latimer was in the past, and that was where he would stay, whether he was at his home or not. Her mind drifted towards his angular face, the greying hair, his smile, the deep blue eyes that could curl her toes when he turned them on her…

She pulled a file towards her and bent her head. Work. That would take her mind off what was in front of her, and off the face she loved. The perfect face. It would have been so easy to send the cheque by recorded delivery.

She lifted her head. In her heart she knew the cheque fiasco was something that Phil had thought about, because why on earth would he want a cheque when he could have received the money straight into his account by bank transfer? It didn't make sense.

And why did he have to respond to her text?

She couldn't wait to leave work, but first she had to risk ringing the Latimers, to inform them of her visit. She stood with the receiver pressed to her ear, listening to it ringing out in the hallway of their Ecclesall home. There was no answer, and the relief was palpable.

Using Rosie Latimer's email address, Liz notified her of the impending visit, and sent it, feeling a shudder coursing through her body.

She desperately wanted to get home to Jake, to hold him, to cuddle him, to enjoy his smell, his warmth, his love. He looked like her; for that she was grateful.

Gareth had never queried his early birth; three weeks early was nothing and they joked that it was a good job he had come early, with a birth weight of eight pounds.

She waved to Karen, who was busy switching everything through to the automatic line, and almost ran up the hill to the tram stop. She took out her book and tried to read, but her thoughts were anywhere but in those pages.

Texting Sadie as she got off the tram, by the time she had walked up the road to the childminder's house, Jake had been strapped into his pushchair.

Liz left quickly, after telling Sadie what was happening the following day, which would enable her to be home a bit earlier, and went through her own front door breathing a sigh of relief.

Dan came out of the kitchen and kissed her. 'You okay, Mum? You look a bit frazzled.'

'It's cold. I wanted to get home quickly. Something smells good.'

'Meat and potato pie, as promised.'

'Brilliant,' she laughed. 'I dare you to put a small plate of salad in front of your dad.'

He returned the smile. 'Great minds think alike. I've already prepared it.'

She lifted Jake out of the pushchair. Dan bent to fold it and placed it in the hall cupboard.

'You settling in at work?'

'Sort of. I thought I would swan back in and it would be all hunky-dory, but it's not like that. I'm working on Tom and Oliver's cases instead of having cases of my own…'

'Mum! You've been back two days! Give it time.'

She nodded. 'Oh, I know you're right. It's me. It's more tiring than I expected it to be, for a start. I'll be home earlier tomorrow, because I'm going to see an old client, so maybe I won't feel so exhausted.'

They heard the front door open, and Gareth's shout of '*yeah, meat and potato pie!*'

Dan and Liz looked at each other and burst out laughing.

4

Liz was grumpy when she arrived at work. Jake had woken twice during the night and she had dealt with him both times. She guessed he was finally feeling teeth breaking through, but Calpol wasn't helping much. Neither was Gareth.

She walked into her office, extracted herself from her thick coat and scarf, and put on a coffee to create something to warm her up. She heard the double buzz indicating Oliver wanted her, so she picked up her notepad, and went through to his room. He smiled when he saw her.

'I thought I heard you pottering about. We really did mean a ten start, you know.'

'I know. I catch the tram and that decides what time I get here. Did you want something?' She waved her notepad at him.

'Yes, to give you this.' He handed her a file. 'Read it, it's concerning a nursing home that's not doing what it's supposed to be doing. I'd like you to handle it all the way through.'

'Oliver, you're a star. This is what I need. Don't forget I'm not in for most of the afternoon. If you need anything doing, make it this morning, will you?'

'I will. You're going to sort out the Latimers, aren't you?'

'I don't know about sorting them out, but I'm taking them a replacement cheque. It's up to them whether they cash it or not. Something about leading horses to water…'

He nodded. 'Strange situation, isn't it? No bank transfer, not querying a missing cheque – and let's face it, Liz, it isn't peanuts. What are they like? You knew them better than anybody else.'

He's the man I came so close to spending the rest of my life with, he's handsome, he's funny, he's unhappy at home. He's Jake's father. He's the love of my life.

'They're pretty ordinary, really. The compensation, if you recall, was from the NHS for a botched operation on their daughter's arm which left her with little use in her left hand. They seemed to me to be normal, although Rosemary Latimer was always a little bit over-protective of Melissa. I suspect that was because she believed she caused the accident that broke her daughter's arm in the first place. It was a bad break, a really bad one – she fell off a slide. They had to operate to set it, and the operation wasn't successful, nerves were trapped and it wasn't spotted that her hand was becoming fixed. By the time the cast came off, she had lost all feeling in the hand, and couldn't move it. It was a fair settlement, agreed by both the NHS and the Latimers, so they had no reason to refuse the cheque.'

'Maybe they'll throw some light on things this afternoon.'

Maybe she will. He won't be there.

'Let's hope so. In fact, let's hope they're there. I've emailed them to tell them I'm calling to bring a replacement cheque, but I've had no reply. There was no answer when I rang, either.'

But there was when I texted. **Okay. I love you.**

'If they're not there, don't mess about. Shove it through the letterbox, and go home. You've booked the taxi through FleetLine?'

She nodded. 'Yes, and I've told them I'll need the driver to wait until I'm ready to go.'

She clutched the file containing her new case to her chest, and left Oliver's office. His eyes stayed on her, unmoving, until she closed the door.

The coffee was ready, and she stood it on the coaster, drawing the file towards her.

At midday, Karen rang through to her to ask if she needed a sandwich bringing in, but she declined. Her stomach was churning far too much to accommodate food.

Karen rang through again at 1.30pm to say the taxi had arrived, and Liz picked up her briefcase and her handbag before heading for reception.

She wanted the journey to take forever, but it was remarkably free-flowing traffic, and Jim, her taxi driver over many years, pulled up outside the Latimer home with ten minutes to spare.

She sat for a moment trying to find some courage, and only moved when Jim turned around and spoke her name.

'Sorry,' she said, and flashed a sickly smile at him.

'You okay? You need me to go with you?'

'No, I'm fine, Jim. I needed two minutes to gather my thoughts. This shouldn't take long, and then you're taking me home.'

She opened the rear door and stepped out. It was bitterly cold, and she shivered. She walked up the long path that showcased the front garden, and knocked on the door.

It opened immediately, and the shock must have registered on her face. Rosie Latimer had aged. Her hair was grey, and her face had thinned and become lined. The biggest change was in her body. Her clothes hung on her. And yet, when she smiled, it was the old Rosie.

'Liz! Come in. It's lovely to see you. Would you like a drink?'

Liz smiled. 'No, thank you, Rosie. I have a taxi waiting outside to take me back to work.' She figured Rosie didn't need to know she was going home; she might press her to have that drink. 'I came to bring you this,' and she handed over the envelope.

'The cheque is inside it,' Liz explained.

'Okay, thank you.' She offered no explanation for the previous cheque not having been paid in, and she stuffed the envelope into her skirt pocket.

'Right... erm... I'll get off then. Good to see you again. Are Philip and Melissa well?'

'They're fine.' Her tone was abrupt, and Liz stepped out of the front door. She walked down the path, and heard Rosie say softly, 'So you've had the brat, then?'

Liz felt sick, and almost fell into the car. 'Let's go, Jim. Straight home, please, not back to the office.'

'You okay?' He could see she wasn't, and he spun round in his seat to look at her. 'A problem?' He had always felt quite protective of his pretty, blonde haired client, and didn't like to feel somebody had caused her pain.

'No, it's fine. I'm still at the same address, but can you drop me here, please?' She handed him a piece of paper showing Sadie's address. 'I have to collect my baby before I can settle down at home.'

Fifteen minutes later, she was pushing Jake and trying not to think about the strangeness of the words that had come out of Rosie Latimer's mouth. Liz felt frozen through, and knew it wasn't to do with the sub-zero temperatures the UK was experiencing.

The house was cold, and she turned the heating up high; after putting Jake into his cot for a nap, she made herself a drink. Comfort drinking – there was something special about wrapping your hands round a mug of tea, and relaxing.

So, you've had the brat, then. The words seemed to echo in her brain. What did Rosie know?

Liz took out the small, non-descript phone, and toyed with it. Should she text him? Would it cause more problems than solve them? Indeed, dare she text him?

Liz could feel a headache starting, and popped two painkillers before picking up the phone again. She typed a message but then deleted it. Indecision. Could she bear to speak to him? Would he want to speak to her? She thought back to that awful afternoon when she had told him of her pregnancy, and remembered his words. *I'll come and get you, no questions asked, and with the same amount of love in my heart.*

In the end, it became simple. No words of love, no 'can we talk' request, just a tight little message; **Does Rosie know?**

She finished her cup of tea, and went to gather up the laundry. With the washing machine drumming quietly, silence from Jake's bedroom, and time to herself before Dan arrived home from school, she moved into the lounge and took the love phone with her – Phil's name for the phones only they used. And it had been about love; even now, after all this time, she missed his touch, his presence, his mind so in tune with hers. There was still no reply, and she sighed. It could never be over; what she would give to feel his arms wrapped around her one more time.

Surely, they had been careful enough... Phil had never expressed any concerns that Rosie suspected he was seeing someone else. And if Rosie hadn't used the word brat, if she had said *so you've had your baby then*, Liz wouldn't have given any further thought to it. There had been venom in the way the word *brat* had been delivered.

Liz hadn't received a reply by the time Dan came in from school. He popped his head round the lounge door.

'Nice and warm in here,' he said, blowing her a kiss.

She smiled. 'It wasn't when I arrived home. We having something warming tonight?'

'Certainly are. Bangers and mash with mashed carrot and swede. That sound okay?'

'Sounds delicious. Your dad will be pleased.'

Dan laughed. 'He's pleased with anything that doesn't contain lettuce.'

He blew Liz a kiss and disappeared into the kitchen. She picked up the love phone one more time, saw that she had had no response, and silenced it before zipping it back into the pocket in her handbag.

A wave of disappointment washed over her, and she knew it would never be over between her and Phil, never.

5

The reply came at 3am.
Yes. I love you.

6

Jake slept well. He went all through the night, finally waking Liz at just after seven. Gareth stirred as he felt her get out of bed.

'Should I get up?' he mumbled, pulling the duvet so that it enclosed his shoulders.

'Might be a clever idea,' she responded. 'It's gone seven.'

He sat up with panic etched on his face. 'I didn't set my alarm, did I? I relied on that nocturnal kid waking at his usual six!'

'Nope, no alarm. You want the shower first, I take it?'

He moved at speed. 'Thanks.'

She heard the water within seconds of him leaving the bedroom.

It was only when both Gareth and Dan had left that Liz took out the phone. She saw the message and felt the blood drain from her face. She had to speak to Phil, she had to know how much Rosie knew, or how much she was guessing.

She pressed speed dial 1 and waited for him to answer. It went straight to voicemail, so she disconnected. He must have switched it off, because she knew he would never ring anyone but her on it. She sent off a small text, and put the phone on the coffee table, taking it off silent.

Ring me if before 3.30 pm.

She hoped he would. She felt a shiver of anticipation as she thought about talking to him again. He had a rich, deep, timbre to his voice, that sounded especially good over the airwaves, and she knew if she did speak to him again, she could easily be lost.

She switched on her laptop and sent emails to both Tom and Oliver, informing them that she was working from home,

23

if they had anything for her that she could deal with. A reply came back with some speed from Tom, reminding her that she was on her day off, and while they were struggling in a coffee-free environment, they would not be contacting her unless her office blew up. Or they needed her.

She smiled. She gave them an hour, and knew something would wend its way through the ether towards her.

She worked on some documentation in the care home case, and after picking up the phone for the fourth time, decided that maybe it wasn't good to work on such a complex issue when her mind wasn't on it. She followed Jake's progress around the furniture as he clung on for dear life, and knew he wasn't so far off being a walking toddler. He was such a cutie, but he truly was beginning to look more like Phil every day. Heartbreakingly, guiltily so.

It wasn't an issue – Gareth would never have considered for one moment that the baby, the unplanned baby, wasn't his. She felt a gentle twang of the heartstrings every time she held her son. More than a gentle twang, a whole symphony of twangs.

'Shall we go shopping?' she said to the little one. He held up his arms at the sound of her voice, and sat on his bottom with a thud. She laughed at the shocked expression on his face, and scooped him up.

'Come on, cosy toes and hands today, you'll have to cope with a red nose.' She dressed him warmly, loaded him into the pushchair, and put the small phone in her pocket. Her iPhone went in her bag.

It was bitterly cold, and she walked briskly, pulling her scarf up over her nose. It hurt to breathe in the frigid air. The whole country had been in the grip of an icy spell for several days, with no end in sight. As she walked, her mind played around with summer holiday spots. It didn't really warm her, but the thoughts were productive.

An hour's walking saw them arrive at the shopping mall, and she went to the stationer's shop. She loaded the pushchair with paper, printer inks and biros – a five-minute search for a pen that morning had caused her to check what supplies were running low.

She directed her steps towards a coffee shop: kindle time, and peace, combined with a coffee. Jake woke while she was enjoying the break.

She handed him his sippy cup, and he smiled, toothlessly. They shared the rest of her cookie, and as she was about to stand to leave, the phone rang.

For a second, she froze. It had been so long since she had heard that ring tone proclaiming Chris Montez' undying devotion in *The More I See You*, that she felt tears sting her eyes.

She pulled it from her pocket and pressed the answer button. Silence.

'Hello? Phil? Is that you?'

Silence.

'Phil? I can't hear you.'

Silence, the silence where you know someone is there, but they're not going to speak.

And then nothing, as the caller disconnected.

No words spoken, no sounds made.

She shivered, and it wasn't from the cold. The phone went back into her pocket, with a hope that he was in a bad signal reception area, and he would call later.

She pushed the heavily loaded pushchair on to the tram, and sat in the small designated seat by the pushchair section, playing with Jake and listening out for the ringtone. It didn't ring, and she walked the short distance from the tram stop with a heavy heart.

It was toasty warm inside the house, and she quickly stripped Jake of all the outer garments she had used that had turned him into a stiff little doll-like figure. He seemed relieved to be a normal child once again, and he crawled rapidly around the lounge in ever decreasing circles.

Liz tipped the small toy box of cars, trucks, dinosaurs, farm animals and assorted Peppa Pig vehicles, switched on Netflix to provide him with back-to-back Peppa Pig, and moved to the small office area they had set up, in order to be ready for her part time return to a job that really demanded full time attention.

With Jake holding a mini Peppa in one hand and a dinosaur in the other, Liz watched for a moment as his eyes followed the fat pigs on the television screen.

She opened her laptop, and logged in, then placed the small Nokia to one side. He had to ring. He had to ring.

She checked her emails, dealt with two that were easy answers, forwarded a file to Tom, the Tom who had said it's your day off, and answered a personal one to Nora, a long-time friend from university days.

And still the phone remained silent. She checked that she hadn't accidentally switched it to that mode, and replaced it by her side. It was just after two, and at half past three the silent aspect would have to be activated, and the phone re-zipped into her bag, away from prying eyes.

Her work completed, she opened a special file, one entitled quite simply *book*. This was a file that gave her a great deal of pleasure, although not opened on any sort of regular basis. She loved history, and one day, while on the tram going to work, had come up with an idea for a book set in France, in the days of the revolution. She was writing it for herself; she loved the research aspect, possibly even more than the writing, and knew it would never leave her computer. It was a project to fill her time, when she had any spare.

She took the notebook out of her drawer, went through the notes she had made, and typed, one eye on Jake as he renewed his acquaintance with Peppa in yet another episode, while chewing on a stuffed dog, and one eye on the computer as she typed in her handwritten notes. There were no eyes spare for the front window, and she missed seeing Daniel walk past it.

She heard his key go into the front door, and she threw her notebook over the phone. A glance at the bottom of her screen showed her it was 15.42; how stupid was she not to have set an alarm?

Dan came through to the lounge and kissed her. 'Good day, Mum?' He bent down and picked up Jake, who giggled at his big brother and waved Peppa in his direction. 'And you, Jakey boy? Good day?'

'We've walked,' said Liz. 'Walked it to Crystal Peaks, bought some stationery I needed, and came back on the tram. It was damn cold though.'

'You're working?'

'I've done a couple of things for work, but I'm adding a bit to the book.'

'The book…' He dramatized the way that he spoke, and Liz laughed.

'Cheeky monkey. Yes, the book. You wait until I'm a famous author and Spielberg wants it for a movie.'

'I thought you said it was being written for you?'

'Okay, I'll have to become a personal friend of Spielberg then, cut out the middleman, the publisher.'

Dan ruffled her hair. 'Good for you. Will it make us rich?'

'Oh yes,' she replied. 'Very rich.'

Dan replaced Jake in the middle of his toys, and walked out of the room. 'Boeuf bourgignon for tonight,' he called from the hall. 'That okay? It's already in the freezer.'

She lifted her head and smiled. What had she done in her previous life that was so spectacular, fate had given her the gift of a chef in the making for a son?

She quickly retrieved the buried phone, switched it to silent and zipped it into her bag. With her hopes dashed, she closed the laptop, and attended to her youngest son's nappy. She took him to bed for a half hour nap, and went back down to the kitchen.

She sat at the table and watched what Dan was doing. A coffee appeared in front of her.

'You okay?'

She nodded. 'Of course. I was lost in the French revolution.'

'So, going back to work isn't an issue, then?'

'Not at all. You know I love my job…'

'But you love Jake more.'

'Stop being grown up, and get back to your cheffing.'

'Just keeping an eye. And I'm only defrosting…'

'Do you really think I'd give everything up for Peppa Pig overdoses?' She sipped at her drink and tilted her head.

'If you're looking at it like that, no. You're good, Mum, I won't check up on you again.'

She picked up her coffee and returned to the lounge. 'Get on with the meal, slave, and stop worrying!' she called. She tidied away the toys, plumped up the cushions, and pulled her bag towards her. She quickly took out the Nokia and looked for messages. Missed call.

Tears sprang to her eyes. Damn. He'd managed to ring again. She allowed herself the luxury of scrolling back through the many messages they had exchanged from the start of the relationship, and went through them a second time as enlightenment dawned.

When Phil had bought them the phones he had made her promise to always delete every text, every bit of evidence of calls between them, in case Rosie or Gareth came across the phones. *We can always say they are phones kept for work calls,* he had said.

But she hadn't been able to delete them. She wanted to keep them. His love had enfolded her through the texts, she couldn't delete them. The texts were the untold story of their love.

The last three or four were different. He had always ended his texts with *love you, sweets*; there wasn't one text from their relationship that didn't have those words. It wasn't on the newer ones.

He wasn't sending them, somebody else was.

7

*G*loomy, always gloomy. The small light that was never turned off gave a tiny glow, enough to see the opposite wall. Phil knew he was in a cellar, chained and attached to a wall. The chain extended long enough to allow him to use an old toilet in the corner, wash in the tiny hand basin next to it, and not an inch further. He hadn't seen or spoken to anyone for a long time – how long, he had no idea. There were steps leading up to a door, but his chain only allowed him as far as the foot of the stairs.

Phil had never seen his captor. In his head, he called him Captor, but he was only guessing it was a man; it could easily be a woman.

The only clue he had about the length of time of his captivity was when he first came around, the weather was still warm. It had changed and Captor had provided two old blankets. Phil shivered through most nights.

There had been no verbal communication, no written messages, nothing other than a dumb waiter that clattered down to the cellar, holding food for the day.

It annoyed him intensely that he couldn't remember getting here. He could only assume that he had been drugged in some way, because he had no injuries, other than a small bruise on his arm. He had tried asking questions, but to no avail. The person at the top of the dumb waiter never spoke, and there was never any activity, until what he presumed was the following morning.

Phil had given up with the questions. The thoughts in his head were slowly driving him mad. Why? Why was he here? Did his kidnapper think he was someone else? Almost all the time his thoughts drifted towards his family; to Rosie, to Melissa – and to Liz.

Rosie had been truly vitriolic when he had confessed to loving Liz, much to his surprise. There had been nothing between them for years, and he had been shocked by her reaction. You're my husband, not hers. She's got her own husband. And does the bitch love you?

At first, he had wondered if Rosie could be Captor, but he ruled it out. She was a gentle soul, under normal circumstances, and he couldn't see her as an evil cow capable of doing this to him. They had simply drifted apart following Melissa's accident, lived together more as friends than anything, so, no, he couldn't see her being this cruel.

His thoughts drifted towards Liz when he heard the rattle as the dumb waiter descended. He stood patiently until the noise stopped, before moving across to it. It wasn't how he imagined a dumb waiter to be, so guessed this had been constructed specifically with his incarceration in mind. It had a small door to keep the contents of the box structure from falling out as it descended from above.

He took out the carrier bag; it contained two sandwiches, two bottles of water and two bags of crisps. It hadn't been any different for the whole of the time he had been there. He heard the dumb waiter rattle its way back to the top, and he opened a bottle of water, and took a long drink.

He was shocked to hear the rattle begin again. He watched it with apprehension, and when it stopped, he moved across to open the door once more. Inside was a second plastic bag, this time a much larger black bin bag. He lifted it out and carried it across to his camp bed.

He had been wearing shorts when he had been taken. This bag contained jeans, a jumper, a couple of T-shirts, boxers, thicker socks – and he groaned. How long did they intend keeping him?

He had washed his existing clothes as best he could in cold water in the tiny hand basin, but they took so long to dry he had almost given up on that idea. Maybe Captor had a conscience after all.

There was an extra blanket and he felt grateful to the unknown person who had supplied him with it. He sat down on his camp bed and gathered the contents of the large bag to him.

And cried.

8

The boeuf bourgignon was beautiful, warming, tasty and eaten. Liz raised her glass of wine. 'To the chef. That was delicious, Dan.'

Gareth nodded. 'So much so, I don't think I could face a dessert.'

'I'll put the apple and blackberry crumble in the freezer then,' Daniel said, smirking.

'Ah... maybe a small amount,' Gareth joked. 'Is it with custard?'

'Would I offer anything else?'

'Not in this house, probably not,' his father said with a laugh.

Liz tried to join in with the banter, but worry had settled over her like a nimbus cloud, and she wanted to be on her own, to think.

She was convinced the texts hadn't been sent by Phil. He wouldn't have sent *I love you* without following it up with *sweets* and some kisses. He wouldn't. So, who had sent them?

Her money was on Rosie. Somehow, she had found Phil's phone. But this raised the issue of where he was – he would not have voluntarily let anyone take it. She had to go and see Rosie again, use some pretext of needing a signature to close the file now the cheque had been paid in – if indeed it had been paid in.

Maybe Phil would be there this time. And if not, she would insist on seeing him to get his signature to sign off the case. She would have to hope Tom and Oliver didn't get to know about it.

One way or another she would see Phil, she needed to get rid of this anxiety, needed to know he was okay.

She stood, leaving the table clearing to Gareth. 'I'm going to bed. I've got a thumping headache, so I'm taking some paracetamol and going to sleep it away.'

'You okay apart from that?' Gareth asked. 'You've been very quiet.'

'It's the headache.' She gave a small smile. 'Don't wake me when you come up, will you?'

'Of course not. I might play the lad here, at that new game he's got.'

'You're not good enough, Dad,' Dan said. 'Go and have a pint instead. I'll look after Mum.'

Liz left them to their chatter and walked up the stairs, holding on to her handbag. She needed to check the Nokia again.

She had a quick shower, slipped into her nightie, and huddled down in bed. She did have a headache, but it was nowhere near as bad as she had said downstairs. She closed her eyes for a minute, and then took out the phone. Nothing. No texts, no missed calls. She double checked she hadn't caught the silent button, and slipped it back into her bag, zipping up the pocket.

And then she had a light bulb moment. Whoever had the phone that had been Phil's, hadn't learned of their affair through that. Phil must have stuck to their agreement to delete everything, because if he hadn't, they would have seen how he ended every text, and copied that. So how did the person, or persons, know about her and Phil? As far as she was aware, nobody knew.

Or had Phil confessed to Rosie? She knew they had a strange relationship, and Phil considered it to be a platonic one, but what if Rosie still wanted him? Could she be sending the texts? And if she was, what had happened to Phil?

Liz tossed and turned, unable to sleep. She tried reading, tried listening to some smoochy Sarah Vaughan, and then gave up. She heard Gareth return, although she knew he hadn't had a lot to drink; he was a loud man when there was too much alcohol inside him, but he merely closed the front door, switched off all the lights and headed upstairs.

Dan was in his room, and she heard Gareth whisper good night to him. By the time he reached their bedroom, her eyes were closed, and she pretended to be asleep. He slid in beside her, and within five minutes was snoring softly.

All was peaceful in the Chambers' household. Liz reached for her kindle and once again tried to read. This time it worked, and fifteen minutes later her eyes closed.

The little Nokia had already received another missed call, and a text that said **Hope our son is okay. Sleep well.**

9

Liz didn't check the Nokia until late Saturday. When she did, she gave a small cry. Dan popped his head around the lounge door.

'You okay, Mum?'

'I'm fine,' she said, a brightness in her voice that was false. 'I read something on Facebook that made me laugh aloud. Sorry.'

'No problem. I'm going up to my room. I won't disturb Jake.'

She smiled. 'Thank you. Where's your dad?'

'Nipped to the shop. Said something about wine.'

She nodded. 'Thanks, Dan. How's the game coming on?'

'Good. I'm sending it to a couple of mates from school for them to give it a go, and give me some feedback.'

'So, what are you doing at the moment?'

'Don't ask me, Mum, and I won't have to lie to you,' he laughed.

'What?'

'Just joking, just joking. I've an essay to do before Monday, so I'm working on that. Mum… are you and Dad okay?'

'Of course.'

'It's just… you're a bit miserable, seem fed up.'

'If I am, it's not your dad's fault. I miss Jake, and it's not been as easy leaving him, as I thought it might be. That's all it is, honestly. Me and your dad are absolutely good.'

'That's a relief. I'm too old to start having uncles.' He flashed his blue eyes at her, and headed for the stairs.

She shook her head, and laughed aloud. Dan could always cheer her up. She put the Nokia back into its pocket, and thought about the strange text. Jake's parentage was something only she

34

and Phil knew about. So, did this mean it really was Phil sending the messages?

She knew it wasn't. Therefore, was the text a stab in the dark by someone playing silly guessing games?

She was stuck until Tuesday; she could do nothing with Jake to look after, she would have to wait until she returned to work. It was so frustrating. Most of what she was thinking was guesswork based on what she knew for facts, but it really didn't help solve anything.

***

There were no more texts or missed calls, and she tried to push it firmly to the back of her mind, but at odd moments it crept through. If she could only speak to Phil once, it would settle her down.

On Sunday, there was a significant snowfall, and Dan built a snowman for Jake in the back garden. He said it was for Jake, but it was a work of art, and she did have to ask the question who it was really for.

She had a long chat with Julia, who filled her in on all of Oliver's faults as a husband, whilst negating any issues she might have brought to the marriage. By the end of the conversation, Liz realised the balance of the marriage wasn't wholly down to Oliver's controlling nature, Julia Hardwick was a truly selfish woman. On reflection, Liz decided, they probably deserved each other.

The sun came out Monday morning, and by the evening most of the snow had gone. The snowman was still standing, but looking a sorry spectacle indeed.

Liz had done some preparatory work for a case that needed sorting on the Tuesday, and she closed her laptop with a sigh. Tuesday meant giving a lot of thought to the Latimer problems; she had to speak to Rosie somehow.

She briefly considered talking to Tom Banton about the whole situation, but she didn't think she could take the condemnation that would inevitably emanate from him. It was against every rule in the book, fraternising with clients, especially married ones.

He would have to dismiss her, and she didn't think she could take that. No, she was on her own.

She dropped Jake off at Sadie's somewhat reluctantly on the Tuesday morning; the tram journey was travelled in silence, and she didn't even bother taking her Kindle out of her bag. She was troubled, but hadn't a clue what to do about it. She was in town for shortly after nine, and decided to go for a coffee before heading into work. She sat at the table in Costa, and took out the Nokia. No messages.

She worded a text carefully and pressed send. **I urgently need to talk to you. Please call 9-5. If can't talk at that time will disconnect and call you back later. Please, Phil.**

Now all she had to do was hope and wait.

Liz finished her coffee and walked down the hill to the office, listening for the ringtone. Nothing happened, and when she was sitting at her desk, she dropped the little phone into the top drawer. She knew she would hear it in there.

She surprised herself by becoming immersed in two separate cases, one of which was her own nursing home case, and it was lunchtime by the time she realised there had been no sounds from the drawer. She took out the phone and checked it. Nothing.

It was a spur of the minute thing to email Rosie. She hadn't thought about doing it, hadn't wanted to do it, but did it anyway.

She told Rosie that she needed confirmation that the cheque had been paid in, the company accountants needed proof as the payment had been delayed for such a long time, and she would be bringing the form out to the house on the Wednesday. She would appreciate it if both parties could be there to sign it.

She signed it *Best wishes, Liz,* and waited for a response.

Rosie's reply came shortly before Liz left to go home. It simply said *Okay, Liz. See you tomorrow.*

She collected Jake from Sadie, and headed back down the hill to home.

The sound of Metallica came from the kitchen, and she called a loud hello, trusting that her voice would rise above the crescendo of the music.

Jake was tired, and had almost been asleep as she had lifted him from the pushchair. She quickly changed his clothes for his sleepwear, and sat on the floor with him to play for a few minutes.

Dan brought a cup of tea through for her. 'I've turned the music down.'

'Doesn't matter. I don't mind Metallica. I don't think this young man will still be awake in five minutes, though, so we'd have to have been a bit quieter then, anyway. You okay with the meal? Need me to help?'

He gave her the look that said keep away from my kitchen, and she laughed. 'I used to cook, you know!'

Dan bent down to kiss the top of her head. 'I know, but let's say you're better at legal issues, and leave it at that.' And then he chuckled as something clearly drifted through his mind. 'That's Jake, isn't it? A legal issue. The issue of a paralegal. Hey, that's cool, Mum.'

He moved out of the reach of her hand, and left her to pick up the grumpy-sounding Jake. She took the sleepy baby upstairs and placed him in his cot.

'Sleep tight, baby boy,' she whispered, and pressed a finger kiss to his lips. 'Love you.'

Quietly closing his door, she headed for her own bedroom, where she lay her head on the pillow for a couple of minutes. She was tired, she was worried, and everything was making her feel a little sick. She was baffled, as much as anything – didn't know what to do, couldn't understand this strange direction her life had taken; and it had all happened because she had gone back to work.

Her eyes started to close, and she forced them open. If she slept now, she would never sleep later. She needed to be alert for work, not staggering around like a zombie.

And the next day, if Rosie's somewhat ambiguous email was to be believed, Liz would see Phil for the first time in eighteen months.

10

*H*e pulled the blanket around his shoulders and sat hunched on the camp bed. So cold, so bloody damn cold. He could tell he was starting with a sore throat, and he prayed it wouldn't develop into anything worse than an irritation.

He heard the rattle of the dumb waiter and waited. He moved as it stopped, always fearful that if he didn't get the food quickly, it would disappear upwards. The carrier bag was bright orange, a Sainsbury bag. Over the months of his imprisonment he had saved the carrier bags, building them up to form insulation underneath his camp bed. The layer of plastic helped stop the cold from seeping up into the canvas from the damp floor beneath his feet.

As always, he waited for the rattle of the dumb waiter as it disappeared upwards, and then he opened the bag. Two sandwiches, two bags of crisps, two bottles of water, a pack of ginger biscuits and toilet rolls. He picked up the ginger biscuits and rolled them around in his hands.

This almost seemed surreal. There had been nothing like this for the entire period of his imprisonment. He hadn't tasted hot food for months, had existed on sandwiches and water, and he knew his health was suffering. Ginger biscuits wouldn't help with his health, but they would certainly help with his taste buds. He picked up the carrier bag and realised there was still an item inside it.

It was a small metal flask. He unscrewed the lid and saw coffee. He quickly poured some into the small metal cup and drank, burning his lips slightly but not caring.

Despite having sugar in it, it was delicious. He opened the packet of biscuits, took one out and tentatively dunked it in the hot liquid. It tasted like heaven. He took out a second biscuit and then sealed the packet tightly. He would ration them; he guessed he wouldn't get this sort of food every day.

He finished the coffee quickly. His experience of metal flasks told him it wouldn't stay hot for long, so he drank it and carried it across to the small sink to rinse it out. He placed it beside the hole where the dumb waiter had been, and hoped that by returning it, he would get a hot drink every other day. He would place it inside the box when he took his next food delivery out of it.

He settled back on to his camp bed and stared at the low wattage light bulb. He had no idea of the time, assumed that when the food arrived it was morning, but it could as easily have been the evening. The only exit from his prison was the stairway; if the light bulb stopped working, he would be in darkness. And still he didn't know why he was here.

He felt comfortable with the hot drink inside him, so he pulled the blankets up around his shoulders, and drifted off to sleep.

Captor watched, and smiled. A small touch of a finger switched on the camera to time how long the prisoner was asleep, and Captor left the stone-built, neighbourless house.

11

Liz spent half an hour putting together a form that required two signatures, confirming that the cheque had been re-issued following cancellation of the first payment, due to non-presentation at the client's bank. She made it sound as official as she could, hoping that Rosie wouldn't realise that there was nothing legal or official about it.

She read it through for the third time, then fastened it into a clipboard, ready for the Latimer signatures. She needed to talk to Phil, and hoped that Rosie would offer to make a drink, and leave them together.

She had already checked the diary and seen that both partners were out for the afternoon; Tom attending court, and Oliver had simply put *home visit*.

She booked a taxi for four o'clock and returned to her work, satisfied that she could do no more.

In a couple of hours, she would see him.

***

Jim jumped out of the car and opened the rear door.

'I'm going for a coffee down the road. When you've finished, give me a call. I'll come and pick you up. And any trouble…'

'There'll be no trouble, Jim,' she smiled.

'You don't like going here. I can tell.'

'I'm fine, honestly. But I will ring. I'm going straight home after this.'

He watched her walk down the path, and didn't move until he saw the door open.

His unease made him decide to drive to the end of the road, switch off his engine, and simply wait for her call. He liked Liz, and knew she had been uncomfortable at her last home visit to this house. He'd keep an eye on things while he was near enough to help, if she needed it.

Rosie didn't look happy, and Liz felt her heart rate accelerate. What was wrong with the woman?

'Hi, Rosie. Are you well?'

'Yes, thank you, Liz. And you? Come through to the lounge.'

Liz followed Rosie's slight figure, and glanced around the room. Phil wasn't there. Liz didn't know whether to feel elated or angry.

'Coffee?' Rosie asked.

'That would be lovely. Is Phil not here?'

'He'll be here in a bit. He's been delayed.'

Liz nodded, and sat in the armchair. 'And Melissa? Is she well?'

'She's really good. Staying at my mum's at the moment.'

Liz watched as Rosie left to make the drinks, and looked around the room. It seemed bare, devoid of the homely bits and bobs that had been there when she'd had to make home visits while pursuing their case in the courts.

Now there were no pictures on the walls, no photographs of the happy family, no ornaments, costly or otherwise.

Rosie returned carrying a tray loaded with mugs, biscuits and anything else they might need for a mini feast. She placed the tray on the coffee table and poured.

Liz thanked her, and picked up a biscuit. She held out the clipboard with the form on it. 'I need your signature on here. Phil can sign when he comes home.'

Rosie nodded, and unclipped the attached pen. 'Is it one signature?'

'It is. It's to prove to our auditors that we don't issue two cheques to the same client without having a good reason.'

Rosie signed her name, then handed it back to Liz.

'Thank you,' Liz smiled. 'I need Phil's now, and I can get out of your life.'

'That will be good.' Rosie's face looked like granite.

'I'm sorry?'

'Maybe you should have thought about staying out of our lives some time ago.'

Liz went cold. She couldn't speak, didn't know how to respond anyway.

'I know,' Rosie continued. 'I know about you and Phil.'

'There is no me and Phil,' Liz managed to stammer.

'There was.'

Again, silence from Liz.

'He told me. He told me all about your affair, where you used to meet, how much he loved you, and then he told me about the brat. How could you, Liz? How could you?'

Liz gasped. 'But he said…'

'He said we were just friends, didn't he? Maybe we were, but that didn't mean I didn't love him. It never occurred to him that my feelings were as strong as the day we married. I forgot how to show them.'

Liz was floundering, out of her depth. There was vitriol pouring out of Rosie. 'Rosie…'

'Just get out, Liz. Leave my home, get out of our lives.'

'I need Phil's signature.' Liz was aware how stubborn she sounded.

'You're not going to get it here. Don't you understand, Liz. He's gone! I haven't heard from him in months. He walked out one day and left. I have no idea where he is, and frankly, I don't want to know, now.'

'Did he leave a note?'

'If he had, I wouldn't let you see it. But, no, he didn't. He took his wallet, his phone, and disappeared. So, your guess is as good as mine.'

Liz stood.

'Then I'll get off back to work, Rosie. I haven't heard from him, so he's not with me.'

'Yes, Liz, you go back to your nice, cosy little family, and live your nice, cosy little life. Obviously, you still have your job…'

Liz nodded at the woman falling apart in front of her. 'I went back after maternity leave. If there's…'

'Don't say anything else. Just go.'

Liz picked up her bag and the clipboard and headed for the front door. Rosie didn't follow her. Liz stepped out on to the path, and fished in her bag for her phone. Before she could ring, Jim was pulling up outside.

She climbed into the backseat without saying anything, fighting to hold back tears of frustration.

'Okay?' Jim asked.

'I'm fine,' she said. 'Just take me home, Jim, please.'

Neither of them heard the crash of breaking crockery as Rosie upended the tray containing the drinks. 'Fuck you, Liz Chambers,' she muttered, and walked from the room.

She picked up the telephone receiver and rang her mother. 'I'd like Melissa home now, please.'

'But she's only been here an hour,' Angela Harmer protested. 'Can't she stay a bit longer? We were going to watch a film…'

'I would like her home, please. She's my daughter, and I make the decisions in her life.'

'Rosie, maybe next time you want to dump your daughter for reasons best known to yourself, maybe we'll have our own decisions to make about whether we can help out, or not.' Angela slammed down the phone, and Rosie burst into tears.

This simply couldn't go on.

12

Sadie Fremantle watched from the bay window as Liz set off down the road, taking Jake home. She felt uneasy. There was clearly something wrong with Jake's mummy, and she hoped it was nothing to do with her. Or Gareth.

Suddenly Liz stopped and turned around; she had felt eyes on her and she caught sight of Sadie in the window. Both women waved, and Liz continued her journey.

Jake crawled happily around, dragging his blankie behind him. The comfort blanket seemed to be an integral part of his make-up, and Liz watched in amusement as he struggled to extricate it from the legs of the coffee table.

'Cup of tea, Mum?' she heard Dan call, and responded with a *no thank you*. She felt she didn't want anything – no drink, no food. She wanted to sleep, to escape from the thoughts running around her head.

She was struggling to accept the idea of Phil walking away from Rosie; the Phil she had fallen in love with wouldn't have done that. Yes, he could conceivably have left Rosie, but certainly wouldn't have done it by disappearing. He would have made provision for Melissa as a priority, and as Rosie didn't seem to have any idea where he was, that provision didn't appear to be in place.

So where was he, this man Liz loved? Even her thoughts came as something of a shock, because she knew that the eighteen months without him hadn't dimmed her feelings.

What had Rosie said? '*He took his wallet and his phone…*'. She knew something was wrong. What if he'd simply fallen, and cracked his head? He could be lying in the woods somewhere, undiscovered… dead. She knew he enjoyed his daily walk through the woods before starting work every morning.

She caught the sob in the back of her throat. But somebody had his second mobile phone. She was getting messages, messages that she knew he hadn't written.

And what about money? Her brain felt as though it was about to explode with all the crazy, inter-connected thoughts tearing through it. He would need money if he was still alive. Rosie had said he disappeared one day.

How could Liz find out if he had accessed his bank account? Ask Rosie? She could imagine what Rosie's answer would be.

And why hadn't Rosie reported him as a missing person? She hadn't, because if she had she would have told the police about their affair, and the police would have been knocking on her door.

Liz saw car headlights swoop on to the drive, and stood. She had to put it to the back of her mind. Gareth was home, and he would soon pick up on any internal turmoil. She scooped up her son, and moved into the hall, where she smiled at her husband.

'Hi,' he said. 'Good day?'

She nodded. 'So so. You?'

'Quiet. Glad to be home.' He took Jake from her, and kissed him. 'And how's our youngest member?'

Jake smacked him in the mouth.

'Oh. You're okay, then,' he laughed. He turned to his wife. 'Any problems?'

'None,' she said, a shade too brightly, and walked into the kitchen, leaving Gareth to handle the wriggling little boy.

None at all.

Liz ate her meal in silence, aware of the general chatter between her husband and her son, but not joining them. She sensed Gareth casting looks in her direction, but said nothing. She would speak when she was ready; Gareth should know that. They had been together long enough for him to recognise when she needed her own space.

'Thank you, Daniel,' she said eventually, standing and pushing her chair away from the table. 'That was lovely. I'm going to check on Jake, he was a little unsettled. Then I might have a long soak in the bath.'

'You okay, sweetheart?' Gareth looked at her with concern.

'I'm fine. Just a little tired. I'll probably have an early night. Will you load the dishwasher, please?'

He nodded. 'Yes, you go and relax.'

She left them knowing their eyes were following her. They knew something was wrong; they knew her.

Her brain was on fire. She was churning the facts around in her head that she had gleaned from everything Rosie had said, and to Liz's horror, concluded that it was possible, even probable, that Phil was no longer alive.

Should she approach the police? If she did, it would blow everything wide open; she could say goodbye to Gareth, and even possibly Dan. And she couldn't do anything to hurt Dan. He needed stability at this point in his life.

Rosie? Could she persuade Rosie to report Phil as a missing person? Again, that could open up the whole situation. And could she even believe Rosie? What if Rosie had killed him after Phil had come clean about their affair?

Liz laughed aloud. Her imagination really was taking her off into the realms of fantasy. Ordinary people didn't do things like that.

She realised how very much on her own she was, and she tried to think logically. The only concrete thing connecting her to Phil was the love phone, and she knew it was somebody else using that. And if somebody else was using it, it meant Phil couldn't. He would never have given up that phone voluntarily, any more than she would part with hers.

Some answers must lie with Rosie, but Liz hadn't a clue how to get her to talk. And really, as far as Liz was concerned, the answer to one question could set her mind at rest. Had Philip Latimer accessed his bank account since the day he went missing?

13

*T*he dumb waiter clanked, and Phil moved across to it, eager to see if he would get a hot drink. The flask was standing by the side of the carrier bag and he grabbed at it eagerly. As he turned to place them on his bed, he noticed a tall brown cardboard box at the back of the cupboard.

He reached in and pulled at it, then decided it was too awkward with one hand. He laid his meals on the bed, and returned to the dumb waiter. He heard the clink as it prepared to rise, and he tugged at the box with some speed.

He managed to get it out with seconds to spare, dropping it on to the floor as he did so. He picked it up and carried it across to the bed.

This was such a break in routine he felt quite sick at the thought of opening it. Nothing on the outside gave any clue as to the contents, and he carefully peeled back the Sellotape sealing the end.

He slid out a camping cooker. In the bottom of the box was a smaller box, holding two gas canisters and two boxes of matches.

He stared at it for some while, conflicting emotions raging through him. What the fuck was going on? Why was he being held prisoner? There had never been any communication, not a word spoken, an utterly silent world, for what must surely be months now. Whoever had taken him had played with his mind; exactly the same unpalatable food and drink, day after day after day, and then suddenly, when he had learned gratitude for being kept alive, Captor had changed things.

Captor was upping the odds; making life a little bit more comfortable. And forcing Phil into making a simple decision. Should he use the cooker to warm the room, in view of the absence of any *cooking implements, or should he conserve the gas and hope for maybe a saucepan or a kettle to be sent down.*

Phil felt almost a touch of panic when he realised he didn't know which option to take. He lay on the bed, forcing his breathing to slow; he made the choice to set up the cooker with the gas canisters, light them to check that the cooker was in working order, and then switch it off and await the next-day delivery. It almost felt like a triumph over Captor, reaching a resolution. It was irrelevant whether it was the right decision or not, it was a decision made by him and not the unknown creep somewhere above.

Phil checked in the carrier bag before opening the flask. There was a small saucepan and a tin of soup. Heinz vegetable soup. With a ring-pull opening top. And a spoon. No bowl, but a spoon. He could eat from the saucepan. He felt tears begin to well in his eyes, tears of gratitude for warm food. He checked further, and found the customary two sandwiches and bottles of water.

He checked the flask – tea today. Again, the rush of gratitude. He drank the tea quickly, allowing himself two of the ginger biscuits.

There was no resentment; he had been enraged when he had first surfaced in his new accommodation, but with acceptance had come a change in attitude. Now it was all about survival.

And that depended on Captor.

14

Rosie felt a surge of anger. She had been going through the household accounts, and things were starting to get a little bit tight, financially. Since Melissa's accident and subsequent issues, she hadn't worked. She knew everything would be solved by paying in the huge cheque from Banton and Hardwick, but every day she hoped Phil would return home. They would need that money to finance a move to a different part of the country, somewhere a long way from Liz Chambers.

Rosie sighed, and placed the cheque in her bag. The following day, she would take it to the bank and deposit it into their joint current account, and then decide what to do with it, once it had cleared. If she didn't, she would have Banton and Hardwick, in the form of Liz Chambers, on her back constantly.

Not for the first time, she wondered about Phil's personal account. He would have drawn on it, he normally only carried around fifty pounds in his wallet.

There was a bang on the front door, and she heard her daughter's voice through the letterbox.

'Mummy, it's me!'

'Where?' she responded. 'I can't see you.'

'I'm outside the front door,' Melissa shouted, rattling the letterbox at the same time.

'No, that can't be you. There's a leprechaun outside the front door, not my Melissa!'

'Mummy, it is, it's me!'

Rosie headed for the door. 'Let me check before I let you in. I don't want any leprechauns in my house.'

She carefully opened the door, and Melissa barrelled in, followed more sedately by Rosie's mother.

Rosie hugged Melissa, and whispered '*welcome home*' into her ear.

She lifted her head. 'Thank you for bringing her back, Mum. I was missing her.'

'No problem,' Angela Harmer smiled; the smile clearly aimed at building bridges with her daughter after their telephone argument. 'I think she was ready to come home. It's been lovely having her, thank you. I'm not going to stay, your father wants to go to the theatre, so we're having a meal in town, and then on to the Crucible.'

'Have a lovely evening, Mum.' She escorted her mother down the path, and watched as she drove away, before returning to her daughter, rifling through the fridge to see what was to eat.

'Is Daddy back?'

Rosie was stunned. 'No, not yet.'

'Is he coming back? Nanny Angela doesn't think he is.'

'We'll have to wait and see, won't we? I'm sure he'll come home one day, when he's tired of travelling.'

Melissa turned to her mother. 'Is that what he's doing? Travelling?'

'I think so. He'll be able to tell us all about it when he comes back to us.'

Rosie was aching inside. She hated lying to Melissa, and in that moment, she realised she had also been lying to herself. He wasn't coming back. Had he had another woman apart from Liz Chambers? It seemed strange because there had only been a couple of weeks between him telling her about Liz, and his disappearance. He had clearly loved Liz; surely, he hadn't found someone in two weeks with whom he wanted to spend the rest of his life?

She stifled a sigh and moved on to the subject of food. They agreed on pizza, and Rosie took one out of the freezer.

'Shall we eat off our knees, and watch a movie?'

Melissa nodded enthusiastically. 'Mamma Mia.'

Rosie laughed. 'We've watched that at least ten times.'

'I know,' Melissa responded. 'Good, isn't it?'

She bounced on to the sofa, leaving her mother to sort out food, DVD and drinks. She was glad to be home, even if Daddy hadn't managed it yet.

Halfway through watching Mamma Mia, Rosie heard the distinctive sound from her mobile phone telling her she had an email. She pushed the fleecy blanket covering both of them to one side, and stood to get the phone from the dining table at the far end of the room.

Liz Chambers. Rosie wanted to smash the phone against the wall, and realised quickly that she probably would have done if Melissa hadn't been there.

She opened the email and saw words that had been on her own mind for weeks.

Did you report Phil as a missing person? If you didn't, maybe you should. It seems strange that there has been no contact from him for such a long time. I realise it is none of my business, but has he accessed his bank account since he went missing?

She pressed the home button and made the email disappear. She didn't want Melissa catching sight of it. Moving back to the sofa, Rosie once more snuggled down beside her daughter. She saw nothing else of the film; her mind was on other things. It was all very well Liz saying report Phil's disappearance to the police, but they would think it pretty strange that she had waited all this time before notifying them.

They wouldn't understand that she had a firm belief that he wanted time out from their marriage; she felt deep inside that he would come home, if not for her, then for Melissa.

The closing credits of the film pierced her brain, and she stood. 'Time for bed, sweetheart. Go get ready, and I'll come and tuck you in.'

Melissa looked a little disgruntled, but knew her mother wasn't as easy to manipulate as Nan Angela; she decided not to try.

'Read to me?'

'Not on your life, young lady. You do your own reading now.'

Melissa attempted a frown, and kissed her mother before going upstairs.

'Five minutes,' Rosie called. 'So, don't mess about.'

She carried the plates and leftover pizza through to the kitchen, scraped the food into the bin, and took out a bottle of wine.

She needed it.

15

Liz received no reply from Rosie; she hadn't really imagined that she would. If the roles had been reversed, she would have ignored such an interfering message.

She returned to work on the Tuesday morning with no further contact on either phone from anybody.

Oliver was waiting in her office; the surprise must have shown on her face.

'Did you want me?'

'No, you're fine. I needed to put some paperwork in the pending drawer. And I wanted to check that everything is working out for you. That it's not too much with Jacob being so young.'

'No, I'm fine.' She smiled. 'Jake's childminder is really good with him, so that fact alone stops the worry. Do you want a coffee?'

'Please. Shall I do them? There's only the two of us; Tom had an early court job.'

She laughed. 'He hates anything before eleven, says he doesn't wake up till ten at least. And thank you, I don't take sugar.'

'I know.'

'Oh, sorry, I say it automatically. I forget how long we've known each other.'

'Twelve years,' he said as he turned away to use the coffee machine. 'You came to me, to us, when Daniel was really young.'

She looked at him, sensing a change in the tone of Oliver's voice, but he said nothing further.

She sat down and switched on her computer. While she was waiting, Oliver finished making the coffee and placed hers carefully on her desk.

To her surprise, he touched her shoulder. She savoured the subtle fragrance of Creed as he leaned towards her. 'Enjoy. I need to go through the Farnsworth case with you later. I'll ring when I get to that point. And is the Latimer money sorted now?'

'Yes,' she said, suddenly uncomfortable. This was a different Oliver. She decided to cover herself.

'I organised getting them to sign a form saying they had received the second cheque, because they hadn't paid the first one in quickly enough. I thought it would cover the practice, just in case. I also thought it might make them get it paid in, and close the file off properly. It's ridiculous having that amount of money and not paying it in. I've no idea if it's been deposited yet, but that form explains what's happened. Was that okay?'

'Yes, of course. Good thinking, as always.' He hesitated as he went through to his own office. 'Did they both sign it?'

'No, only Mrs Latimer. Mr Latimer wasn't there.'

He gave a slight nod, then closed the door.

She breathed a sigh of relief. She had been uncomfortable with the cobbled together paperwork; having brought it into the open, she felt much better. It also covered her for the second taxi journey out to the Latimer home. She opened the pending drawer. It was empty.

That rattled her even more, and for a moment she wondered if Oliver and Tom suspected she had been seeing Phil; she couldn't imagine that being the case, really, they had been so careful.

She opened her emails, and went to work.

The morning flew by and she was surprised by the buzz on her phone indicating Tom needed her.

'You're back? I thought it would be a full day.'

'So did I. All done for today. Back there tomorrow, and then it should be over. I'm letting you know I'm here. Any problems?'

'No, the practice doesn't fall apart because you're in court,' she laughed.

'And here's me thinking it did. I might go home then. And you're okay? Coping with being back here?'

She stiffened. What was it with these two men today? Or was it her guilty conscience reading more into their words than she should be doing? 'I'm absolutely fine,' she emphasised.

'Oops, sorry I asked.' Tom's laughter echoed down the phone as he replaced his receiver.

She stared at her own handset, and frowned. *Get a grip, Liz, get a grip.*

She felt relieved as the clock reached 5pm. The tram was reasonably empty, and she read all the way home. Her reading was interrupted by a text from Gareth saying he had collected Jake, and she said a silent thank you in her head; it was bitterly cold, and it meant she would be in the warmth much quicker.

She managed to check the love phone later, but there had been no activity. She didn't know whether that was good or bad, and the pall of worry continued to hang over her, grey and heavy.

16

*C*aptor watched the screen as Phil moved around, a little sluggishly. The amount of sleeping tablets used the previous day had been enough to knock him out for around five hours, and that was sufficient.

Everything could be moved down in the basement room with time to spare. The decision to do all the goods transference on Tuesday was set, and Captor smiled. Everything was going to plan. Liz's punishment would become so much worse.

Phil picked up a sandwich and stared at it. He felt as if he didn't really have the energy to open his mouth and eat it. He was so tired, and yet he knew he had been asleep.

He sipped at some water, hoping it would revive him. It didn't, so he put the sandwich to one side, and went back to sleep.

17

The weekend passed slowly, and Liz knew she was being unfair. She hardly said anything to Gareth, and Daniel simply took himself off to his bedroom and kept out of the way.

They didn't argue, didn't speak. At one point, Gareth decided to go for a walk and didn't return for some time. Liz said bye as he went, but didn't even notice how long he was away. She felt a sense of relief when Monday came around and Gareth went to work, Daniel to school.

She pottered around, did some laundry, ignored some ironing, read her book; when Jake went to bed she took out the love phone.

Where are you? she quickly typed, and pressed send. She didn't expect a reply, simply had a nagging feeling that she couldn't carry on ignoring the fact that Phil was missing.

***

She dropped Jake off and hurried down to catch the tram. He'd been quite fractious since waking at 6am, and she knew Sadie wouldn't have an easy day. She checked her phone diary and saw that Tom and Oliver would be in, but both had to go out before lunch.

Karen greeted her with her usual cheerful smile.

'Good morning, Mrs Chambers. Mr Banton and Mr Hardwick are in, but they have told me they're going out later. Are you in all day?'

'I am.' Liz handed over a £5 note. 'When Sarah does the lunchtime sandwich run, can you ask her to get me a ham sandwich and something nice to follow that's full of calories.'

Karen wrote the instructions on a list.

'And anything that comes through for either of them once they've gone out, put through to me. I can either deal with their problems, or fob them off until tomorrow.'

Karen mouthed *I will,* as she answered a call.

Liz's desk had a small pile of paperwork on it that was new to her. She glanced through the bundle, then took off her coat. It looked as though it was going to be a long and busy day.

She pulled the pile of papers towards her and went through them more carefully. She was surprised to see a conveyancing file with a yellow post-it note attached to the front, asking her to file, no further action required.

She opened it and saw it related to the purchase of a property at Mosborough, in the south east of the city. She was glancing through it when Tom popped his head around her door to say he was going. 'Have we bought a house?'

'Yes,' he replied, gravely. 'It's for Oliver and I to take our mistresses to, when we've wined and dined them.'

'Yeah, right. I'm sure Chloe will let you do that.'

He acknowledged she might be right. 'It's our second practice, or will be when we've had the builders in. They start in April and gut it. Should be up and running by August.'

Liz stared at him. 'You've certainly kept that quiet.'

'It's because there's nothing really to tell anyone yet. We've been wanting to expand for a while, get out into the suburbs, and this house came up. It's old, and the right price. There will be a lot of discussions that are going to involve you, but as yet there's nothing to talk about. All we've done is buy it.'

She nodded, slowly. 'Thank you for sharing that. I'm not really surprised. I thought you'd be bringing in another partner, way before I left to go on maternity leave. I could see the way this business was building. Congratulations, Tom. I'm really quite proud to be part of this.'

'Good, because the plan is for you to be a much bigger part. But that's enough for now. Mum's the word.'

He closed the door and she stared once more at the file, before taking it to the bottom drawer of her filing cabinet. She would leave it in there until everything was up and running, in case it was needed at any point.

Oliver left half an hour later, and she glanced up as he called out to tell her he was going. Once he'd left she leaned her chin on her hands, deep in thought. Her mind was fixated on the strong relationship she had thought Oliver and Julia had shared; what had happened to break it? Another man? Another woman? Julia had been firm in her denial, saying they could no longer live together, simply incompatible.

She pushed the thoughts to one side, and picked up the paperwork that was her own case. She had to file some papers with the court, and she began.

***

Sadie heard the gentle knock on the back door, and a smile lit up her face. She picked up Jake and popped him in the playpen, before going to the door. She opened it, happy at the unusual afternoon visit.

'Come in,' she said quietly. 'This is an unexpected pleasure.' She smiled at him, and he pulled her into his arms.

'It certainly is,' Gareth whispered. 'Where's Jake?'

'In the lounge, in the playpen. He'll be going for his nap in a minute.'

Gareth walked through and picked up his son, giving him a kiss. 'Hi, Jakey. You being a good boy for Sadie?'

The little boy blew a raspberry at his daddy.

'That's not polite, young man,' Gareth said. 'You might have to be put to bed early because of that.'

Sadie laughed. 'He can go anytime now. I suppose you need a nap as well?'

Gareth had one arm holding his son, and one arm holding Sadie. 'Not necessarily a nap, but a little rest on the bed might be good.'

She took Jake from his daddy, laid him on the changing table and quickly replaced his nappy. 'There we are, young man, nice and fresh again.' She lifted him up and kissed him, then headed for the stairs. Gareth followed her.

18

*C*aptor checked the screen in the room above the cellar, and saw that Phil was sleeping, warmly wrapped in the extra blankets. There were bundles of items stored in the room, and Captor knew they had to go down into the cellar quickly.

The opening of the metal door, for the first time in months, caused it to grate loudly. Captor moved quickly back towards the screen and watched Phil with some concern. His form was still inert on the camp bed.

Twenty minutes later, all the packages had been taken downstairs, and Captor had re-locked the door, resuming surveillance, through the screen, of Philip Latimer.

Philanderer.

Father of the bastard child.

With anger threatening to overwhelm, Captor closed the screens and left the building by the back door. Time to move on to part two of this day, time to step up the terror for Liz Chambers.

Phil woke two hours later, aware of how full his bladder felt. He crawled off the camp bed, and rose unsteadily to his feet. He shook his head, and walked across to the toilet. He unzipped his trousers, placed one hand on the wall behind the toilet, and held his penis as the urine flowed rapidly out of him. A flask full of coffee was clearly having an effect on him, he thought with a wry smile.

And then he froze. One hand on the wall, one hand on his penis. No chain attached to his wrist. No struggling to be in the right position to stop his urine splattering on the floor. He looked down at his left wrist, and could clearly see the scar that the cuff had created over the months. Clearly see it, with a brighter light. He glanced up at the light bulb, and then quickly looked away. Much brighter light.

It was only then that he noticed the packages. He pulled up his zip and walked across to the foot of the stairs. Everything was in cardboard boxes.

He opened the first one and saw tins of baby food, nappies, baby wipes, and other assorted items necessary for a baby. Another one contained a travel cot, along with lots of baby bedding. A third one held a few toys, along with some items of clothing, mainly Babygros. Phil stared anxiously around. What the devil was going on? And when had this lot arrived?

He must have been deeply asleep not to have heard any noise from whoever had delivered it all. Which meant he had missed a chance of escape. A chance to find out who Captor was.

He slammed his hand against the wall in anger and frustration. 'Bastard!' he called aloud. 'Fucking bastard!'

There was no response. Captor was long gone, preparing for the next part of the momentous day.

19

They had reached the talking after bit, the calm contentment following the frantic lovemaking. Gareth pulled Sadie a little closer to him, and kissed the top of her head.

'Thank you,' he said.

'No thanks needed,' she responded with a smile. 'You're welcome, sir. I'm surprised you're here.'

'Unexpected afternoon off. I was supposed to be going to Doncaster, but the customer had to change the appointment. It means I can collect Jake.'

'Then we can stay here for a bit longer?' She reached across and switched on the lamp. 'It's really dark. Hopefully no one saw you arrive.'

'So, what if they did? I'm Jake's daddy, here to collect my son. We're good until Jake surfaces. I'll text Liz in a few minutes and tell her I've finished early, so I'll collect Jake.'

'You know, Gareth, this is wrong on so many levels.'

'You want to stop?' Gareth lifted his head and looked at her. His hand moved, seemingly of its own volition, to her breast, and he rotated the palm of his hand on her nipple. She moaned in pleasure.

'Did I say that? I said it was wrong,' she whispered.

He leaned down to kiss her lips, a kiss that deepened until they were oblivious to anything else; oblivious to the sound of the back door opening, the sound of footsteps moving carefully through the house.

Captor searched for the child in the dark. The woman's car was outside, indicating she was in the house somewhere; it would be good if she was having a nap at the same time as the child. A silent child and a silent woman meant she could live.

Gareth and Sadie broke apart, and Sadie smiled at him. 'Just let me go and check on Jake. I'm not sure, but I think I can hear movement from his room.'

He nodded. 'Okay, but let's hope he's not waking yet.'

She slipped out of bed and crossed to the door, shrugging on her dressing gown; she was still trying to sort out the right sleeve, which was hopelessly tangled, when she lifted her head and saw the figure at the top of the stairs.

Captor's arm reached out and pulled her; a quick twist and she began to tumble downstairs, unable to save herself, with one arm still caught up in the sleeve. She screamed and landed at the bottom with an audible crack as her neck broke, then silence.

Gareth threw back the bedclothes, hurtling out of the bedroom. The scream had been unnerving. He saw the figure, covered in black, holding a silver knife; he momentarily hesitated before launching himself at the hooded Captor.

Gareth's hands clutched the hood, and tugged violently.

He stared in shock at the revealed face, and gasped. 'You! What the fuck…?'

The knife moved easily in between Gareth's ribs, with no clothes to slow down its entry, and he slid to the floor.

Captor twisted the knife before removing it, and wiped the blood from the blade on Gareth's naked leg, before side-stepping around his body and moving further along the corridor. Gareth's dying breaths were loud; there were no sounds from the bottom of the stairs.

Sadie's scream had awakened Jake, and Captor headed for the crying baby's room. The expectation had been that Sadie would possibly have to die, but seeing Gareth had been a shock. Further punishment for Mrs high and mighty Liz Chambers.

Jake was soon strapped into the pushchair that was waiting in the hallway for his departure for home, and Captor wheeled it across Sadie's head to get it over her. Nobody saw the pram's journey as it left Sadie's house, went down the hill and across the tram tracks, to where Captor's car was waiting.

The pram was difficult to close, and Captor finally threw it into the spacious car boot, still unfolded. Within two minutes, the car and driver, along with the baby in a car seat, had disappeared.

It would soon transpire that nobody had seen anything; two people had died, a child was taken, and in the affluent area, nobody took any notice of what was happening in the surrounding neighbourhood.

***

Liz managed to get a seat as the tram carried her homewards. She felt tired; there had been several queries involving cases assigned to the two temporarily absent partners, and she had dealt with them. The worry of the missing Phil was never far from her thoughts, and staring out of the tram window didn't help. All she could see was blackness and her own reflection.

Her headache was worsening, and she leaned her head against the coolness of the glass. Images of Phil flitted through her mind; she had spent eighteen months keeping her memories at bay, and they all came flooding back, bringing with them untold worries. Where was he? Was he even alive? And why the hell didn't Rosie appear to care?

What was worse, Liz couldn't even talk to Rosie about it. She was Phil's wife, for God's sake. Liz couldn't go up to the woman and say where's your husband, because I love him and I need to know if he is still alive.

Liz got off the tram and began the walk up the hill towards Sadie's home. She checked her phone – still no reply to the text she had sent Sadie, telling her she was only ten minutes away, but she guessed she was maybe too busy with Jake to be able to respond.

The house was in darkness, and Liz rang the front door bell. When there was no activity, she rang again, and then knelt to speak through the letterbox.

'Sadie, it's me,' she called, then placed her eye to the aperture.

Sadie was clearly visible, her head on the hall floor with the purple hair spread out like a halo. Her legs were splayed on the stairs, and she was naked except for a dressing gown, half on and half off her.

For a moment, Liz was immobile. She shook her head and looked around her for help. There was nobody. She tried pushing on the front door, but it was locked. Sprinting around the side of the house to try the back entrance, she saw it was wide open.

She was stepping through the entrance when her 999 call was answered. She was almost in tears as she was trying to explain the circumstances in front of her – it was clear Sadie was dead. The operator asked her to go outside, just in case; Liz didn't even think about the term "just in case"; she merely said she had to find her son, Sadie was her childminder, and her baby must still be upstairs having his nap. The frantic panic in her voice left the operator in no doubt as to Liz's priorities.

'Then please stay on the line, Liz. Do not put your phone down, and let me know as soon as you have your baby. Help is on the way, please stay at the property until the police arrive. Are you sure the lady is deceased? If there is any chance…'

'She's dead,' Liz sobbed. 'I'm going to find Jake. I can do nothing for Sadie.' Liz was breathing heavily as she skirted Sadie's body and carefully climbed the stairs. There was a small amount of light casting a glow on to the landing, coming from Sadie's own bedroom at the back of the house.

Liz's eye-level moved past the top tread and she saw the blood and a second body. She stepped upwards and a black mist surrounded her. 'Gareth,' she whispered, and slid down the wall.

20

*C*aptor switched on the garage light, then pressed the remote control to lower the door. The baby was waking, and Captor lifted him out of the car, still in his baby seat.

Jake's eyes moved around, as if searching for a familiar face, but he made no sound as the car seat was placed in the dumb waiter.

Phil heard the rattle of the dumb waiter chains as it was lowered.

He felt perplexed. His food had arrived some hours earlier, so what was being lowered now? He hoped it was a hot drink, then smiled to himself as his brain added the words, 'preferably with a tot of whisky in it'.

He stood slowly, and rubbed his legs to get some feeling into them, before crossing to the little cupboard.

Jake cried, stopping Phil abruptly. A radio? Could Captor be sending a radio down?

He reached the cupboard in two easy strides; if it was a radio, he didn't want it disappearing before he could remove it. The cupboard hit the base with a thud, and Phil smiled. Something heavy was in it. He grasped the handle, and opened the door.

Two things happened simultaneously. Jake lifted his arms to his daddy for the first time, and Phil heard spoken words.

'His name is Jake.'

It was Darth Vader echoing down the chimney-like structure of the dumb waiter housing. Phil remembered the helmet that Melissa had loved, until she had grown tired of it, the one where she could speak in her soft, silvery voice and it would come out as Darth Vader. Did Rosie really think he wouldn't remember the toy?

He lifted out the car seat and risked putting his head in the cupboard.

'Rosie? What the fuck are you doing? Get me out of here!'

The chains clanked, and he swiftly moved his head away from danger. He stepped back and stumbled against the car seat. Jake resumed crying, and Phil bent down to soothe him.

'Hey, little man – that's enough of that. Let's get you out and warmed up.'

The baby was dressed in a long sleeved top and dungarees, so Phil wrapped him in one of the baby blankets that had arrived earlier. He couldn't believe his naiveté. He had assumed Captor had needed to use the cellar for storage, and instead of going through all the boxes he had merely stacked them out of the way – a task that brought something different into his blighted life. Now he saw the truth behind the acquisition of the supplies.

He had no doubt that this baby was his son. He held him close and gradually Jake's sobs subsided. He placed him back in the car seat and went to look further into the boxes. The travelling cot took no time to set up, once he had worked out the complex instructions, and he put as much warmth under the thin mattress as he could; he knew from experience how the cold permeated upwards from the stone cellar floor.

Despite holding the precious child in his arms once again, he felt an anger so intense it was scary. It had to be Rosie holding him there; he knew she had been upset when he had confessed the darkness surrounding him was because he had lost Liz, and that Liz was pregnant with his child, but this was taking Rosie's grief at the news to the extreme. Both he and his son could die in here.

He checked out the box that revealed pouches of baby food. He unscrewed a somewhat dubious-sounding cauliflower, rice and broccoli, and handed it to Jake. He hoped this was the right thing to do. Melissa had enjoyed food out of jars, not pouches.

Jake grabbed at it, and the pouch full of food was soon empty. He tended to eat his own meagre rations when he felt quite hungry, but would that be the way it worked with a baby? He had no way of knowing what time it was, even if day or night. He guessed he and Jake had a learning curve to come.

It was a new experience to him; the first time he changed the little boy's nappy. It was only wet, and he breathed a sigh of relief. He put him in a Babygro, and added a jumper. Keeping him warm was imperative.

They played for a while, with Phil desperately trying to stop his brain from wandering to unanswered questions. This little boy had been taken from his normal environment and dumped with someone he didn't know. It was Phil's priority to rectify that. He could let his mind wander when Jake was asleep.

The little boy's body finally decided enough was enough, and Phil lifted him gently into the travel cot, covering him with layers of blankets. He had placed the cot by the side of his own camp bed; he wanted to be nearby if Jake woke during the night. If indeed it was night…

He watched him sleeping for a few minutes, and inevitably his mind questioned why this had happened. With the arrival of Jake, it pointed to Liz being the person targeted, rather than him.

She must be frantic, his brain was saying, out of her mind. If she had realised he was missing – and he knew there was no guarantee of that – she would be devastated. Their love had been strong, strong enough for him to believe it was still as strong in her, as it was in him.

But losing Jake was another level altogether. This would destroy her.

But… why? Why would anyone hate Liz enough to do this to her? Could it really be Rosie? Despite what he had seen as proof with the Darth Vader voice, it didn't really mean anything. There were probably thousands of the helmets out there, and still freely available. And really… Rosie? Knowing his wife as well as he did, deep down he knew it couldn't be her.

For a start, there was Melissa. Committing a criminal act of this magnitude would always end up with a prison sentence, and he was a hundred per cent sure that Rosie wouldn't risk being locked away from Melissa.

Phil settled himself down for the night and for a few moments allowed a little bit of normality into his life. He watched as Jake slept; his son, sleeping by his side. Under any other circumstances...

21

'Mrs Chambers? Liz? Can you hear me?' Somewhere deep in the back of her brain, Liz could hear the voice. Slowly, so slowly, she emerged from the faint, and groaned.

'Okay, Liz. Don't try and sit up yet. Do you hurt anywhere?'

Liz shook her head, and lifted her hand. It was covered in blood. She groaned once again, wondering what had happened; and her mind cleared.

She spun her head around and gasped. 'Gareth…'

'You know this man?'

She nodded, unable to comprehend what was happening. 'Yes, he's my husband. But…'

'Mrs Chambers, we need to move you. Can you stand?'

Again, she nodded, not sure what to say. The two paramedics helped her upright, and her eyes rested on Gareth.

'Is he…?'

'I'm afraid so,' the tall, male paramedic said. 'Let's get you over here.'

They helped her into the bedroom kept ready should Christian, Sadie's son, need to stay for a couple of nights. She sat on the chair in front of the desk, and her head dropped.

'What's going on,' she whispered, her head reeling with the pain of finding Gareth. 'Where's Jake? Where's my son? Is he okay?' The panic was clear in her voice.

'Your son?'

'Yes, Sadie's my son's childminder.' Liz stood to move out of the door, terror written across her features. The female paramedic stopped her.

'Please wait here, Liz.'

Liz looked up as a policeman came through the door. 'Mrs Chambers? I'm DI Brent. Are you okay to talk?'

Liz nodded. 'Please, get Jake for me first.'

'Jake?'

'My baby. He'll be in the room across from this. In the cot.'

DI Brent looked at the two paramedics, and they shook their heads. 'Mrs Chambers, there's no baby in the house. Bear with me a moment.' He left the room and she heard him speak to someone on the landing.

She tried to stand, to go and look for Jake herself, but was restrained by the paramedics, who pushed her none too gently back on to the seat.

He re-entered, and knelt in front of her. She was shaking uncontrollably, unable to believe what she was seeing on their faces. 'I've asked one of the men to go outside and check the shed and greenhouse, but there's definitely no baby in this house.'

She clutched at his hand. 'Please… he's only eleven months. Please find him. You've got to–' She was frantic, her eyes darting around the people in front of her.

'We will, Liz. I need a description of what he was wearing.' He took out his notebook and wrote down everything Liz told him. 'And did you bring him in a pushchair?'

'I did. It's a Mothercare one. My phone… there's a photograph of him in his pushchair. I don't know where my phone is…' and she wept, unable to conceive fully the horror that had overtaken her.

'Wait.' Sandra, the female paramedic, went out of the door and came back in carrying the phone. 'You talked on it till you reached the top of the stairs, and then you fainted.'

Liz looked at it in shock.

'It's okay, Liz,' Sandra said quietly. 'It didn't fall near any blood, and it's not broken.'

Liz took the phone and scrolled through her pictures with trembling fingers. She handed the phone over to DI Brent. 'That's the best one. If that pushchair isn't in the hall, he will be in it.'

DI Brent left the room once more, holding on to the phone. Within five minutes he was back.

'Mrs Chambers, I need to take you downstairs now. We can let our scene of crime officers do their work. Screens are up, but there isn't much room to squeeze by at the bottom of the stairs. I'll help you.'

Liz looked frantically around the tidy bedroom, as if she didn't want to leave its security. He held out his hand. 'Come on. It will be better for you. My constable is making you a cup of tea, and we can have a chat.'

She felt numb. She knew she would have to bypass two bodies to get downstairs, and… she heard her phone ring. It was still held in the policeman's hand, and she held out her own hand to take it back. He glanced at the screen and said 'Dan.'

'Shit,' she muttered through clenched teeth. 'Dan.' She took the proffered phone. 'It's my other son.' She pressed answer.

'Dan?'

'Mum, you're both late!'

'I know, sweetheart. I'm up at Sadie's. Can I ring you back in a bit? Won't be long.'

'Okay.' She could sense the grumble in his tone. 'I'll keep tea warm, then.'

'Thank you. See you in a bit.'

She went to hand the phone back to Brent, but he shook his head. 'I would normally take it from you, but we seem to have a missing child. Whoever has him may try to get in touch with you.'

She felt sick at the words *missing child*. She moved towards Brent and he held open the door. 'Keep to the right all the way down, and you'll be fine.'

She moaned and stifled a sob as she was faced with a large white screen hiding her husband's body from her; she went carefully down, passing what she knew to be Sadie's body, lying awkwardly at the bottom of the stairs, and hidden from her view by another screen.

They moved into the lounge, and, as promised, a cup of tea awaited her. She didn't want it, but DI Brent handed it to her. 'Drink.'

She sipped at the scalding drink, and waited for him to speak.

'Tell me what you know,' he said.

She took a deep breath. 'I left work at five, caught the tram around 5.10pm. I texted Sadie about 5.25pm to let her know I was ten minutes away – I do that so that she has him ready to go, as soon as I arrive – and reached here about 5.35pm, give or take a couple of minutes. I always collect him via the front door because it's the easiest way for getting the pushchair in and out, but there was no answer, and it all seemed to be in darkness. I shouted through the letterbox, and then looked through it. I saw Sadie, lying at the bottom of the stairs, not moving.' She paused for a moment, reliving the scene.

'I ran around to the back door, hoping it was open. It was. Not unlocked, I mean it was wide open. I was ringing 999 as I went through the door, and by the time I reached Sadie, I was connected to your switchboard.'

Again, she paused. DI Brent waited patiently for her to continue. Her whole body was shaking, and he was concerned he would have to ask a paramedic to take a look at her.

'I could see Sadie was dead. The lady on the phone wanted me to stay with her, try CPR I think, but Sadie was obviously beyond that. I told the operator I was going upstairs to get Jake, and she said to stay on the line. As I went up the stairs, I could see a soft light on the landing, as if it was coming from a bedroom. Then I saw the second body, and lots of blood. I recognised Gareth, and the next person I saw was a paramedic.'

'Did you know Gareth would be here?'

She shook her head. 'No, I didn't. If he finishes early, he texts me to tell me he'll collect Jake. I didn't receive any text. Didn't even receive a reply from Sadie when I messaged her to give her the ten-minute warning. She always responds with 'okay'. DI Brent, Gareth was naked, and Sadie had little covering her. Do you think they had been in bed in that bedroom with the light on?'

'I don't make assumptions, Liz.' He spoke quietly. 'We will be taking in the bedding for testing, and we'll know more then. We'll also be testing the cot bedding; hopefully, whoever has Jacob will have left something of themselves behind.'

'It's just…' and this time she did break down, sobbing uncontrollably. 'It's just,' she spluttered, 'I have to go home, and tell Dan what has happened.'

'How old is Dan?'

'Nearly sixteen.'

'Then tell him the truth. He's old enough to jump to his own conclusions. Make sure he knows the truth, whatever comes out in this investigation.'

'When can I go home?'

'As soon as you feel ready. We'll obviously have to speak more, but for now we need forensics. I'll get somebody to take you home. It's not going to be an easy night, so your family liaison officer will go with you. She'll be here within the next ten minutes. Keep thinking, Liz, in case there's anything that you've missed. Our priority is Jake. We already have officers going door to door, checking on CCTV systems. Your FLO is Tanya Baxter, she'll look after you.'

'Have you come across my handbag? I seem to remember throwing it behind me as I climbed around Sadie.'

'Is it a black plastic one?' The young police officer standing by the door asked, and Liz glanced at him.

'It's a Moschino. Plastic?'

He picked it up from the floor and handed it over, a sheepish expression on his face. She thanked him, and reached inside for a packet of tissues. She blew her nose, then looked up as someone new entered the room.

DI Brent stood. 'Liz, this is your family liaison officer, Tanya Baxter. She'll certainly stay all night and tomorrow, so if you can provide her with a sofa and a sleeping bag, it will help.'

Liz nodded. 'Thank you. We have a guest bedroom you can use, Tanya.' She turned towards Will Brent. 'Thank you. Have you…?'

'No, we haven't heard anything yet. The second we do, I'll inform you. Go home and leave us to do our jobs now, Liz, and take care of your son.'

Liz followed Tanya out of the door, her legs shaking, her heart crying out for Jake.

22

Dan was standing in the bay window, no lights on in the lounge, as he stared out waiting for a parent, any parent, to appear. He saw a car pull up outside, but didn't recognise it. What he did recognise was his mother getting out of the passenger door.

He drew the curtains closed, switched on a lamp, and went to open the front door.

'Mum?'

She stepped inside, and pulled him into her arms. He held her, aware she needed some comfort, and then saw another woman follow her in, and stand waiting patiently for the two of them to move.

He released his hold, and stepped back. 'Mum?' he repeated.

'Dan, come into the lounge. I need to talk to you. This lady is Tanya, she's going to be staying for a day, or maybe two.'

The three of them went into the lounge, and Tanya took off her coat. 'I'll leave you two to talk, but please call me if you need me. I'll find the kitchen and make us a pot of tea.'

Dan sat. He felt sick. Something was wrong, and where the hell was Jake? Hadn't his mum said she was at Sadie's when he rang?

'Where's Jake,' he asked, suddenly sure that this was the problem. 'Is he poorly? Mum... where is he?'

Liz looked down at her hands. She could hear Tanya in the kitchen and hoped it would take a long time to make the tea. This wasn't something she could tell Dan in a few seconds.

She took hold of her elder son's hands and pulled him towards her. 'I don't know where Jake is. Someone's taken him. I don't know why, and I don't know where.'

'Maybe Dad has him…'

'No, he doesn't, sweetheart. I have more to tell you.' She hesitated, unsure where to start. She took a deep breath. 'I went to collect Jake, as normal, from Sadie. When I got there, I could see through the letterbox that she was lying at the bottom of the stairs. I rang for an ambulance and went in the house through the back door. It was obvious Sadie was dead, and I assumed she had fallen down the stairs. As you can imagine, I panicked. I went up the stairs to find Jake, because I didn't know how long he'd been on his own, and as I reached the top of the stairs I saw a second body.'

She watched as the colour drained from her son's face.

'It was Dad, wasn't it?'

'I'm so sorry, Dan, yes it was.'

His face contorted with the struggle to be a man and not cry; he lost the battle.

Tears leaked from his eyes, and he moaned, 'No, no, no. Not Dad.'

Liz pulled Dan close and held him while the grief overwhelmed him. He slowly quietened, and then she sensed a change in him.

'I knew,' he said bitterly. 'I knew he was going up there too often. Is this her fault? Has she killed him, that Sadie?'

Liz stared at Dan, trying to control the shock she felt must be showing on her face. 'What do you mean?'

'I've seen him up there a couple of times. I've seen the car, anyway.'

'But he sometimes collects Jake…'

'At three in the afternoon? And that was the time I spotted the car; I don't know how long it had been there. I asked you the other day if everything was okay…'

'You did, but I thought you meant we didn't seem to talk as much as usual. I didn't know… why didn't you tell me?'

'Mum, are you kidding me? How could I tell you I thought Dad was playing away?' Dan scrunched up his hands and rubbed at his face.

'He's not now,' she said quietly. 'I saw his body, and I fainted. Luckily the ambulance was already on its way. Tanya is our family liaison officer, our go-between for information. Jake wasn't there. There's a massive hunt going on right now, they're checking CCTV all over the place. We have to get our little one back safely, because the alternative isn't to be considered, not ever.' Liz could feel herself getting angry, and the tears began to roll down her face once more. She looked up as Tanya entered the room.

'Thank you,' Liz said. 'Is there any news?'

Tanya shook her head. 'Not yet. I'll let you know if anything happens during the night. Dan, it's good to meet you, even if it's in such awful circumstances. Your mum has explained everything?'

He looked at Tanya for a moment. 'Nothing makes sense. Why would he want her? Sadie? She was nothing compared with Mum. And maybe if I'd told her that I'd seen him up there, it could have stopped all of this.'

'Whoa!' Liz tried to speak calmly. 'Stop that. None of this is your fault, Dan. It's all down to your dad and Sadie, and whoever has Jake. I have no idea why anyone would want to hurt me so much…' Her voice trailed away.

One person wanted to hurt her. Rosie Latimer. And Liz knew that everything would have to come out in the open, because she would have to tell DI Brent of her affair with Phil. And that meant even further heartbreak for Dan; what sort of role models were they for a fifteen-year-old boy?

Would a direct appeal to Rosie help? If she rang her… but not on her usual phone. She didn't want the police checking for phone calls made since the discovery of the bodies. For the first time, she would use the love phone to ring someone other than Phil. If she blocked the number first… Liz felt her head expanding as she tried to work out the best course of action. She would have made a lousy criminal, it was all too complicated, working out a campaign.

Tanya poured out the drinks and handed them to Dan and Liz. There was silence between them, each lost in their own thoughts. Liz felt she couldn't grieve for Gareth, not yet. She had to come to terms with what she was discovering about him. Had she driven him into Sadie's arms? She thought back to the beginning of her affair with Phil – that had been instant attraction, but had matured into so much more. Was that how Gareth had felt about Sadie? Would she have lost him anyway? So many questions. She reached into her handbag and took out a packet of paracetamol. Popping two out of the blister strip, Liz swallowed them, washing them down with the dregs of the tea.

She stood and walked to the bay window, opening the curtains slightly and staring out into the blackness of the night; it mirrored how she was feeling. Where was her baby? Was he crying for her? Was he cold, hungry? She watched as two police cars drove by, before turning up the road where Sadie lived. She wondered if Christian was already on his way back to Sheffield, having been made aware of his mother's death. He was only twenty, studying at Solent University; so young to have to handle something like this. Liz leaned her head against the window pane and sighed.

Dan came up quietly behind her. His voice sounded thick, heavy with raw emotion. 'It was probably a fling, you know. I'm sure Dad loved you…'

'He's certainly paid the price.' She sobbed, and wrapped her arms around her body, seeking any form of comfort.

Tanya stood and led her gently back to the sofa. 'I'm not going to suggest you go to bed, I know you won't sleep, but why not get comfortable on here,' she indicated the sofa, 'and close your eyes. If there's any news, I'll wake you. Oh, and there'll be a technician here any time now. He's going to set up a recording box on your landline, in case whoever has taken Jake decides to ring you. When you go out you need to press a button on it and all calls will be routed to your mobile number. It will record everything, that way.'

'Dan, can you take Tanya up and show her where the spare room is, please? When this chap arrives, I'll let him in.'

Dan nodded. 'And I'll bring a blanket and a pillow down for you. If you insist on sleeping here, you need to be comfortable.'

'Have you eaten, Liz?' Tanya looked concerned by Liz's pallor.

'Mum? I can soon make us something?'

'Dan, take off the chef hat. I don't want anything, I feel sick. You two have whatever you fancy, leave me out of it.'

Dan held the door open and escorted Tanya upstairs and along the corridor to the room in the new extension. Jake's arrival had meant all bedrooms were in use, and they had added a much-needed extension to the property.

Liz realised she wouldn't get a better opportunity to be on her own, and unzipped the pocket in her handbag that held the Nokia. She quickly removed the instruction to show her number, and dialled Rosie's landline.

The call went through to voicemail, and Liz spoke quietly. 'Rosie, if you're there, it's Liz. Please pick up, I need to talk to you. It's urgent. If you get this later, please call me on my landline. It's still the same number. Thank you.'

Within a minute her call was returned.

'Liz?'

'Rosie, thank God. Where's Jake?' As she asked the question, she knew she was being incredibly stupid. If Rosie had her baby, she was hardly likely to admit it.

'What?'

'Jake. He's been taken from my childminder's. Please, Rosie, I'm desperate. If you know anything… imagine if it were Melissa, think how you would feel.'

Rosie spoke slowly. 'Liz, I won't deny I hate the very thought of you, wish we'd never used Banton and Hardwick, but for God's sake, woman! I would hurt **you**, not your baby. Of course I don't know where he is.'

Liz couldn't hold back the sob. 'Oh, God,' she whispered.

'Is this the police incident that's been on Radio Sheffield? It mentioned Gleadless. I don't like you, Liz, don't want anything to do with the homewrecker who destroyed my own life, but I wouldn't wish this on you.'

'Rosie,' again the sob caught in her throat, 'the police incident is a double murder, and a kidnapping. My childminder and my husband are dead, and Jake's been taken.'

There was silence from the other end of the phone for a few seconds; Liz heard a huge sigh and then Rosie spoke. 'Liz... I don't know what to say. I had no idea. I'm so sorry, but I promise you, this isn't the way I would hurt you. I tried to do it through your job...'

'I know. Deep down I knew you wouldn't have done this. I'm clutching at straws because I don't know where to turn. I have to go.' She lowered her voice. 'The police are here. I have to go.'

Liz put down the receiver, then slipped the Nokia back into her handbag pocket. She opened the front door and the police technician walked through carrying a couple of boxes. He worked immediately, and Liz left him to it.

Seconds later, Dan and Tanya walked into the lounge. Dan was carrying a pillow and a couple of blankets. 'You sure about this?' he asked.

'I am. I can't see me sleeping much, and I can get up and make a cup of tea whenever I want. Tanya, is the room okay for you?'

Tanya smiled. 'I spend half my time sleeping in armchairs when I'm working as FLO. Having a room is a real luxury, and yours is beautiful. My phone's set to loud, so if there are developments during the night, I will come and wake you.'

'Thank you. I feel so empty. I honestly had no idea about Gareth and Sadie...'

'And you still don't know for definite, Liz. Whoever murdered Gareth could have removed his clothes. Sadie could have been taking advantage of Jake sleeping to grab a quick shower – nothing is certain yet, so don't jump to conclusions. Now, I know you're going to say no, but I think Dan should make you a couple of slices of toast, whether you want them or not. You're going to need lots of strength over the next few days, don't neglect your health.' She turned to Dan. He nodded and headed towards the kitchen.

Tanya sat down beside Liz. 'Did he take it okay?'

'So so. He'd already seen our car up at Sadie's in the past, and he knows I never take it to work, it's too much hassle getting parked. Oh my God, work!'

'Sssh,' Tanya said. 'Don't worry. We can sort that tomorrow morning.'

Liz's brain went into overdrive. She tried to remember what was urgent, and wondered if she should ring Tom or Oliver immediately, rather than waiting for the morning.

Finally, she took the decision to leave it; one or other of them would shoot across the city to come and support her, and she didn't want that. She needed to be able to sit and wait for news of her baby.

Dan arrived with the toast, and she ate a slice without tasting it. She pushed the other slice to one side, and once more moved across to the window. There was a lot of police activity, but she guessed that would taper off in a couple of hours. She prayed they would have garnered some clues from the door-to-door checks, and she leaned her head against the pane to cancel the reflection that was stopping her seeing outside. Nothing helped.

The technician called her into the hall and showed her what to do if she had a call from a number she didn't recognise, and how to switch the landline number through to her mobile. He explained carefully, and he explained it twice. 'If it is the kidnapper,' he said gently, 'you press this switch, and someone will be listening in. If it is simply a friend, then we don't intrude. Good luck with getting your little one home safe, Mrs Chambers.' He squeezed her hand as he left.

Her eyes filled with tears, and she offered up a small prayer for her baby. He was so little, so cute, such a good little boy – '*please God, keep him safe for me,*' she whispered, almost to herself.

Dan came and stood by her side and put his arm around her shoulders. 'Amen,' he said, 'amen.'

***

She didn't sleep. The sofa was comfortable, she was warm, but she couldn't switch off her mind. She went to the kitchen three times during that long night, making drinks that she hoped would make her eyes close. Nothing worked.

Tanya was downstairs before six. 'No news.' The regretful tone in her voice was obvious. 'Is there anything I can do for you?'

Liz sighed. 'Thanks, but I don't think so. I'll ring work after nine and explain what's happened, and I'll ring Dan's school. I'm reluctant to keep him off, because he's in his GCSE year, but he'll want to be with me.'

'DI Brent will probably want to speak with both of you, anyway, so really Dan has to stay home today. And I can't imagine for one minute he's going to go back to school in the short term; I've seen how close you two are, and he'll consider he has to support you at home. Don't knock it, Liz. He's a bright young man, he'll be fine in his exams. And he needs to grieve for his father. These are horrendous circumstances surrounding your husband's death, and eventually that reality is going to hit Daniel really hard. And you. At the moment, you need to be together.'

Half an hour later, Will Brent arrived. Liz gave her statement, confirming everything she had already told him. He spoke platitudes; they were re-doubling their efforts with the advance of daylight, and he would prefer it if she stayed in the house and had her phone with her at all times.

Dan also confirmed his whereabouts for the afternoon of the previous day; he looked dreadful, dark circles under his eyes and a set to his lips that Liz had never seen before. He had clearly had a bad night, and she ached for him.

Just after nine, Liz rang Karen and asked if either Mr Banton or Mr Hardwick had arrived. Karen confirmed she had seen Mr Hardwick, and she connected Liz with Oliver.

'Good morning, Liz,' he said.

'Morning, Oliver. I'm sorry, I won't be in today.'

'Are you ill?' There was concern in his voice.

'No. I have a problem.' She could feel her voice wobbling. 'Something happened yesterday. Gareth and my childminder, Sadie, were murdered. And Jake was taken.'

There was silence for a moment.

'What?'

She repeated what she'd said, and he let out a long breath. 'I'll be with you in half an hour. I'll give Tom a ring, although he may turn up there as well.'

'Thank you,' she said softly, and disconnected the call.

23

Jake was standing in his cot, staring at his father, when Phil stirred; his head felt strange, fuzzy, and he blinked, then remembered the events of the previous day. Or was it the previous hour?

He smiled at the little boy. 'Good morning, son. Is it morning?'

Jake simply stared at him.

Phil sat up and pulled a blanket around his shoulders. It was cold, so cold. He lifted the little boy out of his cot, sat him on his knee and enfolded him in the blanket.

'You hungry?' he asked, and kissed the top of his head. Jake laid his head against Phil's shoulder, and didn't move.

'Okay, what shall we have? Full English? I might have to rummage through all that baby food for yours though. In fact, Jake, today we're going to go through all these boxes, find out what we've got.'

His heart ached for his son. He must be missing his mummy, and wondering what had happened. Phil cuddled him for a few more minutes, then sat him back in the travel cot.

'Breakfast,' he said. 'Give me two minutes.'

He found a pouch that said it was ready-to-eat porridge, so he handed it to Jake and watched to make sure he ate it. Phil then looked much more carefully through the boxes and discovered cartons of long life milk. He hoped it was okay for Jake – he couldn't for the life of him remember the whole baby milk/cow's milk cut off with Melissa – and he poured some into a bottle, then out of the bottle and into his little pan. He quickly warmed it, and as Jake finished his porridge, Phil handed him a bottle of milk.

'Cracked it,' Phil said, as he watched Jake drain the bottle, before struggling and pulling himself into an upright position. He launched the bottle across the floor.

Phil chuckled at his son, then picked it up and placed it in the small sink. As with the milk issue, he really couldn't remember much about sterilising either, and hoped that washing thoroughly would be enough.

He changed Jake's nappy – still only a wet one – then re-dressed him in the clothes from the previous day.

His search through the boxes had thrown up a few toys and some baby books, so Phil and Jake sat on the camp bed, and Phil read to him. Jake kept trying to put his fingers in his daddy's mouth as he spoke the words, and Phil felt such a pang of longing for Liz, it almost overwhelmed him. This was their child. This wonderful human being had been created by them, and was being held captive presumably because of them.

He prayed Liz was safe; Phil had no way of knowing, and he made a silent vow to her that he would keep their son safe for as long as he could.

The dumb waiter rattled, and he quickly put Jake back into his cot. Phil opened the door and removed his rations for the day, glancing into the carrier bag and seeing nothing out of the ordinary, except for three tea bags. It seemed the flasks were off the menu, he was expected to make his own drinks.

'I like coffee as well, moron,' he growled. He decided to have his drinks without milk – he wasn't sure if they would ever get any more of the long-life stuff, and Jake would need it.

Jake finally dropped off to sleep, so Phil tucked him up in the cot, then moved across to sort out the boxes. Everything in them related to Jake: baby food, clothing, nappies, toys – all there for him, so Phil organised it all, re-stacking the boxes to try and get them off the floor. He placed a layer of carrier bags beneath the bottom ones, and hoped it was enough to protect the contents from the damp.

He then moved up the stairs. His head was finally feeling clearer, and it was slowly dawning on him that the flasks hadn't contained *only tea, there had been some additive that had made him sleep. It seemed that wasn't necessary, hence the cooking stove and the tea bags.*

He reached the top of the stairs, but the door was in shadow. He felt around it but there was nothing. No handle, no lock, no screws, a metal door that he couldn't exit from his side.

He sat down on the stairs, and his head dropped. He didn't know what the hell to do, couldn't see any way out of the situation. And it had become so much more complicated, with the addition of Jake.

'I'll keep him safe for you, Liz, I promise,' he whispered softly. 'I promise.'

***

Captor watched the activity in the basement and smiled. Phil Latimer really knew what he was up against – a door that couldn't be opened, with no other exit from the room, and he had the added problem of the boy to care for, a child he had never met before.

Just how much was Liz Chambers suffering? Her lover had disappeared from the face of the earth, her adulterous husband was dead, and her son had been taken.

Karma.

24

Oliver arrived, followed a minute later by a dishevelled-looking Tom, dressed in joggers and hoodie. Liz couldn't take her eyes off him; she had never seen him in anything but a suit.

'Sorry,' he said as he bent to kiss her cheek. 'I came out as soon as Chloe told me what had happened. I was running...' he finished lamely, indicating the state of his attire.

'I'll make drinks,' Tanya said. 'Coffee, tea?'

They placed their orders, and Liz led them through to the lounge. Dan stood and looked at the two visitors. His eyes showed he had been crying, and Oliver held out his hand. Dan shook it, then turned and shook Tom's hand.

'I'm so sorry, Dan,' Oliver said. 'If you need anything, you and your mum, we're here.'

Tom nodded his agreement. He turned to Liz. 'Is there anything you need, Liz?'

'I need the police to walk through that door and tell me they have Jake. Everything else I can handle.'

Tom put his arms around her and pulled her to him. 'No news, then?' he asked, his voice muffled as he spoke into the top of her head. He felt the sob that seemed to encompass her whole body.

'Nothing. CCTV has caught nothing that's of any help, nobody saw anything. My baby simply disappeared.'

He held her for a moment longer, and then steered her to the sofa. 'Sit down, Liz, and let's talk.'

Tanya brought the drinks through, and for a moment no one spoke. Then everybody seemed to speak at once.

'How…?'

'What…?'

'I…'

Oliver held up his hand. 'Whoa. Let's start again. Is there anything that you need right now? Do you need anything legal?'

'No,' she said. 'I don't think there is. I won't be in work for some time, obviously, but–'

Tom interrupted. 'You take whatever time you need. That shouldn't even have come into the discussion. Can you tell us what happened? Will you be comfortable with that?'

Liz nodded. 'I can tell you everything I know, but it's not a lot.' She talked, covering everything from her leaving work to arriving back home with Tanya. The two men listened in silence, waiting until she had finished.

'Did you know Gareth had been seeing Sadie?' Oliver asked.

'No, I didn't. And apparently, I'm not to jump to conclusions about that – DI Brent said, until the forensics come back on the bedding from the bedroom, and the cot bedding, there is no proof they had been in there. He seemed to infer that maybe the murderer took his clothes, possibly because something of him, or her, had transferred to Gareth's clothes. But Sadie was all but naked, except for her dressing gown, and he didn't take her clothes, then put a dressing gown on her. And I'm sorry I keep saying he, because I'm by no means convinced the murderer is a man. It could as easily be a woman – possibly more so, as my baby has been taken.'

'You think maybe Jake was the target? That Sadie and Gareth were in the wrong place at the wrong time?' Tom spoke quietly, mulling over the possibility.

'I do, and I think that's what was in DI Brent's head when he told me not to assume.'

Oliver joined in the conversation. 'Did they find Gareth's clothes?'

Liz looked startled. 'I don't know. Would they have told me if I'd asked? They seemed pretty keen to get me out of that house, so they could carry on with processing the crime scene.'

'I don't think they'll tell you much until they're convinced you didn't murder your husband and his bit on the side in a fit of jealous rage. When they have time of death, that will clear you. You didn't leave work until five, did you?'

'A little bit after. And I rang the police around 5.40, so it didn't leave me much time to stab them and spirit away my son, did it?' They could both hear the bitterness and anger in her tone.

'I can't listen to this, Mum.' Dan stood, and walked towards the lounge door, his shoulders hunched. 'If you need me, give me a shout. I'll be in my room.'

'Dan!' Liz moved to go to him, and Oliver held her arm.

'Leave him be,' he said. 'He's struggling. He'll turn to you, eventually.'

'This is so hard, Oliver. So hard. Nothing can prepare you for a situation like this. And I haven't a clue what to do.'

'Don't blank your FLO, for a start,' Tom said. 'She's here to support you and your family, so if there's anything you need to know, or you need to speak to Brent, tell her. Hang on in there, Liz. You're one of the strongest people I know. Be brave. And I shouldn't imagine for one minute that you feature in any murder scenario, they have to work through things one step at a time. I've come up against Brent before, and he's thorough. A careful man, doesn't risk losing a guilty verdict with sloppy work. Trust him. And if there are issues, we've got your back. I hope that's understood. Whatever happens, we're both here for you.'

She gave a weak and tentative smile. 'I know. I'm struggling to believe that the woman who got up for work yesterday morning is the woman here, now. I don't feel like the same person. I almost feel like...' She hesitated. 'I feel as if Gareth dying isn't real. I haven't cried for him, and yet we've been together for ever. The only concern is Jake. And as for Sadie... what am I supposed to feel about her? And at some point, I'm going to have to face her son. I'm going to have to tell someone I've never met before, his mother was having an affair with my husband. What a bloody mess.'

'You're jumping to conclusions, again,' Oliver said gently. 'Wait for DNA results, Liz. Until they come through, we can know nothing with any certainty.'

'I know. I know in here.' Liz touched her left breast.

She stood. 'Thank you both for coming, and don't feel offended, but I want you to go. You're forgetting I know your diaries – please go back to work, you're both needed there. I will be back, I don't know when. Is that okay?'

Tom stood and hugged her. 'No time limit,' he said softly. 'We can make our own coffee.' He smiled down at her. 'Take care, Liz. And if there's anything, legal or otherwise, get on the phone.'

'And I echo that,' Oliver said. 'Anytime. Day or night. Remember that.'

'I will. And thank you for galloping to my rescue. I'll keep you informed, obviously, as soon as I have something to tell you.'

She stood at the window and watched as their cars pulled into the traffic, in convoy. She couldn't have had better employers if she'd tried. But she needed space, time out to think.

'Tanya, I'm going for a lie down. If anything happens…'

'Go, Liz. I imagine you didn't sleep at all last night. I'll wake you if you're needed, and any information will be passed straight on. And I won't wake you unless anything is urgent.' She tapped her laptop, open on the kitchen table. 'I have some reports to file, I can be doing them while it's quiet.'

Liz placed the tray of cups on the side and climbed the stairs. The last time she had climbed some stairs… She closed her mind down. These were different stairs, no dead bodies here. No Gareth. No Sadie. And no Jake.

She glanced into Dan's room, and he was reading.

'You okay?'

'No.'

'Need a hug?'

'No.'

'Need to talk?'

'Mum,' he said, exasperation in his tone. 'Leave me alone. This is all my fault. If I had told you about the car being up there a lot…'

'What difference would that have made?'

'Can't you see?' he snapped. 'It would have made all the difference. Dad would have stopped seeing her – he loved you, she really was a fling, I'm sure. You would have stopped Jake going there, and none of this would have happened. Different circumstances.'

'Oh, God, Dan.' She moved across to his bed, and pulled him into her arms. 'You can't think like that! Take it a step further back – if I hadn't gone back to work after maternity leave…'

Dan clung on to her and cried, deep gulping sobs. 'I loved Dad,' he mumbled. 'Why? Why did he do this?'

'He only had an affair,' she explained gently. 'He had no part in anything else. He would have died for Jake, possibly did. We may one day get to know the full story, but don't ever stop loving him, Dan. I won't. He was a good man. And even if they prove he was with Sadie, that love may take a knock, but it won't go away. That's what love means.'

Mother and son laid back on the bed, arms wrapped around each other, and slowly drifted into sleep, both thinking about a man; just not the same man.

***

'Liz? You in the bathroom?'

Liz could hear Tanya's voice through her sleep-induced fog brain. 'I'm in Dan's room,' she whispered, reluctant to wake him.

She slid out from his draped arm, and opened the door.

'Sorry. We cried together, had a talk and dozed off. He's still asleep. Let's go downstairs. Has something happened?'

'Yes. Will Dan be okay if we go down to Moss Way station?'

'Sure. I'll leave him a note. He'll ring me when he wakes. What's happened?'

'We've managed to get some CCTV. I understand it's a bit grainy, but DI Brent wants you to look at it. Apparently, somebody a few doors down from the crime scene works nights; he wasn't in when we did our first sweep for CCTV cameras. We've been back today and there's something on it. It's all we've managed to pick up. Fingers crossed it means something to you.'

'I'll have a quick wash, wake myself up, and we can go. Is that okay?'

'Yes, of course. I'll grab you some water from the fridge, and I can make you a drink of tea when we get there. It's important we go quickly, Liz, in case you can recognise something.'

Liz nodded, headed for the bathroom.

Within three minutes they were on their way to the imposing police station.

Tanya shepherded her straight through, and DI Brent came forward to meet her.

'Thank you, Liz. Come through here.' He led her into a large room, sectioned by screens. 'This is DC Rankin. He's our whizz on computers. He'll take you through the video. It's not a clear picture, but look at everything. The walk, the hold of the person's frame, everything.'

She nodded again and sat down in the chair by the side of the young, somewhat geekish-looking constable. 'Hi,' he said. 'I'm Ian.'

'She looked at him. 'Ian Rankin?'

'Don't ask. My parents are fans.'

Liz nodded a third time. 'Ian, I'm Liz. Show me the movie.'

Pulling her chair closer to the screen, she watched intently. A figure pushing a pushchair came into view, and she gasped. Her stomach heaved, and a figure hurtled towards her clutching a bowl. She tried to swallow, but it was futile. She vomited until she could vomit no more. Her child was on a screen, being stolen.

'Liz?' Brent stepped forward, holding a towel, and a glass of water. 'I'm sorry, I should have realised you would react like this…'

She pushed back her hair, and wiped the towel across her face. 'I'll be fine now. It was the shock… it's definitely my pushchair. The toy dangling from the side of the hood is Peppa Pig. The little hand playing with it is Jake's. And he's awake. He plays with it all the time if he's awake in the pushchair.'

At her gasp, Ian had stopped the video. 'Ready to carry on? We can wait a few minutes if you want to settle yourself.'

'Go ahead, I'm ready. We need to find him.'

'Right, this is crucial now you've established it's definitely your pushchair. I can stop the video at any time you say stop. I'm going to move this on one frame because in this next frame there's a small portion of a face. Look at it carefully. And there's not much to see so don't feel you've let us down if it doesn't mean anything.'

'I understand,' she said quietly, and pulled her chair even closer. 'Go.'

He clicked on one frame, and she stared at the picture. The person's head was encased in a hood, and was looking down towards the ground, clearly aware there may be CCTV cameras that could catch him. All Liz could make out was a brief sliver of skin. It could have been anybody.

There was dejection in her voice. 'No, I can't tell anything from that.'

'Don't worry. We couldn't either,' Brent intervened. 'Ian's going to run the rest of the clip until this person goes out of shot. Watch it through to the end. We can then rewind and take it a frame at a time if you need that.'

She waited, and the video re-started. The pushchair and pusher went across the scene and Liz's eyes never left the screen. This evil monstrosity had killed two people and had her son. Joggers and a hoodie, trainers – unisex wear. Deliberately.

She shook her head. 'I'm so sorry. It means nothing to me. I can't even tell if it's a man or a woman. And I wouldn't recognise any identifiable walking issues because when you're pushing a pram, your gait changes. You're more hunched over. As this person is. The only thing I will say is that whoever it is, is taller than me. The partners in my practice bought us this travel system, and it was really expensive. So much so, that it allowed me to adjust the handle for the comfiest position. This person is bending over. I'm 5'3", so this person is taller than that, but not by a massive amount.'

'I knew I was right to bring you in,' Brent smiled. 'That gives us something to go on. Now, Ian is going to run it one frame at a time. Study each one individually; it will be tedious, but it's so important, Liz, as I'm sure you can appreciate. Then at the end, he'll do one more complete run through. We'll take you home after that.'

Liz settled herself more comfortably on the chair, and leaned forward. 'Go.'

She carefully studied each frame as DC Rankin scrolled through them, indicating when he could advance to the next one. She looked for a longer time at the frame where there was a partial image of the face, then as the screening drew to a close, she heaved a huge sigh. 'Nothing. Absolutely nothing.'

Ian leaned forward and re-started the whole thing. 'Right, one last time. Watch it as if it was Emmerdale, and you're not emotionally tied to it. Watch it as if you're doing a proof on it for ITV, and looking for continuity issues, mispronunciations – look for anything other than that baby being your baby.' He clicked on his mouse and the screening started for the last time.

Liz never took her eyes from the screen, and then shook her head in exasperation at the end. 'I can't help. I noticed the time at the bottom said 16:18, so I presume that indicates my husband was already dead by then? I can't even tell what sex the person is.' She turned to Brent. 'Do you have any thoughts on that?'

He shook his head, his brow furrowed. 'Not really. Everybody wears joggers, trainers and a hoodie, and he or she was careful to conceal with the hood. The timer is accurate – we've checked that out on his set-up. There were three other houses on that road that we thought had CCTV – two of them were dummy cameras, and one wasn't working. This is the only working one between the Fremantle house and the main road at the bottom. Thank you so much for doing this, Liz. Tanya will run you home. I'll probably be in touch later, because we're expecting the DNA results from the bedding. It's the cot bedding I'm most interested in – I don't expect the kidnapper to have gone in the main bedroom, but the little room is a different story. Do you happen to know if other babies are put into that cot?'

'Now there I can help,' she said. 'She had no other children, Tuesday Wednesday and Thursday, just Jake. Monday and Friday, she had a little boy, but he's three and sleeps in that single bed in the same room as the cot, if he needs a nap. In theory, there should only be DNA from Sadie and from Jake.'

Liz placed her handbag on her shoulder, shook hands with Brent and DC Rankin, then followed Tanya from the room.

They walked around the corner to the car park, and set off to head back up to Gleadless. Liz felt frustrated by her inability to come up with anything concrete, and didn't want to talk. Tanya sensed her mood, and kept quiet until her phone rang. She glanced at the display. 'It's DI Brent.'

She pressed to receive the call and Brent's voice filled the car. 'Tanya, are you still with Mrs Chambers?'

'Yes sir, I am. Just going over Birley Lane.'

'I'd like you both to head back here, please.'

'Of course. Ten minutes or so.' She disconnected and looked at Liz. 'Maybe they have another CCTV.'

Liz shrugged. 'Whatever. Let's go back and get it done, then I can go home to Dan. It's starting to feel like a long day.'

DI Brent had been watching for the car; he met them at the door.

'I need you both to come into my office, not the main one.' His expressive face wasn't smiling.

They followed him down a corridor and into an office that bore his name.

'Please – sit down, Mrs Chambers.' Liz felt as if she was back at school. It had been Liz earlier, now it was Mrs Chambers.

'We've had the DNA results back. Rush job, as requested. I'm sorry, Liz, but it does show that your husband and Sadie Fremantle were in that double bed together.' Brent was calling her Liz again, and she felt better for that. His news was as she had expected.

'And what about the cot bedding?'

'There is an issue.'

'Stranger DNA?'

'You could say that. Only two DNA results, one of which is Sadie's. The other one we are assuming is Jake's. We checked it against the DNA result from the main bedding, purely to confirm it was Jake's.'

Liz felt the blood drain from her.

'The thing is, Mrs Chambers, the DNA from the child in that cot is a different DNA altogether to the man in that bed that afternoon. Do you want to tell me why, Mrs Chambers?' He took out a DNA swab from his drawer. 'I need a DNA sample from you, to check we're looking for the right baby. Open your mouth please, Mrs Chambers, and when you close it again, you need to talk to me.'

25

Brent sat back in his chair, and stared at the woman in front of him. Why hadn't she been honest from the beginning? He had no doubt it was her child who was missing, she seemed to have omitted certain parentage details. 'I'm waiting.'

'Am I under arrest?'

'Not yet.'

'Do I need a solicitor?'

'I don't know. Do you?'

She crumpled. 'No, of course I don't.'

'Then start talking. We can't do anything about your husband and Mrs Fremantle, but I believe Jake is still alive. If he or she intended killing him, it would have happened at the house. There's no reason to risk being caught with the baby, if the intention was that he was going to die anyway. So, talk. I need to know who his father is, and everything about him.'

Liz hesitated briefly, mentally shrugged and told her story. 'I had an affair. We had been together six months, and if things hadn't conspired against us, I believe we would be together properly now. It wasn't a fling. We were the right pairing, at the right time. And then I accidentally became pregnant.'

DI Brent waited. She was clearly in a painful place. 'Go on,' he said.

'It forced me to look at what I was doing. I was only five weeks pregnant, so I ended the relationship. I couldn't do it to Gareth, and most of all I couldn't do it to Dan. Added to all of that, he was a client, and even if Banton and Hardwick hadn't sacked me, I would have felt I had to resign. I did the "right" thing and ended it. He didn't agree, not at all, but he respected my wishes and we haven't seen each other since.'

'You haven't been in touch since?'

The hesitation was brief. 'No.'

'We'll need his name and address, please, Mrs Chambers. And his phone number.'

She felt panicked and hoped it didn't show on her face. 'He has a wife and daughter…'

'And?' Brent raised his eyebrows, as he queried her statement.

'And they're going to be upset enough by this, so don't go in with your size twelves, and make everything worse for them,' Liz snapped. 'If I thought for a minute that Phil had something to do with Jake's disappearance, I'd have given you the information long before this.'

Her anger surprised him. 'Liz, I'm not in this job to upset people for the sake of it, I'm in it to solve murders, find missing people – I need that name and address, and I need it now.'

Liz delved into her handbag and took out a small notebook. She quickly wrote down Phil's name and address, followed by his home telephone number. Tearing off the sheet, she handed it to Brent. 'This is his wife's address. Apparently he's left her, and hasn't been there for some time. I can't help with any more details, because I haven't been in touch for over eighteen months. I needed a signature from him, and she was forced into telling me he had left her, but neither of us has heard from him.'

Brent stared at her. 'And you didn't think to tell me this? What if this is a man who simply wants to be part of his son's life? A man who has been discarded by the woman carrying his baby, and who decided to take matters into his own hands.'

He stood and turned to Tanya. 'Get her home, DC Baxter. I'll be speaking further to you,' he said, looking pointedly at Liz. 'Is there anything else you didn't feel it necessary to tell me?'

She shook her head. 'No. And don't speak to me like that. End of.' She stood and picked up her bag. 'I'll make my own way, thank you, Tanya. I need time to think. Tell me, DI Brent, do you have anything that could possibly lead you to where my son is? He's been missing twenty-four hours, and aren't the first twenty-four hours the most important in any missing persons case? Failed miserably, haven't you, you...' she searched desperately for the words she wanted, without using the profanities she needed to use, 'sanctimonious prick.'

Liz closed the door with a bang as she left, and instantly the tears fell. Her world had imploded. She stormed through the lobby and out of the external doors. Standing for a moment and taking in deep breaths of the frigid air, she tried to calm down.

Heading towards the tram tracks, she decided enough was enough. She had felt intimidated by that man, and that was a bad feeling; it wouldn't happen again. And she wanted her car back. They had removed it from higher up Sadie's road, to forensically go through it, but how long was that likely to take?

She wouldn't be catching trams if she had her own transport. That was her priority; no more depending on lifts via Tanya Baxter. There could be nothing in the car to give the police any help. There would obviously be evidence of Jake having been in it, but only around his child seat. She took out her mobile phone and rang Tanya. 'Tanya? Sort out getting my car back to me, will you?'

'It should only be a couple of days, Liz...'

'No, Tanya, I want it tomorrow. It's obvious the damn car wasn't used in any way to commit any sort of crime. It was used to transport my husband to his bit on the side, so expedite it, will you. See you later.'

She disconnected, giving Tanya no time to respond. She reached the tram stop, still feeling as though she was going to cry again. The glow from the tram as it approached cheered her; she would be home with Dan in ten minutes. She had no idea what to tell him. Should she confess? What impact would that have on his relationship with his baby brother? What impact would it have on the rest of his life? The tram picked up speed and she settled back into her seat and switched off her mind.

Ten minutes later she walked down her drive.

'Mum?'

She heard Daniel's voice as she opened the front door. 'Hi, sweetheart, it's me.'

He came out of the lounge and into her arms. She had no time to take off her coat, put down her bag; he clearly needed the comfort of her hug, so she stood and held him.

'Has something happened?' she asked. 'What's wrong?'

'I went in to prepare something for tea for us, thinking it would take my mind off the bad bits. It didn't, it made it worse. I cook for you, Dad and me. Not you and me.'

She held him tighter. 'And Tanya. Although I doubt she'll be here for much longer. We had a bit of a spat. It's why I've returned alone. I've told her I want the car back. I won't be in work for some time, but I'm going to need to get about, and I'll be damned if I'm going to be using public transport.'

Dan stepped away from Liz, and they shared a high five. 'I knew you'd make me feel better. Go you. And get that car. Spag bol?'

'Spag bol,' she agreed. 'She can either like it or lump it, I don't care either way.'

It turned out that Tanya did like it, and in the end the evening passed better than Liz would have thought, especially as Tanya confirmed the car would be available from lunchtime the following day. Dan went up to work on his game, and Liz put Classic FM on to give some background noise. Both she and Tanya settled down to read, but Liz couldn't concentrate on her book. Her mind was anywhere but in those pages, and finally she simply pretended to read, giving her brain free range.

Liz ached for her little boy; she hoped wherever he was, he was being cared for, and not being neglected in any way. He was only a baby... surely his kidnapper would look after him. She checked her iPhone in case she had missed any calls, but there was nothing. No communication from anyone. There had similarly been nothing on the landline.

Why had the kidnapper taken him? Did he or she want money? Had she managed to upset someone so deeply that they felt this was the way to pay her back? Who?

Her job took her into court on a regular basis – had somebody been sent to prison and it had been unjust? Again, who? Maybe she could brainstorm with Tom and Oliver; they knew as much about her cases as she did. And three heads were obviously better than one.

She felt her eyes closing, and Tanya touched her arm. 'Liz, go to bed. You need to sleep.'

She nodded. 'You'll be okay? Help yourself to anything you fancy, although things must be running a bit short. I'll see you in the morning.'

Liz's phone rang as she was climbing the stairs. She looked at the name on the screen and was tempted to reject it. 'DI Brent,' she said stiffly.

'Mrs Chambers. You're not in bed, are you?'

'Just on my way. Why?'

'I need to speak with you.'

She gave a sigh. 'Will it take you long to get here? I am really tired. I didn't sleep last night.'

'I'm outside, in my car.'

Again, the sigh. 'Okay. But can we make it quick?'

'Five minutes.'

She headed back downstairs, popped her head around the lounge door. 'Your boss is here.'

He was standing on the doorstep when she clicked open both locks.

'Come in.' She knew she was being churlish. This man was still working at ten at night, trying to find her son.

She led him into the lounge, and he acknowledged Tanya's presence with a brief nod.

'Is Dan here?'

'He's up in his room. Do you want him?'

'No, I wanted him out of the way while we talk. Can I sit down?'

'Yes, I'm sorry...'

'Liz, stop flaring up at me. I'm on your side, you know.' He frowned slightly as he spoke. 'I've been to see Rosemary Latimer. It appears she is aware of your affair with her husband, and she also knows he fathered Jake.' He held up a hand. 'And before you have a go at me, she volunteered that information. I didn't tell her I knew that he'd left her, I simply asked to speak to him. She became quite upset, and it all came out that he'd left her, but it was some months ago and she hasn't heard from him in all that time. She stressed what a good father he'd been to Melissa and it was out of character for him to not have anything to do with her.'

Liz stared at him. 'What are you saying? That you think Phil has taken Jake?'

'No, I'm not saying that. Mr Latimer hasn't touched his bank accounts, used his mobile phone, contacted a daughter he loves deeply and a wife he still cares about, or work. None of this makes any sense. What I'm really saying is that I think this is all connected, although how is beyond me at the moment. But one thing I am sure of, we're not looking for a missing child, we're looking for a missing child and his daddy, along with a double murderer. From now on, don't go anywhere without me knowing about it, and there will be a squad car parked outside for the foreseeable future. Dan isn't to go anywhere on his own, and neither are you.'

'But...'

He held up his hand as if to shut her up. 'Liz,' he said tiredly, 'for goodness sake, stop fighting me. Go to bed, let me go home to my bed, and we'll look at it with new eyes tomorrow morning. Tanya... be vigilant. If there's anything, any strange noise, you ring the station.'

26

*C*aptor watched the screen with interest. The man appeared to be coping well with the child. The mother was probably falling apart, quite justifiably. She would learn the hard way to stick to her own kin, and not become involved in other families.

The baby cried, and Captor muted the sound. The man, the beloved Phil, went into father mode and picked up the baby. He soothed him, and then picked up a book to read to him.

Captor's mind switched to the news shown that morning. It seemed that the whole country was on the lookout for this baby. It was a pity they didn't know about the missing father as well.

Captor smiled, and switched off the screens, closed the door hiding them, and left the building. The plan was developing nicely – time to sit back and let the main players stew.

Phil was a trifle bored with Peppa Pig, and he swapped the book for one about dinosaurs. The sounds he made caused much giggling in Jake, and he wished he could be as resilient as this young baby. He didn't feel much like giggling, he didn't feel like much of anything, except regaining his freedom, and that of his son.

Since having had the chain removed, he'd taken full advantage of being free to move around, and several times he had climbed the twelve stairs up to the metal door, feeling his way around it. It was in shadow, so he couldn't really see much, but he could touch. There was nothing. It was smooth; no screws, not even an indentation.

There was nothing else, four walls, no window; no escape.

27

For the second night running, Liz hardly slept, despite being back in her bed and not on the sofa. DI Brent confirming that Phil was being treated as a missing person both uplifted and squashed her. The possibility that he was dead made her feel bereft. Heartbroken.

And suddenly Gareth's death had intruded into her thoughts. It was almost as though the discovery of his infidelity had wiped out her good memories of their life together, and she was beginning to remember little things from a happier time; the grief took hold.

She pulled his pillow towards her, and held on to it through the night. His untimely death meant he would never see Dan graduate, never experience the wonders of grandchildren, never walk in snow, kick autumnal leaves; death was hard to accept, especially at three in the morning, when the world outside her bedroom window was sleeping.

Except for the two policemen in the patrol car parked in the layby directly outside her home. The one in the passenger seat held up a thumb to her in query as he spotted her standing at the window. She responded with an upright thumb. 'Everything's okay,' she whispered. 'I want my son.'

Liz went downstairs and switched on the kettle. A cup of tea would calm her frazzled nerves, perhaps help her sleep. She grabbed a couple of biscuits and went into the lounge, nursing the mug of tea. She wondered if Rosie was asleep, or making her own 3am cuppa; two women, both wondering where a man and a baby were.

Liz's arms were aching to hold Jake. She was trying to control her feelings, trying to be strong for Dan, when all she wanted to do was scream at everyone to get out there and find him. Gareth was gone, there was nothing anyone could do about that, but Jake… no tiny body had been found, and she was clinging to that thought with a tenacity she hadn't known she possessed.

Was he crying for her? Was he getting enough to eat to build that little body? Was he being kept clean? She pulled out the photograph album from under the coffee table, where it had lain since she had handed a recent photo of Jake to DI Brent. Flicking through it, she touched each picture of Jake, with a finger and a smile. Her little one; she remembered the tears she had shed on her first day back at work. They were different tears to the ones she was crying now.

She finished her tea and laid down on the sofa, clutching the photo album. Pulling a throw over, she allowed her mind to wander. She replayed constantly the CCTV images she had seen, but still nothing stood out. That the last image of Jake was him being pushed in a pushchair by a kidnapper, distressed Liz beyond anything else, but she still had no idea of the kidnapper's identity, or even gender.

Eventually, her tired brain gave up, the tears stopped flowing, and she slept.

***

Tanya was the one to find Liz asleep on the sofa, and she stood in the doorway looking at her. She felt so sorry; couldn't imagine how Liz must be feeling. The case was complicated enough with the missing baby at the heart of it, but for Liz to lose her husband after he had made love to their childminder – it didn't bear thinking about.

'Liz.' Tanya shook Liz's shoulder gently, and she stirred. She looked up at Tanya initially with a puzzled expression, and then her mind cleared. She pulled herself into a sitting position, and shook her unruly blonde hair as she tried to free her mind from the dark dream she had been having.

'Sorry, Tanya, I was asleep.'

Tanya smiled. 'Good. It's what you need. You want some toast?'

Liz pulled up her legs on to the sofa. 'Just one slice, please. Shall I do it?'

Tanya shook her head. 'No, you come around a bit. I'll do us some toast and a pot of tea, and we'll see what the day has in store for us. Your car, as I understand it, will be back by lunchtime, but don't forget, you're not to go anywhere without taking two police officers with you.'

'Great,' Liz mumbled.

'DI Brent's instructions – don't knock them. He knows what he's doing, and what he's doing is protecting you.'

'I know. I don't like him.'

Tanya laughed. 'You don't have to like him, just trust him.'

'I do. He accepts that Phil is missing for a start, which is more than I could get Phil's wife to do. Although, to be fair, I think she simply buried her head in the sand about it, I don't think she was being devious.'

'And I think you've read her correctly. I'll go and do that toast.'

Liz stood and crossed to the bay window, using her left hand to pull back the curtains, clutching her dressing gown closed with her right hand. At the top of the drive, the two police officers were both out of the car, talking to a young man trying to get down the drive.

Christian.

Although Liz had never met him, she had seen plenty of photographs dotted around Sadie's house.

He appeared to be gesticulating quite wildly, and pushing the two officers away. Liz moved quickly, and opened the front door.

'Christian?'

He turned at the sound of her voice. 'Please… tell them I need to speak with you.' There was a tremor in his voice.

'It's okay,' she said to the two men. 'This is my childminder's son.'

'Sorry, son,' the taller of the two officers said, 'but you're not going in there unless we check you for concealed weapons. We've had our instructions…'

Reluctantly, Christian held up his arms. 'Do it then, before we get an even bigger crowd.' He glared at the small group of onlookers who had stopped to see what was happening.

Liz stayed at the door until he walked down towards her. She touched his hand, then led him into the lounge. 'We're going to have a cup of tea and some toast. Do you want some?'

'Just the drink, please. I don't feel much like eating. I'm sorry, I had to come and see you.'

'That's okay, Christian. This is a lot to take in.'

'You found her? Them?'

'I did. I was collecting Jake.'

Christian dropped his head and mumbled, 'I'm finding it all a bit unbelievable.'

'I'm not giving you any details, and I think we have to put any circumstances from our mind. The big priority is finding Jake. There is some CCTV – the police will probably want you to look at it, in case it stirs anything in your mind. When did you get here?'

'Late last night. I stayed at a friend's house, I still can't get into ours. He says I can stay as long as I want, so I'm okay.'

'This is going to be so difficult for you. You're so young. If you need to talk, we're here.'

Tanya walked in carrying a tray. 'I did extra toasts,' she smiled. 'And you, young man, need to eat something.'

'Tanya is our family liaison officer,' Liz explained to Christian. 'We can say anything to her, and she bats it right back, but makes us think we're not being stupid. You can do the same.'

'I have questions,' Christian said, the simple statement belying the anguish written on his face.

'I'm sure you do,' Tanya said, 'but they'll keep until after you've eaten something.' She handed him a plate with two slices of toast on it. 'Eat.'

And he did, chewing slowly, clearly not wanting it. But the police lady scared him.

He turned towards Liz, unable to wait any longer. 'They found your husband there as well?'

Liz nodded. 'Yes, they did.'

'Why? If he was collecting Jake why was he still there? What's going on?'

She hesitated. Tell it bluntly, like it was, or soften it?

She went for blunt. 'They were having an affair, Christian. I'm sorry...'

'No, I'm sorry.' Once again, his head dropped, the anguish clearly evident. 'Why would she do that? Since she threw my father out all those years ago, she's never had anyone. Why now?'

'Who knows. There's never any real answer to infidelity, Christian. It just happens.' Liz's mind drifted towards Phil. *It just happens...*

'But it doesn't make sense. Do you think she was trying to stop whoever was after your baby? If somebody's out to hurt you, to destroy you, why did they take Mum?'

'I agree,' Liz concurred, 'but I do think one day we'll know. You will meet DI Brent, probably today, and I think you'll then begin to feel a confidence that the truth will come out.'

Tanya stood. 'I'm going to ring the boss now, and tell him you're in Sheffield. He'll probably send a car for you, and you can give your statement and have a look at the CCTV pictures. How long are you home for?'

'I've told them I'll be up here for as long as it takes.' He put down his cup. 'Do you know when I can get into our house? I'd prefer to stay there, rather than on a settee at my friend's.'

'I'll check. But are you sure you'll be okay there?' Tanya voice showed her concern. 'I'll go and ring, get some answers.' She left them and moved into the kitchen.

He ignored Tanya's question, his mind veering off. 'Had they been in bed that afternoon?'

Liz spoke quietly. 'It appears so.'

'Why aren't you ranting about it? Why are you so… bloody accepting?'

'Because it's not a priority in my mind.' Her tone had sharpened to match his. 'My eleven-month-old son is missing, remember? That is of far more importance than my husband having it off with… well,' she finished lamely. This was a twenty-year-old boy who had lost his mother. She didn't need to say what she really thought.

Tanya re-joined them. 'There's a car on its way. Christian, I know you can't tell them much, but say what you can. That will be one more problem out of the way. DI Brent seems to think you can go back home tomorrow, so if you're sure your friend can give you somewhere to sleep for tonight…'

'I'm sure.' Christian stood. 'I'll go and wait outside. I'd like to get it over with. Thank you, Mrs Chambers, and I'm so sorry for everything that's happened. If I can do anything to help with Jake…'

'Christian, please call me Liz. Go and get this business over with, and please feel free to come here anytime you want.'

He nodded, left the room and went out of the front door. They watched him chatting to the two officers still stationed at the top of the drive. Liz ached for him; such a young man to have a heavy burden on his shoulders. A second police car pulled up outside, and the driver got out, spoke briefly to his colleagues and helped Christian into the passenger seat.

Two minutes later he had gone.

'Nice boy,' Tanya said.

'His mum was so proud of him…' Liz felt the tears prick her eyes. She wiped them away angrily. 'I'm going up for a shower. And I'll see if Dan is awake yet, it's not like him to sleep in.'

She went upstairs and knocked gently on Dan's door. 'It's me, Dan,' she called. When there was no response she opened the door.

The bed was untidy, but Dan wasn't in it.

28

Liz stared at the bed, then moved quickly down the landing to the bathroom. She knocked on the door, and called loudly, 'Dan. You in there?'

There was no response, and she pressed down the handle. The door opened inwards; the bathroom was empty. She quickly checked the other upstairs rooms, before almost falling downstairs in panic.

'Tanya,' she called. 'Have you seen Dan?'

'Dan? No, I haven't. I thought he was still sleeping. He's not here?' She took out her mobile phone and pressed for DI Brent. She quickly explained, said *yes* a couple of times, and went out of the front door, still speaking to the DI.

Liz watched her walk up the small driveway to the squad car still parked outside and speak to the two officers. She saw them shake their heads, and she felt sick.

Tanya re-entered the front door. 'They haven't seen anyone leave the house. They also haven't seen anything suspicious. Try not to panic, there may be a perfectly simple explanation…'

'What sort of simple explanation? Even Brent thinks I'm being targeted. Have they taken my other son?'

'They?'

'Figure of speech, Tanya, bloody figure of speech. I've no idea who would want to hurt me, apart from Rosie Latimer, and I'm damn sure it's not her, so where does that leave me and my family? Confined to this damn house, that's where it leaves us.' She broke down in tears. 'Where's Dan?' she whimpered.

'I've spoken to our two officers, and they've seen nothing. Not even a postman has been to the door. That leads me to think that maybe Dan has left out the back. I don't know why he would have gone out, but Dan is a big lad, he would have kicked off if someone had tried to abduct him.'

'If he was conscious,' Liz sobbed. She was trying desperately to stop crying; she wanted to show no weakness.

'Liz.' Tanya held her by the shoulders, and looked into her face. 'Be strong. DI Brent will be here anytime, along with other officers. Don't give up.'

Liz turned away from her. 'I'll be fine. Just give me five minutes on my own.'

Tanya nodded and headed for the kitchen. 'I'll get you some water, it'll help calm you.'

Liz walked towards the bay window, and saw one of the officers get out of the driver's seat. His eyes were trained down the road, and then he moved, quickly. She followed where he was looking, and saw Dan.

The officer reached him, put an arm around his shoulders, and escorted him at speed towards home. Liz reached the front door as he came down the drive.

'Is this the young man we've got half of South Yorkshire Police looking out for?'

Liz raised her hand and slapped Dan across the face, then pulled him into her arms. The tears she had managed to dry overflowed again, and she brought him into the lounge.

'Where've you been? You know we're virtually confined to the house, at the moment?'

'What? What do you mean?'

It dawned on Liz that Brent had issued his instructions after Dan had gone to bed. She groaned. 'You didn't know…' She reached up and stroked the red mark she had left on his cheek. 'I'm sorry. I shouldn't have hit you, I was so scared. The police officers out front are here to babysit us. DI Brent feels we're being targeted and wants us protected. So, where've you been? They didn't see you go out of the door.'

'I went out the back. I dropped down to the playing fields, looking. Looking for the pushchair, Jake's blankie… anything really. I needed to do something to try and get him back. I've been out about three hours, but not found anything.'

The front door opened, and DI Brent came through. 'You're back then. You okay?'

'I'm fine, and I'm sorry. I hadn't been told I couldn't go out. As if I'd upset Mum any more than she already is. I genuinely didn't know I'd cause all this trouble. Mum...'

She held out her hand and clasped his. 'You're safe. Go and have a shower, it'll warm you up. You're freezing.'

They watched as he climbed the stairs, his head bowed.

Liz turned to Brent. 'I'm so sorry. I should have known...'

'I'm pleased he's safe. I've sent everybody back to the station, so there's no harm done. Your reaction was understandable, and Tanya did exactly the right thing.'

'And have you heard anything?'

Brent shook his head. 'Nothing. We're continuing with house-to-house, but so far nobody has seen anything. What we would like to do is a television appeal. We need you to ask for Jake's safe return. We'll show the one piece of CCTV we have, and hope it jogs someone's memory. They'll film it later this afternoon, and we can get it out on the six o'clock news. This will be hard, Liz, but if it brings in something, it will have been worth it.'

'I'll do anything.'

Brent nodded. 'I know. The filming crew will guide you through it, and I'll be there as well, because I'll follow up with a police request for information and the CCTV. The lads who will be on duty at two will bring you down to Moss Way. Will Dan be with you?'

'I'm sure he'll want to. Is that okay?'

'It's fine. It's what we want. I'm heading back now, I was about to start the morning's briefing when Tanya rang.' He turned to go out of the door. 'And Liz, I'm thankful it wasn't anything worse. See you later.'

She watched him speak to his officers, then climb into a car. She felt overwhelmed. Her heart was aching. Where was Jake? Was he still alive? She felt that he was, but was that wishful thinking? Her baby needed to be home with her.

29

*P*hil lay on his bed, watching his son sleep. The child was beautiful; blond hair, blue eyes closed, yet flickering occasionally as if he was dreaming, tiny hands clutching on to the tag that was sewn into the hem of the blanket covering him. He had noticed that a tag calmed Jake down, and Phil handed him one every time he cried.

He lay there for a while, until his own eyes drooped. Captor had sent down a flask of coffee and Phil had welcomed it. He missed coffee. He slept deeply and was shocked awake by the sound of a child crying. For a moment, he was disoriented. He sat up and the room swirled around him; he shook his head, and finally things settled down. Jake was standing, looking over the edge of the cot.

Phil smiled at him. 'Hi, son. How long have we been asleep? You want out of jail? Join the club.'

He lifted the little boy and sat him next to him on the bed. He put on his tiny slippers, more to keep him warm than as cushioning for his feet as he tried to walk.

'There you are, Jake,' he said, and lifted him on to the floor. Jake grabbed for the edge of the bed to steady himself, then turned and looked at this man he had come to accept was part of his life.

Phil stood and moved across to the toilet, then washed his hands. He turned to go back to Jake and Jake was standing, unmoving, not holding on to anything. He lifted his arms and took three tentative steps before dropping to the floor.

'Good boy!' Phil clapped his hands, then immediately his smile disappeared as he realised Liz had missed a milestone in Jake's life. His first steps. She would be devastated.

'God, Liz, our child is bloody amazing,' he said, under his breath. 'And I promise, while ever I live, I'll protect him until he can go home to you.'

Captor watched the scenario that was being acted out on his monitors. So, the child had walked. Another little bit of salt to rub in Liz Chamber's wounds, once the information could be got safely to her. It was time to step up a few things, give a bit of information out to torment her even further.

Plans would be made, and acted upon. Captor switched off the monitors, closed the room door, and left the building. Time to drive her to distraction.

30

Liz broke down in the middle of the filming, and the cameras kept rolling. She was heartbroken, and it showed. Dan tried to comfort her, and the whole world saw it. Brent's face was grim as he outlined the information they needed, and followed it up with the CCTV.

'We desperately need to find this baby. Please think about the CCTV you have seen – does anything about the person pushing the pushchair make you think of someone you know? Is somebody close to you behaving strangely? Out of character? Have you heard a baby crying somewhere where you wouldn't normally hear that sound? The number to call is scrolling across the screen. If you have anything at all, call it in.'

And the picture faded.

Liz and Dan were on the sofa watching the broadcast, Tanya standing behind them.

'That was really good, Liz. Let's hope we have some sort of response from it. Now, you need to eat. Neither of you have had anything today, have you?'

Dan stood. 'I'll see to it. I've all sorts of stuff in the freezer. Tanya, do you like curry?'

'You don't have to feed me, Dan,' she smiled. 'I'll nip to McDonald's or somewhere and get a meal.'

'It's no problem. My freezer portions are always for three people anyway, so do you like curry?'

'Certainly do. Thank you.' She turned to Liz with a smile. 'Why didn't my son have aspirations to be a chef instead of a geologist?'

'I didn't realise you had a son!'

'Yes, he's doing something in Peru, right now, but his job has taken him all over the world. There's just the two of us, although from his emails, I think things are getting serious with a young lady called Hannah.'

'Three of us on our own with a son – you, me and Sadie.'

The landline telephone rang stridently, and Tanya and Liz looked at each other. Tanya moved across. 'It's showing a number,' she said. 'This isn't our kidnapper.'

Liz glanced at the tiny screen. 'It's my friend, Julia. I'll let it go to voicemail, and ring her back after we've eaten.'

***

'Julia? I'm sorry I missed your call. As you can imagine, things aren't normal here at the moment.'

'Oh, God, Liz, I'm so sorry. I've been in Paris for a few days, so only found out about it when I watched the news tonight. Is there anything I can do to help?'

'There's nothing anyone can do,' Liz said quietly. 'The police have nothing to go on; whoever has taken Jake hasn't communicated in any way, and I think the DI in charge of the case is pinning all his hopes on that appeal. I'm not convinced we'll get anything from it.'

'Shit, that's awful. Can I come and see you? You'll need a hug. Has Oliver been to see you?'

'Yes, him and Tom both came up the morning after I found the bodies.'

'You found the bodies?' Julia's voice rose as she digested Liz's words.

'I did. And come up whenever you want, have your mobile phone handy in case I have to cancel. Sometimes they need me at a moment's notice.'

'Give me an hour. We can talk more, face to face.' Julia disconnected.

Liz turned to Tanya with a smile. 'She's a bit of a whirlwind, is Julia. It sounds as though she's back to her usual bouncy self – she's

Oliver Hardwick's soon to be ex-wife. I've known her for years, since school days. She'll be here in an hour, she says, but that could as easily be two hours.'

'Then will you be okay if I go home? I need to check everything's okay, and I'll have my mobile on.'

'Of course I'll be okay. Stay the night, come back in the morning.' Liz held up a hand as Tanya opened her mouth to protest. 'Honestly, I'll be fine. Tell our babysitters outside what you're doing, so they are aware Dan and I are on our own, but I suspect Julia might stay the night anyway. You need time out from this, you know you do.'

Tanya nodded. 'I'll check with DI Brent first. If he says okay, that's what we'll do.'

She disappeared into the kitchen to make the call, and returned a couple of minutes later. 'I checked if there had been any response to the appeal, and they've had a few phone calls saying they saw somebody pushing the pram, but one says it was a man, one says it was a woman, another one says whoever was pushing it, put it in the boot of the car without folding it, after struggling with it for a bit.'

Liz's head shot up. 'That's the one he needs to concentrate on. The pushchair is easy for me to fold, but Gareth never quite got the hang of it. It has safety devices on it, and different levers to release to get it to fold. If you don't know about them…'

'He's given me permission to take the night off, so I'll ring him before I go, tell him what you've said. He may ring you for more information. Are you sure you'll be okay?'

'Tanya, go! I'll be fine.'

Tanya nodded. 'I'll ring him from my room.' She headed for the stairs, almost colliding with Dan as he came from the kitchen.

'Okay, I've set the dishwasher going. I'm off to bed. I was up really early this morning.'

'Julia's coming. You want to stay up to say hello?'

'Julia? You still allowed to be friends with her, then?'

Liz looked puzzled. 'Of course. Why shouldn't I be?'

'I don't think Oliver was happy about them splitting up. Not according to Simon, anyway.'

Liz looked bewildered. 'Simon?'

'Tom's Simon. Simon Banton. He's in my school now, a year behind me. We play football together every day.'

'I don't understand. Why should Oliver and Julia splitting up affect my friendship with her? It hasn't affected my friendship with Oliver, or my working relationship with him. In fact, he didn't mention it. Tom told me what had happened.'

'Whoa! Don't shoot the messenger! I'm telling you what Simon said. He heard his mum say that it was good that you'd given Julia some backbone. Did you?'

'Good Lord, no. All I did was tell her she'd have to make a decision sooner or later, but if the decision was to go, not to waste her time being unhappy mulling it over.'

'So you didn't tell her to leave him?'

'No, I didn't. I like Oliver, and to be perfectly honest, Dan, I wouldn't presume to do anything like that. Marriages are sacrosanct, and only the two people involved can deal with any issues thrown up.'

Guilt, guilt, guilt. Are all marriages sacrosanct? She cringed inwardly at her thoughts.

'Whatever you said to her, she took your advice, apparently. Mum the marriage counsellor. But I'm still going to bed. I need sleep.'

He walked through the door and almost collided with Tanya.

'I'll be back for seven tomorrow morning, Liz, but if you need me…'

Liz smiled. 'I know. I'll ring you. But to be perfectly honest, I'm planning on sharing a couple of bottles of rosé wine with Julia, and then hopefully I'll sleep. Drunk, if necessary.'

'Not really advisable,' Tanya smiled. 'What if they find Jake?'

'You're right, of course,' Liz responded. 'To be perfectly honest, I don't really drink. I'm not keen on the taste, I wondered if it might blot everything out…'

'Enjoy your evening as much as you can, Liz. Is that your friend coming down the path escorted by a policeman?'

Liz laughed. 'She'll love that.'

Tanya exited the door, as Julia entered. Liz and Julia hugged, and then went through into the lounge.

'Proper bummer, this, isn't it?' Julia said, softening her words with a hug.

'You don't know the half,' Liz responded, 'There's so much I need to tell you. But not yet. Dan is probably still awake, and if I can keep this from him…'

'Are we going to need this?' Julia delved into her capacious handbag and produced a bottle of vodka and a large bottle of Coca-Cola. 'That policeman checked my bag before he'd even let me down the drive, and he grinned at me, before he made me feel like an old lady. He called me ma'am!'

Liz collected two glasses from the kitchen, then watched as Julia poured drinks. 'So, I guess we both have some talking to do,' Julia said, as she handed the drink to Liz.

'It was a bit of a shock, hearing that you'd left Oliver.'

'It was a shock to me too, and I went into a shell. I didn't speak to anybody, not even my solicitor, initially. I can only apologise for not ringing you, but I couldn't. Even my mum found out through Oliver, and not me.'

'Why? After we'd had our chat about it, how long was it before you left?'

'The day after. He asked me where I had been. He had called home and I wasn't there. I told him I'd been for a coffee and a chat with you, and he said he didn't want me meeting up with you anymore. He said it wasn't necessary to be friends with you.'

'What? He's never said a word out of place to me.'

'It's the control thing again, isn't it? He made me give up work, said I didn't need to, and for a while that was fine. But then I got bored with being at home all day. Then when my car needed something doing to it, he scrapped it, saying I didn't really need one, I could always use his. Good idea, except it was never there when I wanted to go anywhere. When he said I should drop you, something snapped. I went to bed and couldn't sleep. I was so angry. I thought about what you had said about making a decision but then not hanging around for him to change my mind. He went to work, I packed and moved into a hotel.'

'Did he try to get you back?'

'It took him over a week to locate me. He contacted every hotel he could find. I was in a really small one at Nether Edge, and it was as simple as him ringing them and asking to be put through to Julia Hardwick. They did. My brain was in such a state I never thought to tell them I didn't want anybody knowing I was there. He tried to persuade me to go back, but it wasn't even up for discussion. We ended the call, I packed and checked out. I made it clear at the next hotel I wanted nobody able to find out I was there, and I'm now in a rented house that he has no idea about. Nobody knows where it is, and I'm keeping that to myself, until all financial negotiations for the divorce are settled. Oliver is being quite reasonable, I should add.'

'And according to Dan, Oliver blames me! Although I must say, he has never changed in the way he treats me, so I'm taking what Dan says with a pinch of salt. His words have come via Simon Banton, and prior to that from Simon hearing his mum say something to his dad, about me giving you some backbone. Did I?'

'Somebody did,' Julia laughed. 'I'll never go back to him. It's been nearly five months now, and I feel so much more at ease. I don't want another man, ever, because I won't take that risk of being controlled, but it doesn't matter. I'm happy with my own company.'

'Good for you. And you've got a car?'

'Yes, it's parked somewhere across the road. I feel independent again, ready to get on with life. You did that, Liz, you did that.'

She leaned forward and refilled their glasses. 'Do you want to talk about it?'

Liz looked puzzled. 'Talk about what?'

'What's going on with you. About finding the bodies, about Jake going missing. Is there anything I can do to help?'

'Without clues – although there may be one – there's nothing much anyone can do except trust in the police to find him. Jake going missing has overridden Gareth's death. I can't think about that, about the circumstances. He was having an affair, it seems, with the childminder. Dan suspected, but because it was only a suspicion, said nothing. Me? I suspected nothing. It can only have been a fairly recent thing, because it's only about four months since I first introduced the two of them.'

'That's crap,' Julia said, reaching forward to clasp Liz's hand. 'Why would he want somebody else? You're beautiful, inside and out.'

Liz snorted. 'Don't be fooled, Julia. I know I haven't been quite as... loving... as I used to be, and Gareth obviously felt the need to find someone who was. But it's all irrelevant now, he's gone.'

They continued to chat, with Julia constantly trying to steer the conversation back to the events of the past couple of days. Eventually, Liz said she was tired. 'I can offer you a sofa, if you want to stay.'

'Thank you. I think I'd better – those two officers outside would probably be able to see from my stagger that I wasn't fit to drive.'

Five minutes later, Liz was in her own bedroom, feeling irrationally angry. It was clear that Julia hadn't come to comfort, but to find out the gossip. Liz wished she had offered to send for a taxi, rather than give her overnight accommodation.

Her head sank into the pillow, and yet she couldn't sleep. Talking to Julia had forced her to relive the horrors; the blood, so much blood from Gareth, and yet none from Sadie. The scene was re-lodged in her mind now, and she didn't want it there. She tossed and turned for what seemed like hours; she picked up her kindle deciding not to read the Stephen King she had already started, but to change to something that wouldn't scare her half to death. She chose a debut novel by an author she had decided might be worth the £1.99 she had paid for the download, and began to read.

The book was good; she stayed awake. Finally, she gave in and went downstairs to make a camomile tea. Liz didn't particularly like the taste, but everyone said it helped in getting to sleep. She crept through the hallway, trying not to disturb Julia. It was as she returned holding the mug in her hand that she heard the ping of an incoming text from the lounge. She glanced through the open door and saw the glow from Julia's phone, as it lay face up on the coffee table. Who texted at 3am? Puzzled, Liz went across, making no noise, and glanced down. Oliver.

Julia obviously had a different idea of what *no contact* meant than Liz did. She'd been quite adamant that she hadn't had anything to do with him since they had split up. Any contact had been through solicitors. And yet he was texting her at three in the morning.

Liz quietly left the lounge and returned to her bedroom. There was so much about her life that was full of questions; she could manage quite well without the added complication of Julia's marriage.

She sat up in bed and sipped at her tea, reading the book. Halfway through a sentence she suddenly thought about the love phone. She hadn't checked it once since finding the bodies. She reached across to her dressing table and pulled her bag towards her. She took out the phone, and gasped.

Our son is safe at the moment. I love you.

She felt sick. Nothing made sense. She was still convinced whoever was sending these messages wasn't Phil. He wouldn't be so cold.

And yet it could be him… he had been missing for some months. Could he have planned this? Could he have killed Sadie and Gareth, snatched Jake and hidden him away?

But if it was him, why had he done it?

And she would stake her life on these texts not having been sent by him.

31

Within a five-minute period around eight next morning, several things happened: Tanya arrived, Julia left, the two officers went off shift to be replaced by two more, DI Brent arrived, and Captor knew it was fast approaching the time for the final act.

32

*J*ake was snuffly. He had kept Phil awake for much of the night, with tiny noises and coughs coming from the cot, and Phil hoped it wouldn't get any worse.

He tried getting the little boy to eat breakfast, but he had half the sachet before discarding it. Fortunately, he drank his milk, which gave Phil a small measure of satisfaction, but Jake clearly didn't want to play, and sat with his daddy on the bed. He felt hot, and Phil couldn't help but think his mummy would already have dealt with it via Calpol and Jake would have been feeling much happier.

Phil heard the rattle of the dumb waiter and he quickly put Jake back in his cot before crossing to the hatch. He took out the carrier bag of supplies and closed the door.

Inside, along with his own meagre rations for the day, was a bottle of Calpol. He checked the dosage, filled the syringe, and gave Jake the soothing liquid.

After dealing with his son, he walked with care around the basement prison; he could see no evidence of a camera, yet it had to be there. There was no way Captor could have known of the disturbed night, the baby's snuffly cries, without there being a camera. And if there was one, did it track his movements to every part of the room, or was it static?

Not that it made the slightest bit of difference. He had long since given up on the idea of escape. There was no way out of a stone-built cellar that boasted a metal door with no handle on his side and nothing in the way of a window; just a hole in the wall filled with a dumb waiter. The only person in the cellar that would fit into that was Jake, and although he had taken his first couple of steps, Phil *reckoned that wouldn't be enough to help them, if the baby made the great escape.*

Jake soon fell into a deep sleep, the Calpol obviously doing its job. Phil laid him in his cot, and tenderly covered the tiny body with his blankets. Such a beautiful child; whatever the outcome of this was, he would remember these precious moments always.

His thoughts turned to Melissa, and he felt a tear trickle down his face. What was she thinking. Did she assume that he had upped and left her? What would her mother have told her? And was it her mother holding him prisoner?

He idly picked up a book about Dirty Desmond. He read the two pages, not for the first time, then hurled it at the wall.

'So boring,' he muttered. 'So fucking boring.' He looked up towards the ceiling. 'I know you're filming me. For pity's sake, send me another book!' He spoke quietly, not wanting to disturb the sleeping Jake. He really wanted to scream the words.

Jake slumbered on, and eventually Phil napped, catching up on his broken sleep. He almost missed the rattle of the dumbwaiter.

In it was a small hot water bottle, obviously meant for Jake's cot, and a copy of War and Peace.

Captor had a sense of humour.

33

Will Brent stood at the front of the room. He had called the briefing for 7am; it would have been 6am if there had been anything new to report.

'Right, everybody.' Instantly the room fell silent. 'The lead we had yesterday about the person not being able to fold the pushchair and it being stuffed into the boot of the car – it's okay as far as it goes, but it doesn't go very far. Again, the witness didn't know if it was a man or a woman. Mr Warrender said whoever was pushing the pram took the baby out of it, lifted him into the back seat of the car and strapped him into a car seat, then moved back to the boot where the pram had been left, and tried to fold it. It defeated him or her, so whoever this is, I suspect they're not used to little children. This is a top of the range pushchair, bought for Liz Chambers by her employers, when she left to take maternity leave.'

He looked round at his team. 'It seems he or she struggled for a couple of minutes, then picked up the pram and loaded it into the boot, still in its erect state. This tells us it was a fairly large car, because, although Mr Warrender didn't notice the make, he did notice that our perpetrator simply put it in, then closed the lid. He didn't have to manoeuvre it around, in order to close it. The car was a dark colour, either blue or black. The person then walked around to the driving seat, got in and set off. End of story. We've had forensics on the exact site of where the car was parked, but with no results. Whoever it was, they didn't smoke and discard a convenient cigarette, drop a tissue, or anything helpful.'

There were a few smiles. He continued. 'I want us to repeat the door to door in the proximity of where this car was, in view of this new information. Someone else may have seen something. Any questions?'

DC Lynda Checkley held up a hand.

'Lynda?'

'Sorry, sir… I was wondering if Mrs Chambers had said anything about somebody who might want to hurt her. From everything that we know, surely somebody is pretty pissed off with her, because it strikes me that she is the one being targeted here, not the baby, and not this missing man who might or might not be involved.'

DI Brent smiled at the newest member of his team. 'Is *pissed off* a technical term, Lynda?'

She had the grace to blush.

'The only person Liz Chambers named as holding a grudge against her is Philip Latimer's wife, Rosemary, or Rosie as she is usually known. However, for the time of the murders and abduction, she has a rock-solid alibi. She was at the Children's Hospital with her young daughter, who was having physiotherapy on her arm. We've double-checked this, in view of Mrs Chamber's feelings concerning Rosie Latimer. Rosie and Melissa went straight from school at 3.15pm, arrived at the hospital shortly before 4pm, and eventually got in to see the physiotherapist at 4.15pm. They left the hospital just after 5pm, and went to McDonald's for a treat for Melissa. Apparently, the physio puts her in some pain afterwards. We believe Gareth Chambers and Sadie Fremantle were dead by just after 4.30pm.'

There were several nods of acknowledgement around the room, and then Lynda spoke again. She was clearly giving her mind free rein. 'And Philip Latimer? Is he really missing, or did he do a disappearing act to get away from a wife he'd stopped loving.'

'You mean did he piss off?' Brent kept his face straight as he spoke the words, and once again she blushed. The rest of the team clapped.

'Okay, she muttered, 'I give in.'

Brent smiled at her. 'I hate to think what this lot will give you for a nickname, Lynda, but to answer your question properly, yes, I believe he is really missing. He hasn't touched his bank accounts, or used his phone, for months. I think his disappearance was meant to be the start of Liz Chambers' nightmare, and I believe that's the bit that's gone slightly awry for the kidnapper. Liz didn't find out Philip was missing until she went back to work.'

'And you think he's still alive?' The question came from the back of the room.

'In the absence of a body, I do. I think – and this is only guesswork, because I have no proof – that he was taken so that he could look after Jake once the second part of the plan was implemented.'

Brent looked around the room. 'Anybody else need anything clarifying?'

Several heads were shaken.

'Right – you've all had your instructions for today, so if anything crops up, I need to know immediately. If I'm out, ring me. This case is so bloody short of everything. Lynda – come with me. We're going to see Mrs Chambers.'

Once again, Lynda blushed. 'Thank you, sir,' she said, and followed him from the room.

'Have you been to the Chambers' house before?'

'No, sir.'

'Then I'll drive. You'll drive back.'

They were going up Birley Lane when she spoke again. 'Are we going for any particular reason, sir?'

His answer was almost a growl. 'No, I'm touching base with her and her son, really. Keeping them up to date on what's happening.'

'What sort of woman is she?'

'Fragile, at the moment,' he said grimly. 'Under normal circumstances, I imagine she's a nice person. How she's getting through this, I'll never know. The last few days have seen her world turned upside down. She's lost her husband of around twenty years, her friend, albeit a new friend who proved to be friendlier to her husband than to her, and she has no idea where her baby son is. She's not under any suspicion; her alibi is solid. However, I think she's holding something back.'

'Oh?' Lynda turned to face her boss. 'In what way?'

'I'm not sure. It's why I wanted you to come with me. You're a fresh face to all of it, and I want you to observe. I'm going to be telling her about the lead that hasn't been helpful, and I'm going to try and get her to think if anyone else carried a grudge against her, however small. Whatever it is she's keeping quiet about, she will tell me eventually, I'll make sure of it.'

'Understood. But she's being particularly stupid if it's something that could help us trace her baby, don't you think?'

Brent sighed. 'You're right. It may be that I've read this all wrong, but…'

'She works in a solicitor's office, doesn't she?'

'Yes. They think highly of her. She's a paralegal, and when I spoke to Tom Banton and Oliver Hardwick, her bosses, they said how much they depend on her, and how much they'd missed her when she was on maternity leave. They both seemed dismissive of my idea that maybe some criminal she'd helped get banged up had decided to get his own back. Both confirmed she does more work behind the scenes than in court; they tended to take cases as they reached the critical stage, by her own choice. She preferred the admin side. They couldn't come up with one single name for me to investigate.'

Lynda laughed. 'She really is too good to be true, isn't she?'

'You mean apart from baby Jake not being Gareth's child? The older son, Daniel, doesn't know that little fact, so don't let it slip out at any time. There's no reason for him to know, he's suffering enough with losing his dad and his brother. But maybe you're right, she is too good to be true.'

He pulled up behind the squad car still on surveillance, and climbed out. Lynda got out of the passenger seat and waited for him. He led her down the drive, and Liz met them at the door.

The dark shadows under Liz's eyes told their own story. Lynda knew she had to be tired, she was frightened, and now DI Brent was here, possibly to scare her even more.

'Liz,' he said, as he stepped through the doorway. 'This is the new member of our team, DC Checkley. Lynda.'

Liz nodded at the dark-haired young woman. 'Good to meet you, Lynda. Come through, I'll get Dan to make us a drink.'

They went into the lounge, and heard Dan call out, 'Kettle's on.'

Liz had no sooner closed the door, when there was another knock. This time it was Tanya, returning to duty after her unexpected night off. She followed the others into the lounge and sat on the sofa.

Lynda let her eyes roam around the room; the décor spoke of calmness, peace; quiet that had developed from a happy family life, and she wondered why on earth Gareth Chambers had felt it necessary to have an affair with Sadie. She could sense no discord in the atmosphere, only fear for the child that had vanished into the ether. Had Gareth found out about Liz and Philip Latimer? Was that the answer? Was that his reason for straying? Or was he a man who couldn't keep it in his pants when around other women?

Or was it love?

She had fallen in love with her Andy the first time she saw him, so why was it inconceivable that Gareth would do the same? Just because Liz Chambers appeared to be such a lovely woman, didn't mean she was.

Dan pushed open the lounge door with his bum, his hands occupied with carrying a tray of drinks.

Liz smiled at him. 'Thank you, Dan. Lynda, this is my son, Dan. He's been my rock.'

Dan acknowledged them all, simply by glancing around the room. 'Why are you here?' His tone was blunt.

'Not for any bad reason, Dan.' Brent's voice was firm. 'Come and sit down with us, if you like. We're bringing your mum up to date on the investigation, but there's really nothing new to report. It was more of a touching base exercise, I don't want your mum to feel left out of the loop. Your brother is still missing, and is our priority. Find your brother, and we have your father's killer.'

Dan hesitated. 'Nah, I'm good. I've some work to do upstairs. Has Julia gone, Mum?'

'Yes, sweetheart. About ten minutes ago. She said to say bye to you.'

He nodded thoughtfully, and left the room.

'Julia?' Brent asked.

'My schooldays friend, and Oliver Hardwick's soon-to-be ex-wife. We drowned our sorrows last night, and she slept on the sofa. It's not the comfiest of places to sleep, so I think she was quite thankful to be going home. So, what do you have to tell me?'

'Very little. Although it seems the sighting of the pushchair being put in the car unfolded was the person we're looking for, the witness couldn't tell us anything. Big car, dark colour, not sure if man or woman. We're concentrating our door-to-door enquiries on that area where the car was parked, trying to track down any CCTV footage, but for now it seems to be a dead end.'

Liz stared at him, waiting for him to go on.

'We need more, Liz. I need you to really think. We still believe you are the target, someone is intent on hurting you very badly indeed. There has to be something in your past that will take us deeper into this. I don't believe you are in physical danger, but Dan could be. Whoever this person is, they want you hurting, not dead. Dan must not go out unaccompanied, until this person is behind bars for good. So, start thinking. And I mean really thinking. If necessary, we can have you taken to work if you need to go through past files.'

She shook her head. 'No, I can access everything from here. I work from home on my days off, if I need to get stuff ready for court, or anything like that. I'll go through everything, see what

I can find, after I've emailed Tom and Oliver to tell them what I'm doing.'

'Thank you. It will be a massive help. Any little thing, make a note of it. What may be slight to you, may be massive in their mind.' Brent put down his cup. 'Thank you for the drink, Liz. Our little chat hasn't triggered off any thoughts? Oh, and before I forget, I need to take your phone. You'll have it back by tomorrow. It's not so much for any calls, we can get those from your provider, it's more for your photographs. Our tech guys will download them and we'll go through them. They'll pull out any pictures where we need you to identify people, particularly in the background, in case there's anyone who shouldn't be there. I know it sounds as if we're clutching at straws, but we are.'

She reached into her bag that was standing on the coffee table, and handed the iPhone to him.

He briefly looked at it, then dropped it into an evidence bag he produced from his pocket. 'Is this your only mobile phone?'

Lynda's eyes were on Liz's face. She saw hesitation, before Liz said, 'Yes, it is.'

'She's lying,' Lynda said, moments later, as she climbed into the driver's seat. 'She's got more than one phone. And my guess, with no proof, is that it is one she shared with Philip Latimer only.'

'Is that what people who are having affairs do, then? When I asked her, I meant did she have one that she used for work.'

Liz put the car into gear and pulled out into the traffic before answering.

'They do if they're already married, and it's important it stays secret. If she does have another phone, and her reaction says she does, that could be so important. If it was a work phone, she would have said she had it.'

'You're right. I'll speak to Tanya when I get back. Maybe she can throw some light on it, or get Liz to acknowledge she has it.'

They drove in silence for the rest of the way, and as Lynda pulled into the car park, he turned to her. 'Good work this morning, Lynda. You did exactly as I asked, picked up on the phone issue. Thank you.'

She laughed. 'Just my job, sir. A job I've wanted since being at school.'

'You'll go far.' He climbed out of the passenger seat and was already dialling Tanya's number as he entered the building.

***

She had to hide the love phone. Liz had seen Lynda watching her, and knew she had been a heartbeat too slow in her response.

She sat on her bed and took the little Nokia out of the zippered pocket in her bag. She stared at it for a moment, and then realised there was no need to hide it anymore. Thanks to the DNA results, the police were fully aware of her liaison with Phil, and Rosie had confirmed it anyway.

Liz sighed and carried it downstairs.

Tanya was sitting in the kitchen, working on her laptop. She lifted her head and smiled. 'Hi, Liz. You okay? I know they couldn't tell you much this morning, but to use the cliché, no news is good news.'

Liz held out the phone. 'Is this what you've been told to watch out for?'

Tanya took it from her and looked at it. 'Yes. DI Brent guessed you had a second phone.'

'Phil and I had them. We called them our love phones. I'm not sure how it can help – I initially kept it from you because nobody knew about us, but now everybody knows. There are things that don't add up on it. I think I need to speak with DI Brent again. Can you run me there?'

'Of course. I'll notify him we're coming. I'll get one of the surveillance team to come inside with Dan while we're away.'

'You think he's in danger in the house?'

'Gareth and Sadie were.' Liz let the words sink in, and nodded. 'I'll tell him to come downstairs until we get back.'

***

Brent took the phone from her, and stared. 'Why didn't you hand this over at the beginning?'

'How could I?' Did this man deliberately go out of his way to annoy her? 'Nobody knew about us, and certainly nobody knew Phil was the father of my baby. I wanted to keep it that way.'

'And now we've wasted days. Your baby could be dead, Mrs Chambers.'

'He's not.' She was defiant, yet in control. 'He's not dead. I'd know.'

'So,' he waved the phone in the air, 'this is the phone you used to communicate with Philip Latimer, and only Philip Latimer.'

'Not quite,' she said. 'Let me show you. I've saved every text he ever sent me. And don't say a word, DI Brent, these were private texts between me and the man I loved. I'm going to explain things through showing you those texts.'

She took the phone from his hand, scrolled back to the beginning and patiently led him through all of them, one at a time. She tried not to blush, and he didn't comment on the content. And then she reached the ones that still said he loved her, but without the term of endearment he had used on ever other message.

'Stop,' Brent said. 'There's a difference.'

She nodded. 'I know. It took a couple of texts before I realised they were being sent by someone else. And it's pure luck you can see that difference. When Phil bought us the phones, he said we must delete every call, every text, then if someone else found the phone, we could say it was for work. There would be nothing on it to prove otherwise. Phil obviously did that, because wherever he is, the person holding him doesn't know what he called me.'

'And you couldn't delete yours?'

'No. They meant too much to me. I kept the phone safe in the bottom of a deep zipped pocket in my bag. It's why I bought that particular bag.'

'Okay,' he sighed. 'And I do agree with you. Whoever sent these few texts at the end, they're definitely not in love with you. I'm going to send this to our tech lab to see if they can pull anything from those; fingers crossed they can. Is there anything else you've forgotten to mention, Mrs Chambers? Like a video of somebody stealing your child?'

She bristled. 'Don't be so bloody sarcastic. And when this is over, after the court appearance, I want that phone back. And I want it exactly as it is now.'

He picked up the phone, dropped it into an evidence bag, and glared at her. 'Then stop pissing us about, and start being honest. And remember, once this goes to court, your other son will hear all the details of stuff on this phone. I suggest you be honest with him, as well.'

Liz felt tears threatening. Determined not to show weakness in front of this irritating man, she turned and left the room. Brent nodded at the silent Tanya, and she followed Liz out of the room.

'He's doing his job,' Tanya said to the angry Liz.

They went out to the car park, and Tanya returned Liz to Gleadless. 'They're reducing my hours with you so I'll be dropping you off and heading back to Moss Way. If you need me at any time, you have my number. I'll collect my stuff, and get out of your hair. I hope next time I see you, you have Jake back with you, Liz, I really do.'

Liz felt her eyes fill with tears again. She hated this; every little thing that was said reduced her to a gibbering wreck. 'I try to switch off from it all,' she said quietly. 'I try to give Brent the benefit of the doubt, try to pretend he's not a dickhead and he'll bring Jake home to me, but it's hard. And now, it seems, I've a really difficult conversation to have with Dan. I have no idea how he'll take it.'

'Come on, I'll make you a cup of tea before I go. Give yourself a break. you've had a stressful morning, but the phone is where it should have been.'

They opened the front door, and the police officer went past them on the way back to his surveillance duties in the squad car.

'Bloody kid's brilliant on that game of his,' he grumbled. 'I need a copy of that.'

'I'll talk to him,' Liz smiled. 'Is everything okay?'

'No, I lost,' he said, and they watched him walk back to the squad car.

'Is he really that good?' Tanya asked.

'Clearly,' Liz responded. 'Gareth always said he was, but my technology knowledge is limited to what I need to know for work. I wouldn't know where to start with doing what Dan does.'

The two women went through to the kitchen and Tanya turned to Liz. 'A word of advice, Liz. Don't fuck around with DI Brent. If there's anything else he needs to know, make sure he does. He could so easily have charged you – withholding information is a serious offence, particularly so in a murder case.'

'And what would you have done, Tanya?' Liz retorted. 'Dan's father has been brutally murdered. The last thing I need is for him to find out his mother's been having an affair, and his brother is only his half-brother. I realise I'm going to have to tell him, but believe me, my head's been all over the place.'

Tanya switched on the kettle. 'I do understand that, but if this phone gives out any tracking details, it will mean we could have got Jake back much sooner. Do you think Phil Latimer has him?'

Liz shook her head. 'If the person pushing that pushchair has Jake, then it's not Phil Latimer. He's tall, quite well-built, muscly. That person wasn't. Even with a hoodie on, there would be no doubting the fact that Phil is a male figure. No, the only way Jake is with Phil, is if whoever has taken Jake, also took Phil. But Phil has been missing for so long...'

Tanya touched Liz's hand, a sympathetic gesture of appeasement not lost on Liz. 'Don't give up hope. If anybody can get Jake home, it's DI Brent. Trust him.'

She made their drinks and they sat at the kitchen table. Dan looked in on them to say he was going back upstairs now the babysitter had gone back to his police car.

'He wants a copy of your game,' Liz said.

'I know. He was getting the hang of it when you came back. I don't really want to do that though, I'm not far off sending it somewhere.'

'Then don't,' his mother smiled. 'Your game, your decision.'

He gave a thumbs up, and disappeared back to his room.

'Nice lad,' Tanya said as she sipped at her tea. 'He'll go far with two strings to his bow.'

'It will be harder for him without his father here. And while I'm still coming to terms with Sadie's actions in all of this, I can't help but feel sadness for the situation Christian's now in. He's going to have to mature really fast.'

'Mmmm. Sadie…'

'She must have been lonely,' Liz said. 'They certainly clicked pretty quickly. How long is it likely to be before we can lay Gareth to rest?'

'It won't be long. When the post mortem is over, and the forensic side is finished with, they usually release the body straight away.' Tanya took her cup and placed it in the dishwasher. 'I'll go and get my stuff from upstairs, and then head back to Moss Way. If you need me at any time, you ring me.'

Liz nodded. 'Thank you. And thank you for getting me through these last few days. It would have been a nightmare without you.'

Ten minutes later she was alone. She switched on the television, saw it was Bargain Hunt and switched it off again. She picked up her kindle, but couldn't get into her book, so gave up on that. She was almost relieved when her mobile phone rang. 'Julia?'

'Hi, Liz. I'm back home now. Thank you for last night. Despite both our lives being a bit bleak at the moment, we were there for each other, and that's good. The wine was good too.' She laughed throatily.

'Too good. I'm about to take some tablets and go and sleep it off.' Liz hoped Julia would take the hint that she didn't want to talk.

'I wanted to let you know I'm here for you. Give me a call if you need anything.'

Liz sighed. 'I need Jake.'

'I know, honey. I'll speak to you soon. Bye.'

Liz put her phone down, thankful that Julia hadn't rung for a mammoth chat session. Liz needed some thinking time. She had a conversation to have with Dan; she couldn't begin to imagine how he would react, but she knew he would have to be told.

34

Watching the activity in the cellar, Phil cuddling the baby while he cried, Jake's snuffles apparent even through a camera lens and microphone, Captor knew time was running out. It was almost welcome. The scene had been set, the picture complete; endgame was in sight.

It was a relief to have reached this stage. The screen showed baby Jake lift his hands to touch his father's face, and Phil gently stroke his son's face in response.

The whisper echoed clearly through the receiver. 'Love you, Jake.' Phil bent his head to kiss his son. Captor winced.

So much love. Phil for Liz, Liz for Phil, Phil and Liz for Jake, Jake for his daddy, love everywhere but in Captor's own life.

The anger surfaced yet again. Angry all the time, hiding it behind a gentle smile, kind words, actions that nobody would query; actions ending in death.

Sadie's death had been half-planned; if she had come upon any part of the abduction of Jake, she would have died. But Gareth – he was an unexpected bonus. Liz must surely be on her knees now. No husband, no lover, no kid. Just Daniel.

Just Daniel. In that moment, Captor made the decision to leave Liz with her first-born. He would be the constant reminder to her for the rest of her life of everything she had lost.

The meddling, interfering bitch would never know peace again, Daniel would always be there, the taunt to tell her life had changed irrevocably.

The cameras were switched off, the dumb waiter lowered for the last time. Slightly more rations than usual, enough for two days, *but would Phil realise that? Or would he assume Captor was being generous?*

Captor smiled. Did it really matter either way?

Before anybody realised where they were, they would be dead.

The voices and angst inside Captor's head would soon be stilled; the longer Phil and Jake were kept hidden, the closer discovery was, and to Captor, a prison life was out of the question. There had always been the knowledge that death would be Captor's own endgame; the time was close.

Phil heard the rattle of the dumb waiter and placed Jake quickly in his cot. He opened the small door and took out his rations. Carrying the bag back to the bed, it occurred to him it felt heavier.

He had two of everything. At first his heart lifted; maybe hunger wouldn't be the thing that stopped him sleeping that night; but a warning light came on in his brain. Maybe Captor was unable to visit the following day. Phil stashed away the secondary items, and decided to stick with his normal offerings. If his rations arrived as usual, the next day, he could still eat his small stash.

He felt uneasy. Something wasn't right; he prayed it would have no impact on the tiny child in his care. His son.

35

Oliver popped his head around Tom's door.

'Busy?'

'So so. Missing Liz's input.'

'That's what I want to talk to you about. Obviously, we give her whatever time she needs to get through all of this, but I think we need somebody to help out, even if it's with general typing and filing duties. What do you think about Karen?'

'I think she'd jump at the chance. She's wasted on reception. We'll get one of the youngsters out of conveyancing swapped to reception duties, and bring Karen in here, perhaps with a view to training her up for when we open the new offices, and Liz moves there. Karen can use Liz's office until she comes back, then we'll sort something. I think it has to be something permanent, a step up for her. Do you agree?'

'Fully agree. Can I leave it with you?'

Tom nodded. 'I'll sort it today. They can both start their new positions from tomorrow. I'll give Liz a ring and explain what we're doing, so that she doesn't get ideas about coming back because we need her.'

'Does Liz know we want to put her in overall charge at Mosborough?'

Tom shook his head. 'No, I gave a tiny hint we needed to discuss things, but that was all. I wanted to give her time to settle in after her mat leave, before I zapped her with a change and a promotion. We'll put the conversation on hold until she's ready. How are the plans going?'

'I'm meeting with the architect next week, so if you want to be there…?'

'No, thanks. Bring me in at the end when I need to sign the cheque. You're the imagination man, you'll know what we want. How long before it's up and running?'

'Oh… I should think early November. Don't quote me on that, though,' he said with a laugh. 'We'll certainly be in by Christmas.'

He closed the door and returned to his own office. Picking up the photograph of Julia, he stared at it, tracing her face with his finger. Her lovely face. A face he missed being on the pillow at the side of him when he woke in the morning.

He knew she wouldn't come back. His middle of the night text to her, where he spoke of his deep love and wanting her to return to their home, had been replied to with vitriol in every word. Words like manipulative, bully, control freak, ownership, Liz, divorce, point of no return, Liz, all used with a depth of animosity he had never before seen in Julia. And yet he loved her. Longed for her. Craved her.

He opened a drawer and dropped the photograph face down in it. He had to work, not spend all day wishing her back with him.

Tom rang through to the conveyancing department and asked for Bella to be sent to him.

When she arrived, a timid knock on his door heralding her appearance, she looked scared.

'Bella, you take over on reception when it's Karen's lunch break, I believe?'

'Yes, sir.'

Tom hid his smile. Was he really so scary? Or was it only to his sixteen-year-old employees?

'How would you feel about taking the job on full time, for a year? We'll then give you the option of moving on to whatever department you would like to be in, or staying where you are.'

Her smile appeared from behind the cloud that had been there.

'Really? I'd love that.'

'Then don't say anything yet, I'll confirm it with you as soon as I've spoken to Karen. She will be moving in here, pending Mrs Chambers' return to work, which could be some time away. I have to get Karen to agree, and if she does, you'll be on reception from tomorrow. I'll leave Karen with you for a day, to give you the basic training, and to show you the other jobs that she does which you won't have come across in your hour a day, and then from the day after you'll be on your own. How does that sound?'

'It sounds brilliant. Thank you so much.'

Karen was shocked. The proposition was a step up she had never envisaged, and she could feel herself tremble as she said yes to everything Tom Banton asked of her. He requested that she not contact Liz until he had spoken to her, but then he was sure Liz would be at the other end of a phone or email if Karen needed clarification on anything.

She did a little dance of delight when she reached her workstation in the reception area, and smiled all afternoon.

Tom made himself a coffee before ringing Liz. He didn't want to rush the conversation, he wanted her to know how much support she had, from both him and Oliver.

She answered almost immediately. The stress was obvious in her voice.

They talked for fifteen minutes, and he explained the new arrangements made to accommodate her enforced absence.

When they finally said goodbye, she put down the receiver with a feeling of relief. Tom was right – she had been worrying about work, on top of all her problems.

She sat, letting everything wash over her. Not only was there a calmness engendered by Tom's phone call, she also welcomed the sense of liberation since Tanya, who had done an excellent job of supporting her through the initial first few days, had departed for pastures new. Now Liz could give in to the grief; Gareth's death was finally implanting itself in her mind, and even Jake, who she firmly believed was still alive, created a similar feeling within her.

She missed them. Having met Gareth at such an early age, at school, it seemed as if there had never been a time when she hadn't been with him, and despite his adulterous fling with Sadie, he had been a fantastic husband. And now he was gone.

Liz brushed away a tear that had trickled down her cheek. Dan was her priority. She had to somehow tell him about Jake, about Phil, even about Rosie. Dan had always been grown up; he had been pretty perfect as a child, and teenager, but she doubted he was mature enough to cope with what was coming next.

She put off the inevitable for a further hour, then went upstairs with a heavy heart; she felt sick.

36

Dan's chin dropped down until he was staring at his legs. For some time, he didn't speak. Couldn't speak.

Finally, he raised his eyes and looked at his mother. 'I think I knew.'

'What?'

'You and him, I think I knew. You changed, laughed a lot, and then suddenly you told us you were pregnant. In the end, I put the change down to you and Dad getting closer, resulting in Jake being born. I didn't think anything of it after that. It all makes sense now. Did Dad suspect?'

She shook her head. 'No, I'm sure he didn't. Phil and I were careful.'

'Not careful enough if Jake was the result,' Dan said, more than a touch of bitterness in his voice.

'I meant we were careful not to let other people know. We couldn't – Phil was my client. I would have lost my job; Phil's marriage would have fallen apart… it was all too much to contemplate.'

'And you loved him? No wonder you haven't cried for Dad.'

She knew Dan was deliberately hurting her. 'Dan, if you think I haven't cried for your dad, then you couldn't be more wrong. I miss him so much, yet he was the one who strayed in the end.'

'Of course he did. Dad wasn't stupid. He can do maths. He goes away for six weeks, comes home and then you announce you're pregnant. The baby arrives early with a healthy weight on him – no, Dad wasn't daft. I bet anything this was payback time for him.'

She stared at him, this son who had become a stranger in such a short space of time.

'And what about his wife? Rosie did you say? And his little girl?'

'He thought his marriage was over.'

'I bet his wife didn't.' Dan paused and stared at Liz. 'Mum, leave me alone. I need to digest this. I'm assuming you've only told me because this is going to come out if it ever goes to court?'

She nodded, misery etched across her features. 'Please, Dan…'

'Go, Mum. I've things to do. I need to think this through. On my own.'

She stood and looked at him, his arms wrapped around his knees as he sat on his bed. 'I'll be downstairs. If you want to talk…'

The look he gave her wasn't a good look.

She closed the door quietly behind her, and headed downstairs. She picked up the receiver and rang Brent.

'Liz?' DI Brent answered at the first ring.

'I've told him.' She knew her voice sounded dead.

'And?'

'And he's thinking things through, on his own, in his bedroom. We'll get through it… I hope. I rang to see if there's any news.'

'Only that we can release your husband's body. I haven't told Christian Fremantle he can sort out his mum's funeral yet, so don't make it public knowledge.'

'I won't. I contact a funeral director?'

'Yes, it becomes a more normal death. You simply do anything you would have done if Gareth had died of, say, a heart attack. The only difference with the funeral is that there will be an undercover police presence, unless we track Jake and Philip Latimer before that.'

'You definitely think they're together?'

'I do, but I'm pretty sure they've both been taken. I don't think Latimer took Jake. He hasn't used any banking facilities for months, hasn't used his phone… no, somebody else has them both. Whoever has them is no dumbo. The couple of calls made to your phone, and the texts we believe have been sent by the kidnapper, have all triangulated on the city centre. A smart move. It tells us nothing.'

She sighed. 'Thank you for updating me. Every day I wake up and think this is the day Jake will come home, and I'm slowly losing heart.'

'We're doing everything we can. I believe this one will be solved by technology – he or she will slip up one day, and we'll track the error. We have some smart cookies on our computers, so don't give up on your little one, Liz.'

'Thank you,' she responded quietly. 'I'll be in touch when I've sorted out the funeral date.'

She stared out into the darkening sky, and slowly sobs engulfed her. She leaned her brow against the window pane, her hands on the window sill. And then she felt arms go around her and hold her.

'Come on,' Dan said. 'We'll get through this. Together.'

She turned around and held on to him.

One of the surveillance officers turned to the other and nodded towards the bay window of the house they were watching. 'Wouldn't want to be in their shoes for a million pounds.'

'Me neither,' the other one agreed. 'Fancy some pizza?'

***

Christian Fremantle felt sick. He had been told he could return home, and from the outside it all looked normal. Once inside, he realised life would never be normal again. His childhood home felt strangely bereft.

The stair carpet had been lifted and taken away. He had been warned to expect that, but even so, it came as a shock. He had dismissed his family liaison officer within a day of her arrival, but he wished he hadn't been quite so hasty. He was truly on his own, and maybe a little company would have eased his return.

He walked around the house, feeling as if he didn't know it at all, despite living in this same place all his life. His bed was rumpled, and he assumed somebody had sat on it during the investigation. His mother's bed had been stripped of all bedding, as had the cot she had used for Jake. He had decisions to make. Sell or keep?

He doubted it would sell – not at the moment anyway. Who would want to buy a house where there had been a double murder? Maybe in a few years, but certainly not now. And maybe in a few years it would form part of any decisions he would need to make, after finishing at Solent.

He gathered up his duvet and pillow and took them down to the lounge. He would text the friends who had given him sleeping space over the last few days, thank them, and say he was back at home. That night, he would be on a different sofa – his own.

After checking the contents of the fridge, he walked down to the shops. Two people spoke to him as he headed down the road, expressing their condolences; he responded with a nod, a smile and a thank you. His brain wasn't engaged enough for any more than that. It was only as he passed by Liz Chambers' house that he faltered. He looked over towards it, hesitated, then crossed the road. The shop could wait a few minutes.

Liz saw him speak to her bodyguards, then walk down the drive. Her door was open before he reached it.

'Come in, Christian,' she said quietly. 'How are you?'

'That's what I came to ask you,' he said equally quietly. 'I'm going to the shop…'

'Have you time for a drink?'

He nodded. 'Just water, thanks. How's Dan?'

'He's doing okay. We both had a bit of a meltdown last night, but it seemed like a turning point. We'll get past this, somehow. How are you?'

He sat down on the sofa, and shrugged. 'I've stopped feeling so bloody angry.'

'Good. You've been back home?'

He nodded again. 'It's awful. And I do realise your memories of how it looked must be really bad, but that was my home. Now it's empty. Who would have thought a missing stair carpet would make all that difference?'

Liz sat down by his side. 'It's not the missing stair carpet, Christian. It's the missing mum. The stair carpet can be replaced.'

'I know it can. It seems to symbolise everything.' He looked so miserable; Liz placed her arm around his shoulder and pulled him close.

'If I can do anything to help…'

He gave a short bark of laughter. 'You've lost even more than me. Is there any news…?'

'On Jake?' She shook her head. 'Nothing. He's alive, though. I know he's alive.' She stood. 'I'll get you that water. Have you had breakfast?'

'Not for about four days, no,' he smiled.

'Bacon sandwich?'

'Thank you.'

The smell of the bacon grilling brought a sleepy-eyed Dan downstairs, shocked at cooking being done by someone else.

'Mum…?'

'Don't panic, Dan,' she smiled. 'Bacon sandwich? I'm already doing one for Christian. He's in the lounge.'

Dan rubbed his eyes, stared at his mum and headed for the lounge.

Liz could hear the two of them talking. Two young men who had shared massive trauma in their lives; they were uniting over bacon sandwiches.

She carried their breakfasts through, and then excused herself. 'I need to do something normal. I'm going up to strip the beds, now Tanya has left us.'

'Don't do mine, Mum. It's got notes all over it. I'll sort it today, I promise.'

She smiled as she walked upstairs. She could hear the two young men speaking and knew they would have things in common. Probably gaming.

Fifteen minutes later, post bacon sandwiches, she heard them continuing the conversation while climbing the stairs before going to Dan's room.

Dan's voice was then most noticeable as he explained things to Christian, and then there was silence, interspersed by cries of success or failure as they worked their way through various levels.

Liz couldn't for the life of her understand the attraction of gaming, but right at that moment she felt grateful for anything that took their minds off the tragedy of the situation they found themselves living in, through no fault of their own.

She finished making up Jake's cot, then carried all the bundles of laundry downstairs.

She fed Christian at lunchtime as well, and when he went home mid-afternoon, he apologised.

'I'm sorry,' he said. 'I blamed you and your family for all my troubles, but I was wrong. You're as much innocent of anything as I am. The man who killed your husband and my mum is to blame.'

'You think it's a man?'

'Only because it's normally a man. It seems, according to DI Brent, that there's no clear indication of either sex. Would a woman do this?'

'Possibly,' Liz admitted. 'Some of my cases have been women who killed. Don't close your mind to the killer being female.'

'But why kill two people to get one baby? Surely, with a baby, it's pretty easy to grab them from a pram? Or am I wrong?'

Liz smiled. 'I think you'd still have to kill whoever was pushing the pram. If somebody tried to snatch Jake from me, they'd have to kill me to stop me fighting back.'

Christian frowned. 'So, have you upset somebody?'

'Not that I know of. We've been through files from work and I've wracked my brain to think of anybody who has cause to hate me, but come up blank.'

'Rosie hates you,' Dan called from the kitchen.

'Rosie?'

'Phil Latimer's wife,' Liz said. 'And she doesn't hate me. I almost think she understands…' Her voice trailed away as she realised Christian knew nothing of the complications surrounding Jake.

He waited, but when she didn't continue, he turned to leave.

'Thanks, Dan,' he called. 'See you soon.'

She watched as he crossed the road, finally heading towards the shop. She knew one day he would get on with his life, probably leave Sheffield behind him, but he still had to reach that stage. For now, he was hurting.

37

*D*arkness had fallen. Captor hesitated before leaving, turned, and headed back towards the dumb waiter. Loading everything available into it, the contraption moved for the last time downwards.

Phil heard the clank of the chain, and put Jake into his cot. He crossed to the cupboard door, and quickly removed everything that was in it. Several bottles of water, three packets of biscuits, even a bar of chocolate. Teabags, four milk cartons, baby food… He stared in horror at the assortment of goods.

It felt like the last supper.

The contraption clanked as it returned to its normal level, and Phil automatically stored away the goods, his mind spinning. This shouldn't have happened until after Jake's next sleep, a long sleep which told Phil it was night-time.

***

Captor parked in the lay-by and sat for a moment in the car. Contemplation of what was to come was inevitable, but not scary. It would be far scarier if a long prison sentence came into the equation. Affairs had been put in order, the time was approaching, and an extra five minutes added on to life was acceptable.

Finally, reaching into the boot, Captor picked up the small backpack, strapped it onto both shoulders, and left the warmth and comfort of the car behind. The path had been walked several times over the last couple of weeks; the way was known. One glance *backwards, as if maybe a consideration of a mind change, then endgame.*

The keys to the small locked room housing Phil Latimer and his son sailed through the night air and landed high in a tree. The rain was relentless, and Captor pulled up the hood and walked.

Liz Chambers, payback time.

38

Tuesday morning saw Liz wake up with a banging headache, and a sick feeling in her stomach. Today was the day when she had to make the arrangements for Gareth's funeral, and she wasn't convinced that Dan would want to go with her.

She peeked through the bedroom curtains before heading to the bathroom, saw it was raining heavily, and almost went back to bed.

She stood under the shower for longer than normal, allowing the water to batter her head and face, and felt marginally more like a human being once dressed. She could hear Dan having a shower, so waited until he joined her downstairs before asking if he was still okay to go with her.

'Of course I am.' He gave her a hug. 'You don't seriously think I'd let you go through this on your own?'

They didn't talk much over breakfast; neither of them wanted the bowl of cornflakes, both of them forced it down their throats.

They left the house, despite Liz's protestations, in the back of the police car. The two officers said they would feel happier with both their charges in the back seat, than if they had to follow Liz and Dan through innumerable sets of traffic lights as they travelled in Liz's car to the funeral home. They did give Liz the option of checking it out with DI Brent, but she wisely declined and gave in to their requests that felt like instructions.

A little over an hour later, they were back home; Gareth's body had been collected the day before and was in the funeral home being prepared for viewing. Liz arranged to go to the Chapel of Rest the following day, and to her relief, Dan declined to accompany her.

He said nothing until they were back in the house.

'I can't go to see Dad, Mum.'

'That's fine. be sure, is all I ask, because after next Tuesday you won't have that option.' She touched his cheek lightly. 'Your decision, my love.'

'I'd rather remember him how he was.' Dan's tone was quite abrupt, and she watched as he left her to go to his room. He was angry. It wasn't directed at her, more at the world, and how it all seemed to have gone pear-shaped at once.

She took drinks out to the two officers, who she had to accept, reluctantly, had been the best option for getting to the funeral home; her head was everywhere, and she wasn't really fit for driving.

Liz was walking past the phone when it rang. She glanced at the number – she had long since ceased to expect it to be the kidnapper.

'Hi, Tom,' she said. 'Is everything okay?'

'Kind of. Can you and your phenomenal memory remember anything Oliver might have been going to do today?'

She briefly glanced at the calendar to make sure she was linking her mind to an accurate date. 'Not as far as I am aware. I take it he's done his usual thing of not putting it in my diary?'

Tom laughed. 'Yes, he's not been in today. I've tried his mobile, but I know he switches it off when he's with a client, or in court. It's not urgent, I don't want to waste my time trying to find him if he's not contactable for a specific reason. So, how are you?'

'I'm okay. Aching to hold Jake again. Gareth's funeral is next Tuesday at ten, Abbey Lane Cemetery. There'll be drinks and a lunch afterwards, but I don't know where, yet.'

'We'll be there, you know that, don't you?'

She stifled a sob. 'Thank you. That means a lot. How is Karen doing?'

'Very well. A little nervous, but that will pass. I seem to remember you being nervous, once…'

'A long time ago,' she said drily.

'I miss you – we both do. But your job is safe, never doubt that. We have plans for you. At the new place.'

'Tell me more,' she said, trying to sound enthusiastic.

'Not yet. But better times are coming, hold that thought. If you need either of us for anything before next Tuesday, simply pick up the phone. Are you listening to me?'

'Yes, boss. Speak to you soon,' and she replaced the receiver, her lips curving into a smile for the first time that day. Tom Banton had always been able to cheer her up.

Lynda Checkley rang later, ostensibly to ask if she was okay. Liz told her she had been to arrange Gareth's funeral, and she was feeling far from okay, but coping. Lynda's next comment surprised her.

'I've been thinking…' She hesitated. 'I know we've all checked your files for any low-life folks who may have felt angry at you for them being in prison, but has anybody asked you if you've ever managed to upset somebody at work? Or anywhere else for that matter? People can bear grudges for a long time.'

'At work?' Liz paused for a moment, letting her mind roam back over the years. 'There was only one – somebody who I upset by being promoted into Tom and Oliver's next-door office. She thought she should have had the job. But she's dead now anyway, died of cancer about three years ago. I really can't think of anybody else.'

Lynda sighed. 'Okay, it was merely a thought. This is such a frustrating case. Nobody saw anything, nobody is reporting anything out of the ordinary, nothing.'

'I'll get my boy back, you know.' Liz's voice was strong. 'He'll come home to me.'

'We're all hoping for that outcome. Me especially. I have a son of the same age. I suffocate him with cuddles these days. It's all too easy to think "there but for the grace of God"…'

They disconnected the call, and Liz switched on the television. There was a small piece about the ongoing investigation; it was dying a natural death, through lack of results. She wanted to scream at them, to force them to keep Jacob Chambers' name in the forefront of everyone's mind; she didn't want him forgotten. She switched it off in anger, irrational anger; she knew he wasn't important to the rest of the world, just her and Dan, but she needed the rest of the world to keep searching for him.

It was fully dark, and she stared through the lounge window, watching the two officers watching her. They must have had a shift change because they were different to the two escorts of that morning. She saw them sit up a little straighter, then both got out. Brent climbed out of the car that had pulled in front of them. He spoke briefly, and they returned to their vehicle.

Liz moved to the front door, dread in her heart.

She opened the door, wordlessly. 'Hi, Liz. Take that look off your face. I'm not here with news of Jake.' He watched her face crumple, and tears flowed.

'Hey,' he said. 'Bad day?'

She nodded. 'Bad day.' She pulled her tissue from her sleeve and mopped ineffectually at the tears. 'Are you here for a reason?'

'I am.'

She saw his eyes change, from caring to professional. 'It's concerning Oliver Hardwick.'

'Oliver?' She looked puzzled. 'He's not arrived at work, then?'

'You knew he was missing?'

'Sort of. I knew Tom Banton couldn't track him down. I didn't know he was missing…' Her eyes widened as she took in the implications. 'Oh my God, you think he's been taken as well, don't you?'

'He's connected to you, we can't discount that there's a link.'

Fear flashed across her face. 'But why? What have I done to bring all this down on people that I love?'

They moved into the lounge and sat down. Liz was tearing her tissue into shreds. 'Have you checked with his wife? With Julia?'

'She's the one who has officially made him a missing person. Ordinarily, we wouldn't even be considering it at this early stage, but in view of his link to our investigation, we're taking it seriously.

Apparently your Mr Banton has been ringing his mobile phone all day, with no success. He eventually rang Julia Hardwick, who knew nothing of his whereabouts, but by this time alarm bells were ringing in Mr Banton's head, and he asked Julia, as Mr Hardwick's next of kin, to report him missing. They're being interviewed right now, in the hope we can get some lead on him.'

'He lives alone…' she started to say.

'We know. We have no idea when he was last seen. His wife hasn't seen him for some time, although they have infrequent conversations by text. She's almost of the impression he's doing it to get her back; apparently, he was devastated when she left him, and it's been pretty constant, the barrage of texts telling her he wants her back in his home. I don't think that's the case. I think he's been taken. I need to ask you a question. Have you and Oliver Hardwick ever been anything other than employer / employee?'

'My God, no!' Her answer was emphatic. 'I have only ever slept with two men in my life, Gareth and Phil. Yes, Oliver was a friend as well as an employer, but that's all.'

Brent nodded. 'Does his wife know that?'

'What? There's nothing for Julia to know, or even query… I'm not really sure what you're getting at.'

'I'm getting at Julia Hardwick. Have you ever managed to cross her, either knowingly or accidentally?'

'We've been friends for years. Since junior school. Met up again when I started work for Banton and Hardwick because I recognised her from the photo on Oliver's desk. For fuck's sake, I wouldn't sleep with her husband.' He could hear the anger in her voice, and knew there could be more to come. He had to push her, to make sure she was telling the truth.

'You slept with Phil Latimer,' he said. 'I don't imagine Rosemary Latimer was too pleased about that.'

'I loved… love… Phil. I didn't love Oliver. Simple.' Her tone was scathing. 'Now back off, and go and find the bastard who is doing this to me. And get those two gone from my driveway, I don't want any protection from now on. Let whoever is taking them come and get me. At least I'll see my son again. I mean it, DI Brent. Get them out looking for this kidnapper, instead of guarding me.'

'That's against my wishes, Liz.'

'Do I care? I'm going to see my husband in the Chapel of Rest tomorrow, and I'm going alone. If they're still at the top of my drive blocking my car's exit, I'll ram them. That's a promise. Tell them to go when you leave here. Now, is there anything else?'

'Not at the moment. Can I send Tanya back to you if you don't want the lads in the car?'

'No. Leave Dan and I alone. We'll look after each other.'

He nodded. 'As you wish. I'll be in touch.' He stood. 'I'll see myself out.'

Her anger was evident in the way she held her head, the stiffness in her frame as she stood. 'Find my son,' she snarled as he exited her house.

39

The density of the cloud cover effectively blocked out the moon, and the night sky was black, dense like velvet. The wind had increased slowly through the day to howling level; the rain was torrential. A bad night to be out, and few people had ventured far from their homes. The attractions of a fire proved to be much better than ferreting out the wellies and going to the pub, or to bingo.

Dog walkers let their shivering, reluctant pets out into the back garden, instead of taking them out for their night-time perambulations. In the darkness of the woodland, a tree branch creaked as the wind, slightly less strong in the more sheltered environment, caused the weight attached to the limb of the tree to move.

It swung, it spiralled. The bowels and bladder had long since evacuated, the eyes stared. Rainwater dripped off the dangling fingers; the hair was flattened to the scalp.

Oliver Hardwick was not destined to join Phil Latimer and Jacob Chambers in the cellar. Endgame was underway.

40

Liz waited until seven before ringing Tom. He was already in the office. From the noise, she guessed he was in her room, using the coffee maker.

He sounded subdued. 'Liz?'

'Tom – any news?'

'No. I couldn't sleep…'

'Me neither. I've waited two hours before ringing you…'

'Where can he be, Liz? He's so predictable. Does everything by the book. If he had planned this time out, he would have cleared it with me. I know he's been really down over this split from Julia, but…'

'Tom, DI Brent thinks it's connected to Jake's disappearance. He doesn't think Oliver has walked away, he thinks he's been taken.'

'But that doesn't make sense, or am I missing something? Oliver is your employer, not your lover or your child. He's not, is he? Your lover, I mean.'

'No, he's not. Definitely not. But I do care about Oliver, as I care about you. Brent is convinced that all of this is to punish me, to make me suffer, and it's bloody working. We can't work out who would want to do that.'

Tom hesitated. 'Rosemary Latimer?'

'No, she has an alibi for the time of the murders. And she loves Melissa too much. That child comes first with her; she wouldn't risk prison, risk losing everything. Yes, she's mad at me, would probably like to see me dead even, but she wouldn't do anything about it.'

He sighed. 'You're probably right. I was clutching at straws. I'm going to ring Julia now, see if she knows anything. I'm assuming

Brent will have her as first port of call, as they're technically still married. I'll ring you later.'

She put down the receiver and walked into the kitchen. It was still dark, the rain bucketing down, lashing against the window.

Slowly, over the next twenty minutes or so, the sky lightened. Her mood didn't.

She dressed carefully, knowing this would be the last time she would ever look on Gareth's face. She thanked God for all the memories they had created over their joint lifetime, and knew she would always miss him.

When Dan joined her, he was dressed in his suit. 'I've decided to go with you.'

'Have I forced you into this?'

He shook his head. 'No, you haven't. I think I'm scared of seeing a dead body, but he's my dad. He never hurt me when he was alive, and he wouldn't hurt me now he's gone. Is his face…?'

'It's untouched,' she said gently, and pulled him close. 'It will be like seeing him sleeping.'

She felt him nod.

He moved away from her, and headed for the kitchen. Removing his suit jacket, he called, 'Want me to cook the cornflakes this morning?'

She smiled. 'Make mine Coco Pops. I need chocolate.'

***

Dan clung tightly to Liz's hand as they were led into the room where Gareth lay. To Dan's horror, he realised that 'looking as if he were asleep' was a mile away from how his father looked. He looked dead.

He choked back a sob, and she released his hand, pulling him closer to her, her arm around his shoulders.

'I'm here for you,' she whispered. 'Don't be afraid. Your dad wouldn't want that.'

They stood for a moment without moving, and then Liz released her hold on him and moved forward. She touched the back of her hand on Gareth's brow.

'I love you,' she whispered. 'Fly with the angels, Gareth.'

Dan moved to join her, then leaned down and kissed his father's head. 'Love you, Dad. I'll take care of Mum, I promise.'

They stayed a few minutes longer, then left, once again holding hands.

Liz felt numb. She knew one day the grief would hit her, but while ever Jake was out there, unfound, she couldn't give in to it.

They climbed back into her car, and she set off for home. Back to the real world – the world where three people who belonged, one way or another, to her, were all missing.

She would have to say goodbye to Gareth, but she knew it wasn't time to say goodbye to the others. It was all she had to cling to – her hope, her belief that Jake and Phil were still alive somewhere, and possibly joined by Oliver.

Whoever was holding them was pure evil, but it had to be someone who knew what would hurt her the most. And it had to be someone who knew her, really knew her. This wasn't some stranger, this was someone close to her.

She drove the car on to the driveway, and almost ran the few steps to her door. She let them in, and gave her son a kiss on his cheek.

'Thank you,' she said. 'Don't feel you need to stay with me – I heard what you said to Dad, but I don't need looking after. It's still my job to look after you. Go to your room, and make us lots of money with your game. I don't need baby-sitting, honestly. Besides, I have some thinking to do.'

He nodded. 'If you're sure...?'

'I am.' Her tone was firm. 'And thank you. I wouldn't have let you know, but I was dreading going to see your dad on my own. You give me strength, Dan.'

He returned her kiss, and headed up the stairs.

She moved into the kitchen, sat at the table and took out the small notebook she carried in her bag.

The list started with Rosie Latimer's name.

Rosie Latimer

Tom Banton

Chloe Banton

Julia Hardwick

Christian Fremantle ???

And then she stopped. Did she really only have this small circle of people who knew her well? And should she put Phil Latimer on that list? Should Christian be taken off it? She had no idea what Sadie had told him about her, if anything, so she left him on the list, and left the question marks in place.

Could Phil be behind all of this? If he was, he had played it cleverly, laying false trails with the phone, not using his bank card... but she couldn't see it. They had loved too intensely, the kind of love that would endure through everything. No way would Phil cause her distress or pain.

She could almost sense him beside her, so extreme was the feeling she knew still lived in her. His face – the eyes that smiled all the time, the hair she had run her fingers through, before, during and after making love. The laughter, the quietude, the times they didn't need to speak. No, Phil shouldn't be on the list.

So that left four people – she couldn't really count Christian, she had never even spoken to him, before the murders had joined their lives.

She started a new page and wrote 'Rosie Latimer' at the top.

1. Discovered affair by Phil telling her.
2. Knew about Jake being Phil's baby.
3. Strange behaviour re cheque – never explained.
4. Alibi for time of murders. Assume police have triple checked this.
5. If she didn't commit murders, she didn't take Jake.
6. Could she have a partner? Has Brent looked into this?

Liz stared at the points she had made, then turned over to the next page. She would go back and continue with the bullet points if anything else occurred to her. She moved on to Tom Banton.

1. Boss. Known me 12 years.
2. Did he know about my affair?
3. If he did, why would it upset him to this extent? Effect on business?
4. Is he happily married?
5. Does he have an alibi for time of murders?
6. He isn't the right build for the person on CCTV. He's too tall.
7. Need to check with Brent if they've looked at Tom.

On her next page, she wrote 'Chloe Banton'. She was undecided whether or not to include Chloe – she had known her for a long time, but only on the periphery of Tom's life. They had shared phone calls when Chloe had called her husband and Tom had been out of the office. They had met up at the annual Christmas event that Banton and Hardwick hosted for their employees, but Liz knew she couldn't really call them close, Chloe and she had never been best buddies – unlike her and Julia.

Liz left the page with Chloe's name on as a blank page, and headed up the next one with the name Julia Hardwick.

1. Wife of Oliver, close friend. Knew about Phil.
2. Asked me if Jake was Phil's baby, so obviously suspected. I did not confirm.
3. No babies of her own. Is this significant?
4. Drinks heavily now.
5. Refuses to consider going back to Oliver.
6. There was a barrier between us the other day. Coldness.
7. Does she have an alibi?
8. Right size for CCTV pics.
9. Where is she living? Oliver still in marital home.
10. She could get close enough to Oliver to disable him. Syringe? Drugs?

Liz leaned back on the sofa and closed her eyes. Was she letting her imagination run riot? Her notes pointed to Julia – Julia, who she had known since they were children at school. Liz thought about all the late-night chats, the shared drinks after work, the chatter between them, and she realised she knew little about her. Did she not want children, or was there some medical problem between them that stopped them having a family? Could she have taken Jake to bring him up as her own?

Liz leaned forward and jotted down the additional thoughts that she had worked her way through. Then she headed up the next page with Christian Fremantle's name, but could find nothing to write on it.

She stared long and hard at the page dedicated to Julia. Where the hell was she living? Did it have a secure room in which she could keep two men and a baby, locked up with no means of escape? It seemed a ridiculous, improbable thought.

Liz knew that neither Phil nor Oliver would give in to imprisonment, they would seek freedom. She took her mobile phone out of her bag and hesitated a moment before pressing the number that would connect her to her friend. She had to be careful; had to act exactly as she usually did, when she rang purely for a chat. This time the chat would be her commiserating about the disappearance of Oliver, and the call would be from a solicitous friend.

She pressed the button and Julia answered almost immediately.

'Liz?' There was an obvious catch in her voice.

'I'm here, Julia. Is there anything I can do? Have the police found him?'

'No, no sightings, nothing. He's not used his phone, his cards, and heaven knows where his car is. I'm so scared.'

'Hey… he may have taken off for some time out. I know his split from you really upset him…'

'But where is he? Why hasn't he rung me to let me know he's safe? He's quick enough to text at other times, but now, nothing. The police seem to think it's connected to Jake and Phil Latimer's disappearance, but I'm not buying that. He doesn't really have any connection to them.'

'Have they told you that, or are you adding two and two and making five?'

'They hinted at it. Seemed to suggest he might have been snatched, exactly as they think happened to Phil.'

'Julia, I hate to think you're on your own. Tell me your address, and I'll come over and see you.'

Liz was shocked when Julia gave her the information. She had half expected her to procrastinate, find some excuse for not passing on the address. It was a stone-built detached house, Julia explained, with inadequate car spaces, so Liz might have to park and walk.

Liz didn't want to go, but she seemed to have talked herself into it. She explained to Julia she would check Dan was okay, after the morning's activities, and she heard Julia's quick intake of breath.

'You two have been to see Gareth, haven't you? Oh my God, Liz, I'm such a shit. Stay with Dan. If things go pear-shaped with Oliver, I'll need you then, but for now, Dan is more important. Stay with your son.'

'If you're sure…'

'I'm sure. And as soon as I hear anything, I'll give you a ring. If things get desperate, I'll nip over to see you.'

Liz nodded, then realised Julia couldn't see her. 'Okay, we'll leave it at that. Ring at any time, Julia. I'll be here for you.'

She stared at the now-silent phone, and threw it on to the sofa. Result. She had the address.

Going to the foot of the stairs, Liz hesitated. *Screw your courage to the sticking post, or whatever that crazy saying is,* she mumbled softly, and climbed.

41

*P*hil felt the first stirrings of panic since waking up on that awful day, when he'd realised there was no means of escape. Over the months he had come to accept he would have to sit it out until either he was killed, or someone found him; he couldn't escape on his own.

But now it felt different. There was no dumb waiter delivering anything, not for him, not for Jake.

Phil spread out one of his blankets on the floor, put some toys on it and sat Jake amid them.

'Hey buddy,' Phil smiled, 'playtime. You want porridge for breakfast?'

The little boy grinned at him, his one tooth showing clearly. He picked up the set of plastic keys and threw them at his daddy. With a laugh, Phil threw them back.

'Oh, if only these were real ones,' he said. 'If only, Jake.'

Phil checked through the pouches until he found a porridge, screwed off the top and handed it to Jake. 'I promise, Jakey, when we get out of here I'll make you some real porridge, in a bowl, with a spoon that you eat it with. In the meantime, you'll have to make do with a pouch.'

Jake didn't care. He quickly finished off his breakfast, and Phil handed him a bottle of warmed milk. The small cooking stove warmed the air slightly, and Phil was reluctant to turn it off, but he only had three gas canisters left and no guarantees he would get more; he warmed his hands, then quickly turned off the gas before his brain could say leave it on for a bit.

Jake drained all his milk, and threw down the bottle. Phil picked it up and carried it across to the small washbasin. He washed it as well as he could, and stored it in what he called his pantry, the heavy-duty cardboard box the nappies had been in when they arrived.

Phil looked across at the dumb waiter; had he slept through its arrival? Had it been taken back up without his knowledge?

For the second time he moved across and opened the small cupboard door. Nothing.

Jake pulled a small, bright yellow, play computer towards him, and hit assorted keys with his tiny fingers. A is for... here we go round... N is for... the number three... here we go round... how many elephants...

Phil turned, leaned against the cupboard door, and watched as his son played. He had tried desperately to keep Liz out of his mind, but every day he had physical proof that she was still as firmly embedded in his heart as she had ever been. He couldn't begin to imagine the devastation she must be feeling, not knowing where Jake was, and he knew he would give up his own life to save their son, to get him back to her.

He straightened up and felt the room go slightly out of kilter. Food. He needed food. He had to remain healthy for Jake. He looked at the meagreness of his supplies, and once again panic threatened to override everything. He ate half a sandwich, then snapped open the chocolate bar. He removed one small chunk and bit down on it, saving a small piece for Jake.

'Here, Jake. Try this, but don't tell Mummy I gave it you,' Phil smiled. 'I'm not sure how she'll feel about you having chocolate.'

Jake ran his tongue around it, took it out of his mouth, stared at it for a moment, and popped it back in.

'That settles that,' Phil laughed at his son. 'We don't tell Mummy. What happens in the cellar, stays in the cellar. High five, Jake,' and he held up his son's hand as they shared their sweet secret. Chocolatey secret.

42

'Tibby! Tibby!'

May Fraser hadn't felt this worried since Fred had walked out on her all those years earlier. Where the hell had Tibby got to? In the fifteen years he had lived with her, first arriving as a tiny kitten bought to replace the errant husband, he had never so much as left the back garden. For the past week, he hadn't been well.

She had asked neighbours to check their gardens and sheds, but he had neither arrived home, nor been reported as a lifeless body. She was on day three without him, and fearing the worst. What had that young woman at number two said? *Cats go away to die, if they're ill.*

She didn't want that for her Tibby, she wanted him at home with her, where she could give him a proper burial in her back garden, when the time came. The nearby wood had seemed the most logical area to search once she had covered the neighbours.

'Tibby. Come to Mummy,' she called, then mewed the sound that always brought him running for his food. She stood and listened, hoping to hear an answering mew. She rattled the small box of dried cat food she had brought with her – he recognised that sound, that should bring him back to her, if nothing else did.

Creak...

She whirled around. 'Tibby? Is that you?'

Creak...

She stepped carefully around the tree roots, heading towards the sound.

Creak...

The wind was strong, although not as bad as the day before, but it was still raining. She hoped the sound was coming from Tibby. She navigated a tree, holding on to the trunk for support, and stepped into an even darker area.

She didn't scream. It took more than a swinging body to cause that reaction in her. And the poor fellow hanging there wasn't going to hurt her.

She took out the mobile phone given to her by her niece, tried to recall Siobhan's words on how to use it, and hit the 9 button, three times.

43

'The lady over there, a Mrs...' Lynda checked in her notebook, 'Mrs Fraser, found him when she was trying to find her cat. He's gone missing. The cat...'

Brent smiled at her. He could hear the tension in her voice; the scene of crime was cold, dark and extremely wet. The body was on the ground and it was, without doubt, Oliver Hardwick. The tent had been erected over it in an attempt at preserving any forensic evidence, but he doubted much would have been saved. The body had clearly been out here for some time, in gale force winds and torrential rain.

'Do you think he killed himself, sir?' Lynda asked.

'No idea. Looking at the set up, I would say yes, but that could so easily have been staged. We'll not pre-suppose, Lynda, we'll wait for the experts to tell us whether it's murder or not.'

Brent was looking at a substantial evidence bag with a backpack in it. 'We need them to get that back to the station, check what's in it, and get it logged in. Then we can have it, see if there's anything helpful to our investigation in it. The wallet in here,' he held up a smaller bag, 'indicates it is Oliver Hardwick. If it is murder, it wasn't because of theft. There's quite a bit of money in it, all his cards, a picture of Mrs Hardwick...'

'The wallet was on him?'

He nodded. 'Yes, in that pouch thing of his hoodie top. We had to check in that for ID, but I can't open the backpack because I don't want to contaminate any evidence. I'm hoping whatever is in it will be dry, not damaged by all this bloody rain. I'll go and have a word with Mrs Fraser, get her escorted home and then we have the job of telling Mrs Hardwick. I want you with me, Lynda.'

'Yes, sir.' Lynda acknowledged his words, her face grim.

Brent spoke briefly to May Fraser, asked one of the attending constables to take her home and make her a cup of tea, and returned to watch the white-overalled forensic workers assiduously doing their jobs.

They stayed another quarter of an hour, then left the body removal to the people who knew how to do it. He and Lynda drove to Julia Hardwick's home.

She saw them arrive, watched as they parked four car lengths away from her front door, and went to meet them.

'You're wet through,' she exclaimed, as they entered the hallway. 'Let me get a couple of towels.'

'No need, Mrs Hardwick. We'll be fine. Can we go through to the kitchen, we don't want mud on carpets.'

She stared at them 'You have news…'

'The kitchen. Is it through here?' and Brent led the three of them down the long hallway.

'Please…' Julia said, almost in a whimper.

Brent waited until they were all seated. 'We believe we have found your husband, Mrs Hardwick. I'm sorry, there's no easy way – he is dead.'

Her eyes widened. 'No… did I hurt him that much?'

'You're assuming it's suicide?'

She let the words sink in. 'What are you saying, exactly, DI Brent? Murder? Accident?'

'I'm saying we don't know. It looks as though it could be suicide, but we still have to wait for forensics on it. We are sure it's your husband though. We found his wallet in the front pocket of his hoodie.'

She frowned, looked puzzled.

'In what?'

'He had on a dark grey hoodie, black joggers, trainers.'

'But… unless he's had a personality transplant, he's not my husband.'

'What do you mean?'

'My husband only ever wears suits. He doesn't possess any leisure wear, not even jeans. When we go on holiday he takes shorts for during the day, lightweight suits for the evening. He wouldn't be seen dead in joggers…' and she stopped, all too aware of what she had said.

The tears ran down her face, and Lynda reached out and grasped her hand. 'I'll make us all a cup of tea,' she murmured.

Julia's head dropped to her arms, resting on the table. 'And Jake? Liz's baby,' she mumbled, barely audible.

'No, just your husband. We firmly believe Liz Chambers is being targeted, and Oliver's death is a possible escalation.'

The kettle started to hum; Julia's mind went into overdrive. 'Does Liz know?'

'Not yet. Our priority was to notify you. We will need you to identify the body, possibly tomorrow. In the meantime, is there anybody we can call for you? You shouldn't be alone.'

'My sister, Catherine… I went to her when I first left Oliver. She's speed dial 1 on my phone.'

Brent nodded to Lynda as she handed out the mugs of tea, and she went down the hall in search of the phone. They heard her lowered voice as she explained the situation.

'She'll be here within the hour,' Lynda said as she returned to the kitchen. They quickly finished their drinks, Julia not saying much, trying to take in the enormity of the situation.

'We will need to speak with you, again.' Brent stood to leave. 'Ring me if anything occurs to you, but let your sister take care of you. I'll go and see Liz and Tom Banton, so no doubt they'll be ringing you later. Give yourself an hour's break from it, before the rest of the world knows. I'm really sorry for your loss, Julia; I know you were separated, but he was still your husband.'

She wiped away a tear. 'I didn't stop loving him, I stopped being able to live with him. He controlled me, controlled our lives. Which is why I'm querying the clothing you say he had on. That wasn't the Oliver I've known for twenty years. If that Oliver had been around during our marriage, we would still have been together. Leaving him wasn't a decision I took lightly. I had long conversations with Liz about it, and I suppose really it was her who gave me the courage to walk away. She basically said I had to be true to myself.'

Julia followed them to the door, then closed it softly as they left.

Lynda's thoughts were racing. Liz had advised her friend to leave her husband, and Julia had acted on that advice.

'Sir…'

'I know what you're going to say. It's another link, isn't it? Liz advises Julia to leave Oliver, and she sticks with that decision, doesn't go running back to him at the first hurdle. She's got a lovely home, all on her own; Oliver must have been resentful if Julia was silly enough to say "*well Liz says*"…'

She frowned. 'But it's Oliver who's dead.'

'Then let's pray Phil Latimer and Jake don't quickly follow. I was dreading telling Julia Hardwick, but telling Liz Chambers is going to be worse. And that's not because Oliver is dead, it's because she's going to make the jump to who's next.'

He put the car in gear and pulled out into the traffic. 'Let's go and get this over with, then we'll head back to the station. I'll tell Liz first, then I'll ring Tom Banton.'

***

Liz was horrified. Oliver dead? She stared at Brent, disbelief written across her face.

'So, you no longer believe his disappearance is connected to Phil and Jake's kidnapping? Is that what you're saying?'

'No, I'm not saying that. We can't form any theories until we hear from the pathologist. He will confirm time and manner of death. I didn't want you to hear about this on the news, didn't want you jumping to conclusions – which you are doing.' He frowned at her. 'We have no results yet, Liz. I can't stress that enough. Nothing was clear at the site, apart from it was dark, wet and muddy. Our forensics people wouldn't even speculate to me, they told me to go and they'd let me know as soon as possible, but would prioritise it.'

She gave a huge sigh. 'I'll ring Julia. She'll be devastated.'

'Catherine should be with her now. Did you tell Julia to leave Oliver?'

'What?'

'Liz, help me out here. I'm trying to make sense of this. If this death is murder, then all our previous thoughts still stand. If it's suicide, which is how it's meant to appear, then it brings into question Oliver's mental state. And that, I suspect, would take it away from the investigation into Jake and Phil's disappearance. So, I'll ask again, did you tell Julia to leave Oliver?'

'No, of course I didn't.' God, how she disliked this man. 'I told her to be true to herself, and to come out of his shadow. I didn't even know she'd left him until I went back to work after maternity leave. They were both secretive about it. If she interpreted my words as I must leave him, then so be it. But that's not what I said. I tried to empower her enough to stand up to him, not to walk away.'

Five minutes later, Lynda and Brent were on their way back to the station. Liz was in tears, wondering when all this was going to be over. So many tears. Oliver – dead. Unthinkable.

And Tom. How would he react? Brent had asked her not to contact him for an hour, he needed to speak with him first. But she guessed Tom would take it badly. They were friends as well as business partners; he would take it very badly indeed. And he would, eventually, place the blame at her feet.

***

Tom didn't ring. He arrived at her front door, his face like thunder.

'Tom, come in.' Her voice was quiet.

'We need to talk.'

'I know.'

'There are things going on that are coming to the surface, things involving Philip and Rosemary Latimer. Start talking, Liz.'

'I had an affair with Phil.' The statement was bald, uncompromising. 'I loved him. I stopped it for two reasons – I was pregnant with his child, and I was putting my position at work in jeopardy. The main reason was Jake, though.'

Tom stared at her. 'Liz Chambers, you're a bloody idiot. Why didn't you come to me at the beginning? Did Oliver know?'

She shook her head. 'I don't think so. If he had known, I would have been finished, I suspect. There was no bending with Oliver.'

'This takes us around in circles, then. Who did know?'

'Nobody at the time. Phil told Rosie after we had split up.'

'She knows? And she's not been taken in for questioning?'

'She has an unbreakable alibi for the time of the murders. I've gone over and over this in my mind. I can't believe Oliver committed suicide. Why would he? Okay, Julia had left him and made it clear she wasn't going back, but he would have got over that, eventually. He had a more than successful business with you... none of this makes sense. DI Brent is convinced I am the sole target, somebody wants to hurt me so badly, but I've even made a list, trying to work things out.'

She reached into her bag and took out the small notebook. She opened it and handed her notes to him.

He was quiet while he read them, and then looked up at her.

'Julia? You think Julia killed Gareth and your childminder? How does Brent feel about that?

'I haven't said anything to him.' Liz dropped her head. 'It was an exercise in bringing my own thoughts into focus.'

'And?'

'Julia has been my friend for years, Tom. How can I think that of her? How can I say to Brent that she could be holding my baby because she doesn't have any of her own, or she wants me to suffer for some reason? None of it makes any sense.'

Tom reread her notebook and sighed. 'This was why I became a solicitor, and not a policeman. You're right, of course, none of it makes sense, and I'm sorry I was so damned angry when I arrived here. Maybe we should go have a chat with Rosie Latimer. Do you think that would help? This all seems to hinge around Phil Latimer. He disappears, and bad things start to happen.'

'But the police have CCTV of whoever took Jake, and while nobody seems to know whether it's a man or a woman, it definitely clears Phil. And you, for that matter.'

'Me? You've seriously considered me?'

'No, of course not, any more than I would seriously consider Oliver. But Phil is tall, he's over six feet, and quite broad. That person pushing Jake down that road was slim, medium height... nobody would place either you or Phil in that category,' she finished with a smile. 'I'm going over and over everything, every day – it's a proper living nightmare. And now losing Oliver...'

Tom's eyes dropped to the floor. 'I have to go back to work and tell them. Karen knows, but I've asked her to say nothing. I think this needs to come from me. My God, Liz, he was such a good friend. What's happened to him? Why has he done this?'

'I don't think Brent is convinced it was suicide. He kind of hedged his options when he was here. If it is murder, if somebody killed him and then hung him from that tree, it has to be whoever has Jake. But if it's suicide, then why? After talking to Julia, I got the feeling that it was salvageable. I don't believe for one minute that their marriage was finished. She still loves him, I know she does. He needed to soften, to stop the control. Julia's not a child, she's the same age as me, and he gave her no room to be herself.'

'You think?'

'I'm sure. So, we have to look further afield if it is suicide. Maybe he's left a note.'

'The police have already gone to his home. We have to wait; Brent said he'd be in touch once he knew more.'

Tom stood. 'I'll get back to the office. And I'll ring Chloe – I've already told her, she was sobbing when I put down the phone. Then I'll have to tell the staff. God, this is hard.'

'I know.' Liz touched his hand. 'I'm sorry I'm not there supporting you.'

She followed him to the door, and watched as he drove away. She felt strangely uneasy; he had been really angry with her when he arrived; in all the twelve years she had known him, he had never so much as raised his voice.

She turned to go back into the lounge, and saw Dan.

'I didn't want to interrupt...' he said. 'Are you okay? He sounded a bit stroppy.'

'He's angry because he's lost his business partner and best friend.' She paused. 'Dan... can you find plans of houses on the internet?'

He tried not to smile. 'I can find plans of the Pentagon on the internet.'

'What?'

'Oh sorry, I shouldn't have confessed that... what do you want to know?'

'If I give you an address, can you find plans for the house?'

'Yes.'

'Is it legal?'

'Fudged.'

'What? What does that mean?'

'Mum, give me the address.'

She tore a page out of the notebook and wrote down Julia's address. She handed it to him, and he glanced at it. 'Give me an hour. I've got something running that I need to finish first.'

He went to head back upstairs.

'Can you really get the Pentagon plans?' she called.

'Of course.'

She shook her head and smiled. She hoped he was joking.

44

*P*hil was hungry. Working on Jake's sleep patterns, he reckoned it was two days since the dumb waiter had last arrived.

This was scary. He was concerned about the intermittent pains he was experiencing in his chest, the prolonged ache in his back, the weakness he felt generally. He was rationing milk, nibbling at food – what he wouldn't give for a big fat juicy steak. Jake was okay; he had enough baby food for a month or so, but without an adult to give it to him…

Had this been Captor's intention all along? To get father and son in this cellar, before walking away? To leave them to die?

Whoever Captor was, the planning was incredible. Phil had no idea how long he'd been held, but knew it must be months. He had never heard any voices other than Captor's own disguised voice, so obviously nobody knew of the existence of this prison.

Phil took a small bite out of the stale sandwich, and chewed it slowly. When his own food was all gone, he would have decisions to make about the baby food.

He needed to live to keep Jake alive.

45

Rick Naylor walked into DI Brent's office carrying the backpack and wallet. He was tall and starting to carry a little too much weight to be healthy. Brent looked up as the door opened.

'Rick! Didn't see you at the crime scene.' He held out his hand to shake Rick's. 'Seems ages since we've been out for a drink.'

Rick grinned. 'About six months, I reckon. I got out of the crime scene job. Was a bit wild and woolly, I understand. Everybody came back wet through. Anyway, brought these up for you. The report's been emailed to you, but it basically says it was suicide. That backpack has a note in it, explaining why. I brought it straight up here because it gives you even more problems. It makes everything that's happened in your murder case so far, look like trivialities. It's all been logged, and the victim's fingerprints are all over the note. It seems he climbed up the tree, tied a rope round his neck and jumped. Deeply disturbed chap.'

'Sit down for a minute. Take me through it.'

Rick opened the bag and withdrew a small plastic bag with a letter inside it. He passed it across to Brent.

'This is the main item. It's dated two days ago.'

Brent took the handwritten letter from Rick and read.

DI Brent

I am possibly making assumptions, but I am presuming that you have, by now, worked it out that I am the one who killed Sadie Fremantle and Gareth Chambers. If you hadn't have reached that conclusion, it would have only been a matter of time before you did.

I cannot, of course, go to prison. Therefore, as you are reading this, I am dead. That solves that particular problem.

Brent lifted his head and stared at Rick Naylor. 'Shit.'

Naylor nodded. 'Thought you might say that. I'll leave you to it then,' and he stood to leave Will's office.

Brent held up a hand. 'Hang on, Rick. You've read all of this?'

Naylor nodded again.

'Then don't go. I can't miss anything in this, any little nuances there might be. Let's go through this together, if you can spare me the time.'

Naylor let out a small whistle. 'Bloody 'ell, Will. We've never had a DI before who knew the word nuances, never mind knew what it meant.' He retook his seat opposite Brent and waited.

Brent picked up the letter again and continued to read, this time aloud, so they missed nothing.

Elizabeth Chambers has caused so much heartache, so much pain in my life, she has had to be punished. I only intended taking her baby; that was the plan. I would keep him for a few weeks, then leave him somewhere he would be found. I wanted her to know that she couldn't interfere in, and subsequently destroy, other people's lives.

But then Rosemary Latimer came to see me. She was distraught. She told me her husband, Philip, had been having an affair with Liz, and the baby was her husband's child. Not only was Liz forcing her way into my own life by dripping poison into Julia one drop at a time, she had destroyed another family.

Julia ultimately left me, and there is no hope left in me of a reconciliation.

Brent paused again, while he digested what he had read aloud.

'It gets better,' Rick said. 'Or worse, depending on which way you look at it.'

'This man is seriously disturbed,' Brent growled. 'He's changed from being a solicitor, to take on the role of judge and jury.'

I decided to set up the place where I would keep the baby, but after Rosemary had told me about Philip, I knew the man had to be the first. If Liz loved him as much as Rosemary said she did, it would wound her deeply to know he was missing. I followed him one day, dressed as a jogger. He was walking in Ecclesall Woods. It was early in the morning – I didn't sleep much, and I had sat in my car, near his home, all night waiting for him to go out. It was a regular routine for him to walk every morning.

It was simple. I stabbed him in the neck with a syringe of Rohypnol, and he fell to the floor. I dragged him back to my car and within an hour, before he recovered from the drug, he was in my place of captivity. He is still there. I removed his watch, his wallet and two mobile phones before locking him away.

The significance of the second mobile phone, a Nokia, was revealed when Liz Chambers tried to contact him. I decided to use that phone to let her think she was speaking to her beloved Philip.

I fed him inadequate amounts daily, via a dumb waiter I constructed. I watched him the whole of the time via CCTV cameras I rigged up. At first, he was angry, but every so often I would do something decent, like providing an extra blanket, and he would cry with gratitude. I was playing with his mind.

'Dumb waiter? Is he holding him in a cellar then? Or a bedroom? This man is a psycho… I feel like a complete idiot. I've interviewed him twice, not because he was a suspect, but because it was part of the general routine, really. He came across as one smart guy, polite, friendly, and extremely professional. He also came across as clearly being fond of, and supportive of, Liz Chambers.'

'That type of persona was what gave Harold Shipman credence. The professional bit. Don't beat yourself up about it, Will, it seems he's fooled everybody, not only you. Nobody from his practice has raised any queries, have they? Not even his partner?' Rick could see Will was winding himself up over it.

'Shit,' Will groaned. 'His partner. I've to tell one of the most respected solicitors in Sheffield that his partner has murdered two people, kidnapped two more…' and then realisation hit him.

'Where are they, Rick? Is it at the end? We need to get officers to wherever it is, and get that baby back to his mother.'

Rick shook his head. 'Don't bother rushing with reading it – he makes it clear he's not going to tell anyone where they are.'

Brent felt numb. Could the day get any worse? He returned to reading out the letter. Rick sat forward, listening intently. He had read it, but listening to Will's audible version of it made it… different.

Then I became even nicer to him. I sent hot drinks down to him.

'Down to him… so he definitely has them in a cellar. The dumb waiter is travelling down, not up.' Brent wrote *cellar* on his notepad.

He slept more, because I thoughtfully put tablets in the hot drinks, medication supplied by my doctor after I told her I couldn't sleep following the break-up of my marriage. I soon learned how many tablets he needed to put him out for three hours, and during one of these lengthy naps I moved everything the baby would need into Latimer's prison room.

Then I stopped giving him the medication, he needed to be alert enough for a young child. He didn't seem to understand. I think he thought it was merely some stuff 'Captor' (that is what he called me) needed to store.

Are you following all of this, DI Brent? Everything happened as I expected it to, until the day I snatched the child.

I knew there was always the chance I would have to kill the woman. The child was never in danger. I had the address from our taxi service records. Their driver took Liz from Rosemary Latimer's direct to Sadie Fremantle's to pick up the child.

What I hadn't counted on was Gareth Chambers screwing her on the afternoon I turn up to get the child. I had taken a knife in case I had to dispose of her, but I have to tell you, DI Brent, if I could have done it without killing, that is what would have happened.

She appeared at the top of the stairs, naked except for a dressing gown she was trying to put on. I was holding the knife, but managed to grab at her and throw her down the stairs. She screamed, but initially that didn't worry me.

Gareth Chambers then appeared out of the bedroom door, naked, and recognised me. I stabbed him.

I took the child, climbed over the woman and strapped Jacob into his pushchair. I had parked my car on the service road that runs parallel with the main road, and I strapped him into the rear seat. I couldn't fold the pushchair, as you probably know, so I threw it into the boot still fully assembled.

I then drove to the prison room, and sent Jacob down to his father in the car seat, via the dumb waiter.

Will stopped speaking and stared at his friend. 'Fucking heartless, absolutely fucking heartless. What sort of bastard are we dealing with here?'

'A dead one,' Rick responded drily. 'But carry on, and you'll really learn what a bastard he was.'

They bonded as if they had always known each other. Latimer treasured that child; what a pity he hadn't treasured his own wife and child as much. He is still looking after him now, but this is where things get difficult, DI Brent.

You don't know where they are, and this letter isn't going to tell you. This letter is all about me, about why I did this. When I made my plans, I knew I would have to die, but to be perfectly honest, I have nothing left to live for. I love Julia. I adore Julia.

Liz Chambers took that relationship away from me by poisoning my wife against me, advising her to be strong, to walk away. She destroyed Rosemary Latimer's marriage, and her husband's relationship with Melissa, his only child.

Now she will pay.

Phil Latimer has little food, maybe enough for a couple of days. He has approximately four small bottles of water, although he does have access to a wash basin with running water.

Jacob has enough baby food for about a month.

When Phil Latimer becomes disoriented and weak from lack of food, he will be incapable of feeding the child. Or changing nappies.

There are no clues. I don't want you to find them. Maybe if Julia had come back to me, the outcome would have been different. But she didn't.

I will be avenged.

Oliver Hardwick

Brent threw the letter on to his desk, and clenched his fists. 'This was written two days ago, which means Phil Latimer may already be out of food, unless he's been really careful, and has clicked on there's no more coming from the dumb waiter. Let's think this through.'

'I already have,' Rick said. 'I'm glad you asked me to stay while you read it. The key to their survival is if Latimer can stay alive. If he can ration that baby food so that they eat one portion each per day, it may give you an extra two weeks.'

He stood and shook Will's hand. 'Good luck, pal. We'll have our drink when this is over.'

The office felt empty once Rick had left, and Brent picked up the letter and quickly reread it. He walked into the main office, looked around at his team, and waved the letter at them.

'If anybody's booked any leave in the next three weeks, forget it. I want everyone on the team here in thirty minutes for a briefing, and I mean everyone. If anybody is out interviewing, or door-knocking, get them back here. Lynda, Tanya, can I see you in my office please?'

The two women looked at each other, both briefly wondering what they had done wrong and deciding nothing, then followed their boss into his office.

'I want you to be prepared, by reading this before the briefing. You both know the Chambers family, and we have a massive problem.' He turned around, walked to the photocopy machine, and ran off two copies of the letter. He silently handed them to the women, then went back to the machine to run off extras for the briefing. He printed twenty more, and decided he wanted all twenty back in his hands at the end of the meeting. He didn't want this getting into the papers, either by accident or design.

Tanya and Lynda read through the letter, and for a moment both were silenced.

'Murders solved then,' Lynda finally said. 'The absolute bastard.'

'We have to tell Liz,' was Tanya's initial response. 'Maybe she can think of somewhere that she can connect to Hardwick. She's known him for a lot of years – maybe he has a holiday home? Maybe his parents left him property? Liz, and Tom Banton – and Julia Hardwick, of course – know the most about him.'

Will nodded. This was what he hoped would happen after the briefing – a fast and furious exchange of thoughts. He had a good team; they would be horrified when they read the letter, but it would energise each and every one of them.

'Thank you, ladies. Keep thinking. After the briefing, I'm going to see Liz. I want you two to filter all the ideas coming from everyone at the meeting, get things up on that white board. We're against the clock. We have to find this prison, and fast.

46

D an clattered downstairs, carrying printouts. He handed them to Liz, and she quickly scanned them. Then she spread them on to the coffee table.

'Are you legally getting these?'

He shrugged. 'You are. I gave them to you.'

She thought through his logic, and shook her head. 'I'll take the blame if anything should come of this.'

'And I'll let you,' he said with a laugh.

'Right, talk me through them.'

'First, did you know who owned the property before you asked me to get the plans?'

She shook her head. 'No, I know Julia is renting, until she finds the right house to buy.'

'Then that's even more strange. It's owned by your Mr Hardwick.'

'What?'

'That's what it says.'

'I'm 100% sure that Julia doesn't know that little fact. She put her name with several estate agents, and waited to see what they all could offer. This one was in the right area, at the right price, although she's paying a ridiculously small amount of rent for a Victorian stone built property in that area. That explains the low rent, doesn't it? He's manipulating her once again. Do I tell her, or not?'

'How are you going to explain that you know who her landlord is? You can't say you've seen these. She'd think it pretty weird that you wanted plans of her house.'

Liz shrugged. 'I have no idea. She's obviously going to find out though, because Oliver's death means she inherits; they're still married.' She shook her head, showing the despair she was feeling. 'Perhaps the answer is to say nothing, then when she does find out, be the caring friend. That way, I keep her friendship, instead of being in a potential "don't shoot the messenger" situation.'

'I think you're right. So, what next?'

'Let's go through these papers, see if there's anything suspicious. We're looking for a cellar, an attic, an outbuilding that could conceivably house Jake and Phil.'

The house had four levels: basement, kitchen and living area; three bedrooms, and an attic level. Liz dropped her head, after putting on reading glasses. Over her years at Banton and Hardwick, she had seen hundreds of sets of plans, and blessed that fact as she pored over Julia's house plans, understanding everything she was seeing.

She started with the basement – it was split into two areas, one that had originally been used to house coal deliveries, and the other for storage, wine cellar – whatever the owner needed. The entrance to the basement was a door leading off the hall, with twelve steps going down.

'Look at this,' she said to Dan. 'We have to go see Julia. You up for it?'

'Give me two minutes.' He stood, and the doorbell rang. They glanced out of the window and saw Will Brent's car.

'Damn,' she swore quietly. 'It's Brent and Lynda. Let them in.'

'What about these?' He pointed to the papers on the coffee table.

'I'll think of something.'

The two police officers moved into the lounge and Brent asked Dan to give them half an hour.

'Mum?'

'It's okay, Dan, if I need you, I'll call. I make decisions about our lives, not DI Brent.'

Ouch. Brent felt the pierce of the barbed comment. She really had taken against him.

'Liz, drop the antagonism. We're here with news.'

'Jake?' Her eyes lit up briefly, then dimmed again when Brent shook his head.

'Only partly. We believe him to still be alive, as is Philip Latimer. However, we don't know where they are. I have something I would like you to read, but I will be taking it back after you've read it.'

She felt afraid, truly, darkly afraid. She took the photocopied letter from him, and began to read.

As she reached the end, she was reading it through tears. Lynda passed her a tissue, and squeezed her hand.

'No. He had this so wrong. I had finished the affair with Phil, given him back to Rosie. It was Phil who told Rosie, she didn't find out by accident. We were discreet always. And I spent the best part of a year listening to Julia pour her heart out about the restrictions on her life, how he wouldn't let her go to work, drive her own car, have any say in the home… and still I encouraged her to think twice before walking away. Just one time I told her she had to decide, whether to go or stay. And really, I only said that because I was hormonal, feeling sick all the time, and fed up with her problems at home. I can't believe that these terrible happenings are because Oliver had me all wrong! He was so good to me.'

'He clearly wasn't good to you, Liz. It was all an act. The entire team now has something to work with, and they're following different leads. We're hopeful we'll get them both free before much longer.'

Liz felt anger bubble up inside her. 'And I was beginning to think Julia was behind it all. I even got this,' she indicated the papers on the coffee table, 'to see if she could be holding them at her house.'

'House plans? Can I look?'

She nodded. 'Of course. Look at the basement. It's split into two halves. Plus there's an attic. And she had moved into this before I went back to work, before Jake was taken. She moved in round about the time Phil disappeared. But this is all no longer relevant following Oliver's confession, is it?'

'We can't ignore it, Liz. Does she own this house?'

'No, that's the strange thing. Oliver does, but I'm pretty sure she doesn't know that. She obtained it for rent through an estate agent. An estate agent who is probably a friend of Oliver's.'

Brent took out his phone. 'Tanya? I need a search warrant.' He read out the address, and she promised to ring him back as soon as it was done.

'Come on, Lynda, let's get over there. We may be clutching at straws, but let's clutch sooner rather than later. Can I take these?' He bent to pick up the plans.

She sighed. 'Yes. Provided you ring me immediately if he's there.'

'That's a promise.' He sounded grim. He was going out of the door when he stopped. He looked back and winked. 'Just for the record, where did you get these plans?'

'I found them on the mat this morning,' she said drily.

'Thank Dan, will you?'

***

Julia felt bewildered. Her house was full of police officers, searching everywhere. DI Brent was with her, having shown her the same copy of the letter he had taken back from Liz, and she knew her world was about to implode.

Oliver had murdered. She had been married to a murderer. And the police were searching her house, her house that she had been told Oliver owned. It seemed that Oliver's house, their marital home, had already been searched following the discovery of his body, but another group of officers had been despatched to do a second search. They were taking no chances. Time was against them.

'Does your husband have any other properties?' Julia shook her head to bring everything back into focus. 'I have no idea. I didn't know this one belonged to us!' She gave a short, sharp laugh. 'It appears I'm paying rent to myself, DI Brent. How crazy is that?'

He could hear the hysteria in her voice. Time to inject a note of calm. 'Okay, we have two missing people who are going to die if we don't find them soon. I need you to think. Have you ever driven by any properties he's taken an interest in, noticed any unusual payments into the bank account…?'

'Bank account? We have one, do we? I simply get an allowance. I know nothing of how much money we have, any properties we may own, and do you think he will have made it easy for me to find out? Try asking Tom Banton. Maybe he'll know. Don't forget my husband would be more than capable of doing his own conveyancing on any properties he bought, so they could be well hidden in his files.'

'We have our tech guys going through his computer. We found a desktop and a laptop at his home. Do you know of any others?'

'He had an iPad as well. But there's also his work computer. Liz would know more about that than me.'

Brent nodded. 'Thank you. I'll check we've found the iPad. We already have his work computer.' He could see she was beginning to be marginally more amenable, and he asked Lynda to get them a pot of tea. He needed to have her thinking clearly, if she was to help them. He knew they wouldn't find anything here, Oliver wouldn't have been able to hide Phil and Jake in this house, not and keep Julia in the dark.

'Okay, Julia. I need you to go back to when you first met Oliver. Where was he living?'

'With his father. His mother had died recently, and he put off moving into a place of his own while his dad was still grieving. Six months later his dad died, and he remained in the house, buying his brother out of his half share.'

'Brother? Can you give me more information, please?'

'Not really.' She looked unhappy. 'I know little about him. I knew at the time that Oliver was buying him out, but I never met him, and I've never heard of him since. He was older than Oliver by about ten years, and they simply drifted apart. I don't really think they fell out or anything, they didn't move in the same circles, and I never heard Oliver speak of him again. His name was Jared, but that was his second name. I can't remember his first name, but I know it begins with O. It's why he insisted on using Jared, so that mail didn't get directed to the wrong O. Hardwick. Oscar? Owen? Otto? I really can't remember, I'm so sorry.'

Julia was babbling about trivialities, embarrassed that she knew so little of her husband, a man she had been married to for over fifteen years. 'I'm sorry,' she apologised once again, looking down at her hands. 'I'm not much help, am I. How is Liz? I assume she knows about this new development?'

'Yes, she does. She's hurting, she's in panic mode, she probably needs a friend. That's if anybody can get past bodyguard Dan. That boy is amazing. If I ever have a son, I'd want him to be like Dan. But it's her other son we need to concentrate on. And I believe your husband stashed them in a property he owns, hidden away where nobody is likely to visit it. He may have owned it for years, and now found a use for it. We must find it. We'll be out of your hair shortly, Mrs Hardwick, but if you think of anything…'

'Of course. The only thing I can add to what I've said is that I understood his brother was in construction, in case you need to find him to tell him about Oliver. That could be a starting point.'

'When this news breaks, it's quite possible he will contact us.'

Brent made a note on his pad. O. Jared Hardwick. Construction. He stared at it for a moment, wondering if the elusive brother was still in construction. And did he too have properties? Properties that Oliver Hardwick had done conveyancing on… after all, with the excessive costs relating to buying bricks and mortar, it would make sense to contact a long-lost brother if he was a successful solicitor with his own practice. His mind was racing with the possibilities opening, following that simple statement from Julia, that Oliver had bought his brother's half share in the family home.

Two members of Brent's team appeared at the door and shook their heads, indicating that nothing had been found.

Brent and Lynda finished their drinks and stood. 'Thank you, Julia. I know how you must be feeling, and this will come to an end.'

She nodded, and followed them to the door. 'Just as a matter of interest, how did you find out Oliver owned this house?'

'Oh, we have our ways,' he said with a smile. 'I need to know of any others now, so keep thinking, please, Julia, let's get Jake back with his mummy, and Phil Latimer back to his family.'

Julia stood at the door until every officer had left, then closed it firmly, locking it behind them. She sank to the floor, and sobbed. Oliver was gone, and despite the evidence in the letter, she could never have seen him as a murderer. She had loved him for so long, waited patiently for his controlling side to ease as he became more confident that she wasn't wanting to go off with other men, and now she had truly lost him.

She sat there for a while, letting the tears flow, then stood. She picked up the phone, and dialled the estate agents. The lovely Mr Bloomfield could get ready. He might have been Oliver's friend, but he was about to find out just what it meant to make an enemy of a woman.

47

*P*hil stepped back after taking stock of the baby food. He would have to limit both himself and Jake to one pouch each per day, once his own meagre rations had gone. He still had half a sandwich, six ginger biscuits, half the bar of chocolate, one packet of crisps and unlimited water, thanks to the small hand basin.

He had a box full of baby food pouches, and after counting them was relieved to see thirty-seven assorted foods, some savoury, giving more vital nutrients to them, and some sweet. He knew he wouldn't be choosy one day, it would be a case of keeping alive to keep Jake alive. He also had seven cartons of long life milk, maybe not the most nutritious in the world, but it would fill Jake's stomach, settling any hunger pangs. Nappies wouldn't be an issue either; by the time the last nappy was to be used, they would both be dead. He could no longer dispose of them, but he had hundreds of carrier bags he could utilise, and he could stash the bags in the dumb waiter while they waited for rescue.

Rescue. What an awesome word. He now had no doubt that Captor had disappeared for good, abandoning them to whatever fate had in store for them.

He knew the whole country would be looking for the two of them, but he had no way of knowing how far on the journey of discovery the police had travelled. He had realised long ago that maybe Rosie had assumed he had walked away from her and Melissa, and therefore hadn't reported him as a missing person, but that would not have been the case with Jake. That would have been instant news. He had no idea how long Jake had been with him, but surely every day was a day nearer being found.

He would do his bit to buy the police time, by keeping the two of them alive.

Jake stirred, and Phil waited for that first delicious after-sleep smile from his son. The blue eyes, so like his own, flickered open, then closed, then opened once more.

The smile came. The arms raised, and Phil lifted him out of the cot.

'Okay… you hungry, little man?

He handed him a bottle of cold milk, having decided to limit his use of the gas to once a day, for warming milk. It didn't seem to bother Jake, and he drank it with relish.

Phil decided to do without anything, and after Jake had finished his milk, they settled down under a blanket to read.

Please, dear God, send us some rescuers soon, Phil thought, even if it's so we can get some new books. Peppa Pig is such a spoilt brat.

'Peppa,' Jake said.

48

There was an air of hope in the briefing room; Brent had updated them all on the morning's activities, and had told them he wanted information on O Jared Hardwick, possibly, but not necessarily, in the construction business. He also wanted reports on the computers, including the iPad recovered from Oliver's house, and he wanted them fast.

For the first time, he read through the pathology report on Oliver Hardwick, and knew that no matter how bad things got, he would never have the balls to climb on to a tree branch, loop a rope around the branch, the other end around his neck, and jump.

The man's mental state must have been slowly deteriorating for months, and yet not one of his acquaintances appeared to have noticed it. There was no suggestion it could have been anything but suicide; the facts, combined with the letter left by him, cleared that up.

Brent typed up his own report: two murders solved, one perpetrator dead, two victims still missing.

***

Brent closed down his computer and went into the briefing room. Nobody held up a hand indicating they had something to tell him, so he walked amongst them. Everybody seemed to be on the phone. The noise was at a level he hadn't seen since the beginning of this investigation, and it gave him a considerable buzz.

He leaned over the computer of the young constable he could never remember the name of, and asked him what he was working on.

'O Jared Hardwick, boss.'

'And?'

'There's a construction company called Hardwick, but it doesn't list an O J, or even a J, as one of the directors. I'm running a search through Companies House to see who the directors are, because the business is Chesterfield based, close enough to be a consideration.'

'Thanks, er…'

'DC Peters, boss, Steve.'

'Oh, right. Thanks, Steve, and welcome to the team.' Brent wandered over to the next desk where Lynda was reading through notes. 'Anything new?'

She shook her head. 'No, but I'll keep going till I've read everything. We have to find this little one, sir. Do we need to re-interview Rosie Latimer and Tom Banton, in view of the letter?'

'Tom Banton's in court till three. I'm going down to see him after that. I'm going up to see Rosie Latimer from there, and then Christian Fremantle. That's everybody seen then, who's on the need-to-know list.'

'We've not found OJ then?'

Will smiled. He knew the team had taken to calling Oliver Hardwick's brother OJ; he hoped he wouldn't use it, if and when he eventually got to meet the man.

'Not so far. We don't really know where to start, he might not even still live in the country. Fingers crossed we get a lead soon.'

Brent headed back to his own office, and poured himself a coffee. Thinking time. He could do nothing else for an hour, when he would have to leave for his appointment with Tom Banton. He had liked Tom the first time they had met, and Brent wondered how he would react when he saw the letter. He not only had to take the facts on board, he also had to tell their not inconsiderable staff. In addition, he had the business to sort out, distance himself from the evil that was Oliver Hardwick. He hoped the practice would survive.

His thoughts drifted to Gareth Chambers, and the upcoming funeral. Even though they had found the murderer, he would still be at the service, watching, looking for strangers, doing the policeman sort of things everyone expected at a not quite normal funeral service. And supporting Liz and Dan.

He took a sip of the coffee, and watched through the window separating his office from the main room. This case had dragged on for some time now, and he felt they were no nearer getting their missing persons back. Phil must be really bonding with the little boy, and Will wondered what the future would hold for the child, once they reunited him with his mother. Phil would most likely insist on being a part of his life, but would Liz be able to handle that? Would Rosie and Melissa?

The whole thing was such a mess; convoluted lives, insecurities – everything that could go wrong, had already done so. Could it ever be put right?

He pulled the letter towards him once again, and read it through in its entirety. If he hoped for enlightenment that hadn't been there earlier, he was disappointed. It still wasn't there. The worst thing was that he could hear Oliver's voice reading it aloud. The phrases, the overall tone, it was all Oliver. Slightly pompous, not too friendly, the one in charge.

He rolled the letter in its plastic cover and put it in his jacket pocket, ready for showing to Tom Banton. He looked through the inner window, caught Lynda's eye and pointed to the outside. She nodded, closed her computer and joined him.

'Tom Banton?' she asked.

'Yes. Let's go and get it over with. This poor chap doesn't know what's coming his way.'

***

Tom was already waiting for them. They walked into his office, and he offered them a drink. Both declined, and he wasn't impressed. He'd deliberately waited for them before getting himself a drink, thinking they would join him, and he had to miss out by being polite.

'You have some progress?'

Brent nodded. 'Yes, sir, we do. I have something I want you to read. It's your partner's suicide letter.'

'So, it was definitely suicide? Shit. I've known him all these years, and never saw anything that would lead me to think he was falling apart.'

'There's a lot more to this letter than simply falling apart, Mr Banton. Be prepared. It's not pleasant reading.'

Tom took it from him, and smoothed it on to his desk top.

He said nothing until he got to the end, then went back to the beginning and read it again.

'How did I miss this, DI Brent?' he said eventually. 'How can I have known this man for all these years, almost loved him as a brother, and not known he was capable of this? How can we possibly carry on as a business which deals with the law, after this? He's not only killed two people, kidnapped two more, and killed himself, he's potentially put twenty people out of work, with all the problems that will cause.'

Brent didn't know what to say. Lynda did.

'Maybe we should have the coffee, now.'

Tom picked up the phone. 'Karen, can we have three coffees, please? And then I need you in here when DI Brent has left, please. We have things to organise.'

'Your secretary can't see the letter, Mr Banton. That won't be in the public domain for quite some time, if ever. Obviously, this will never go to Crown Court, just the Coroner's Court. When you tell your staff, give them the bare facts. No reference to Hardwick's state of mind, tell them it was suicide.'

Tom nodded. 'I understand. I have to tell them today. They have to know what we're facing.' He handed the letter back to Brent as Karen walked through the door, holding the tray of drinks.

As she turned to go, she asked how Liz was.

'She's okay, missing her little boy,' Lynda responded before Brent could answer. 'I'll tell her you asked about her.'

Karen smiled. 'Thank you. Give her my best wishes.'

Nobody spoke until she had gone. And then all three spoke at once.

'What…?

'When…?

'If…?'

They all smiled, and decided not to bother. The coffee was too good to spoil with conversation, and the two police officers realised Tom needed to think.

He ran his fingers through his unruly ginger hair, and frowned. 'It's too much to take in, isn't it?'

Brent nodded. 'Couldn't agree more. When it was first handed to me, I read it aloud to one of our forensic chaps. He'd already read it, and I asked him to listen to it being verbalised. Sometimes you can pick things up by listening, instead of reading. I found it so disturbing, I felt physically sick. Like you, I wouldn't have believed it of Oliver Hardwick. However, it leaves us with a massive problem.'

'You don't know where he's stashed them. Latimer and Jake, I mean.'

'It seems Mr Hardwick has properties even his wife didn't know about. Did you know he owned the house Mrs Hardwick is currently renting?'

'What? No, I didn't. And he's charging her rent? I take it she didn't know.'

'No, she didn't. She was none too pleased, I can tell you. And did you know his brother?'

'I didn't even know he had a brother. This is ridiculous. Do you know how long I've known him? It seems I know nothing. Who's this brother?'

We're not sure. Julia… Mrs Hardwick, seems to think his name is Jared, but she also thought that was his second name, and his first name begins with O. He was considerably older than Oliver, she thought about ten years. She did say she'd never met him, and that Oliver bought him out of his half-share in the family home, when the parents died. He apparently had a construction company, but that was many years ago.'

Tom carried his coffee to the window, and stared out at the darkening sky. 'What a shitty winter this has been. We were so looking forward to having Liz back with us. She's so efficient, funny, and an absolute star at generally dealing with problems. Oliver clearly didn't feel the same.'

'Did he ever suggest he didn't want her back?'

'Never. He was the one who insisted she started at ten instead of nine, he bought the new coffee machine to make life easier for her – nothing would have suggested this level of hatred. To take her child…'

'He made sure she was never in danger.' Lynda spoke quietly, bringing a level of sensitivity to the discussion. 'He wanted her to live, to know that the man she truly loved, Phil Latimer, and her baby, had both been taken. There can be no worse punishment, I could tell that the first time I met her. She's a caring person, not only for her family, but for her friends too.' And then a small smile lit up Lynda's face. 'In fact, she cares about everybody except DI Brent.'

Tom returned to his desk. 'Oh? You've upset her, then?'

'Only every time I see her,' he said ruefully. 'She doesn't half bawl me out. I can't do right for doing wrong, as the saying goes. I guess we rub each other up…'

Tom looked at the policeman. 'Never, in all the twelve or so years I have known Liz have I heard her raise her voice. I've heard the odd *bugger* but that's as far as it goes. She must really have some issues with you.'

He shrugged. 'I'm here to do a job. Half of it is done; the murders are solved. I need you to give some thought to any properties Hardwick may have owned, or rented, or anything else. This could go back many years, so don't dismiss anything. Where would he keep deeds? There's nothing at his house, but if I was the one in his situation, I would have made damn sure those deeds were well locked away, and out of sight.'

'We have archives in our basement here, and we store many sets of deeds for clients. Can I tell Karen what has happened? I'll ask her to take time away from what she's currently doing, and go down into the storage room and go through everything. It would be logical to hide them in plain sight, wouldn't it? And Oliver was always logical, if nothing else. You can, of course, send one of your officers to do the job, but Karen will be able to recognise anything out of the ordinary much easier than your people. She's not been here long, but she's worked for solicitors, and the courts, over many years. Her knowledge is pretty impressive.'

Brent put down his empty cup and stood. 'Thank you, Tom. That will be helpful. Will she be okay to start in the morning? Time is of the essence, as I'm sure you'll realise.'

Tom looked at his watch. 'It's four now. We'll both work until as late as we can without falling asleep. We can send out for a pizza or something to keep us going. There's a lot to look through, but we'll be meticulous. I feel as if I should be apologising to you for what he's done…'

Brent shook his hand. 'Don't take that on board, for God's sake. This is entirely down to Oliver Hardwick, not you, not your practice. Yes, your business will take a knock, but it won't last forever. You have an excellent reputation, and that will save the jobs. Tell Karen everything, but she can be the only one. The others can know he committed suicide, until we find our two missing people. And thank you, Tom, for doing this search.' He handed Tom a small piece of paper. 'This is Julia's address. If you look for this first, and find it, I think that's a pretty good indicator that any more properties he owned will be there as well. This one, by the way, doesn't need to go on any list, it's already been checked.'

Brent and Lynda left the warmth of the solicitor's office, and stepped out into the freezing early evening air. Lynda shivered. 'Nice man,' she said. 'Let's hope he finds something, because if he doesn't, what do we do?'

Brent gave a deep sigh. 'Something will come from somewhere. I'll not let them down. And that you can believe.'

Lynda nodded. She believed.

Tom watched from his office window as they drove away, then he pressed the intercom for Karen. She answered immediately.

'Karen, do you have anything to rush home for?'

'Not if you need me.'

'I do. We have to go into the basement, stay down there for a few hours, and look through some of the most boring files you'll ever come across. There'll be the two of us, but I will buy you a pizza. How does that sound?'

'Delightful,' she said drily. 'And will there be spiders?'

'Not many.'

'Oh, deep joy. I'll cancel my date for tonight then.'

'Did you have a date?'

'No, I didn't want you to think I'm a sad old woman who has nothing in her life but boring old files. Are we going down now?'

'Half an hour. I want some time with the rest of the staff. I'll fill you in fully later, but the rest will be told that Oliver committed suicide, and we don't know the reasons fully, yet.'

'But we do?' Her tone was sombre, the banter had died.

'We do. DI Brent has asked that I don't reveal details to anyone, but I think you're excluded from that. You deserve to know the truth.'

'Go and do what you have to do, Tom, I'll finish off in here. Maybe you should send everyone home, after you've finished telling them. I imagine there will be some upset staff tonight. As soon as we've locked up behind everyone, we can start on those files.'

By half past four they were downstairs, and holding the deeds to Julia's address; Tom began to talk.

49

Rosie Latimer opened the door as soon as she heard the doorbell chime.

Her hair had turned an even dirtier shade of grey, causing a haggard look; without make-up to help, her skin was sallow.

'Mrs Latimer? Thank you for your patience. We were with Tom Banton longer than expected.'

'That's okay, DI Brent. I didn't have anything else to do. Melissa is with my mum – in fact, Melissa almost seems to have moved in with them. I don't blame her, life's not a bundle of joy anymore, is it?'

'Can we sit down?'

She led them into the lounge. It was cold, and she bent down and switched on a gas fire. 'I've stopped using the central heating. It costs too much to heat a house this size, so I heat whatever room I am using.'

It was a miserable looking room. It had no atmosphere, no colour, no warmth, and Rosie knew why Melissa was usually to be found with her grandparents.

'Lynda,' Will Brent said. 'Perhaps Mrs Latimer might like a cup of tea.'

'Oh, no…' Rosie started to say.

'Mrs Latimer, have the cup of tea. You will need it, I'm sure. We have some news.'

'Philip? Is he…'

'No, he isn't.' He waited while Lynda went in search of the kitchen, and then took out the letter from his jacket pocket. 'The man who murdered Gareth Chambers and Sadie Fremantle, and who currently is holding your husband and baby Jake, committed suicide. It's Oliver Hardwick. He left a note.'

Brent handed the letter to Rosie. Oblivious to the sound of the rattle of cups and saucers, the kettle as it boiled, she was lost in the words of a dead man. She read it in its entirety once, then read it again as if unbelieving of the contents she had read the first time around, before handing it back to Brent.

'Pure, pure evil.' She took a tissue from her sleeve, and dabbed at her eyes. 'Do you have any idea…?'

Brent shook his head. 'We have a couple of leads, that are really nothing much more than ideas, but other than that, we're struggling. He hadn't even come on to our radar as a suspect, he was a clever man. I must ask you not to leak any of this, we don't want the investigation jeopardising by any information being out in the public arena. Did you know Oliver Hardwick?'

She nodded, her face a picture of misery. 'I did. I went to see him. Prior to that we had only dealt with Liz Chambers, throughout our compensation claim. She handled all of it. When I found out about Phil and Liz, and that the baby was his, I was so angry I went to see Mr Hardwick. I told him. This would have been June or July. Shortly after that, Phil disappeared.'

'Did you tell Phil you had been to see Hardwick?'

'I did. It's really the reason I didn't report him as a missing person. I thought he had simply left me, that what I had done, in trying to get Liz the sack, was the final nail in our marriage's coffin. It was only when Liz started making waves, wanting to know where he was, that I realised that something may have happened to him. He hadn't contacted us in any way, not even Melissa. I can cope with him having stopped loving me, but he adored our daughter. He wouldn't have walked away from her.'

Lynda came back into the room and handed Rosie a cup of tea. Rosie raised her head and thanked her. 'You two aren't having one?'

'Our bodies won't take any more,' Brent smiled at her. 'During investigations, we drink so much tea and coffee we become waterlogged. It's the go-to thing to do, and I bet you feel better for simply holding that cup, yes?'

Rosie nodded. 'Yes, I do. I'm not eating properly... I just want to know he's okay. If he wants Liz, that's fine. I don't want him to be dead.'

'We're doing our best, Rosie. We won't let this go. You stay there, we'll see ourselves out.'

She heard their car pull away, and stood to lock the door. She walked into the kitchen, went into the cupboard and took down a chunky candle. She placed it in a storm jar and stood it on the windowsill of the bay window, before lighting it.

'Come home safe, Phil,' she whispered. 'I'll keep this lit until you do.'

***

He went on his own to see Christian, and handed him the letter.

'Oliver Hardwick, the solicitor Liz works for.' Christian frowned. 'This man, this upholder of the law, he killed my mother, without any thought as to the consequences.'

'He did. It seems his somewhat unfounded hatred for Liz was what drove him to it; he was quite deeply mentally ill, Christian. No excuses, he knew what he was doing, but I think his entire view on his life, at that moment, was well skewed.'

Christian repeated the actions of everyone who had seen the letter; he read it through once, and then, as if unable to truly believe what he had seen, he read it once more. 'He's a fucking maniac. I lost Mum cos he couldn't hang on to his wife?'

'I know. Murders are often committed for far milder reasons than that, trust me. You know as much as anybody else with close links to this case, and if you want to talk at any time, you have my number. You're a bright lad, Christian, and this is a tragedy. But don't let it stop you living the rest of your life to its fullest. I'll be saying the same to Dan. You've both got a lot of living to do yet.'

'Unless we come up against another Oliver Hardwick.' The scorn was evident in Christian's voice.

'Not likely, believe me.' He stood. 'I'll be at your mum's funeral on Wednesday. You'll have people there to support you?'

'Mum's parents, and her sister and brother, are all coming the day before. They live on the south coast – one of the reasons I chose Solent. I guess from now on, my life will be with them. I'll sell this place as soon as possible.'

Brent held out his hand. 'Good luck, Christian. I'll see myself out.'

He was halfway to the station when he realised he had forgotten to pick up the letter from the coffee table. He turned the car around and headed back.

Christian saw him pull up, and went out to meet him, holding the letter.

'Guessed you'd be back,' he said with a smile.

'Thank you,' Brent called, and set off for the second time.

He headed along Birley Lane, and thought about the two young men involved in all of this. Both Dan and Christian were good lads, and he wondered how the hell you simply 'got on with your life' after nightmares of the sort they were experiencing.

Christian went inside, and picked up the copy he had run through his printer. He didn't know why he'd done it, just that he had. It might come in useful, at some point. He hadn't written his eulogy for the funeral yet…

***

They finished checking the files at 10.23pm. Tom pulled the list towards him and sighed. 'I'm knackered.'

'My bum's numb,' Karen countered.

'Shall we ring Brent now?'

'I think so, and tell him I'll email them in about ten minutes. I need to learn to walk again first, so I can get up those stairs.'

'And I don't want to see you in work, tomorrow. What you've done tonight is way beyond your job description.'

'I'll be in. He may need additional information. Don't argue, Tom. I'll come in a bit later, but that's all. Now come on, let's get back in the office, and get this sent off. You ring him, while I'm typing up the list of houses.'

They checked that all the cabinets were locked, before unlocking the door. The stairs leading up to the offices were steep; to Karen, they felt like a mountain. She waited halfway until Tom had locked the door behind him, and then continued up.

There was a ping as Tom picked up his receiver, and pressed for the outside line. Powering up her computer, she typed from the list in front of her.

She heard Tom confirm that they had six addresses, all owned by Oliver Hardwick. They were scattered in various parts of the city, and yes, Karen was typing them on to an email as they were speaking.

Karen was also praying that in one of those addresses, a small baby was sleeping, waiting to be reunited with his mummy. She double-checked the list, then hit send.

'It's gone,' she called through to Tom's office.

Tom repeated the phrase, and then put down the phone. 'He says thank you. And he realises it's an inadequate word. Now, I'll drop you at home. Let me ring Chloe, she's a bit frazzled by everything that's happened. I can tell her I'm on my way, she'll maybe stop worrying, then.'

Half an hour later, he went through his own front entrance, threw down his briefcase, and pulled Chloe into his arms. 'What a shitty day,' he murmured into her ear. 'Do not, under any circumstances, offer me a cup of tea or coffee, I want the biggest glass in the house, and I want it full of whisky.'

She held him tightly. 'Or do you want to cut out the middle bit and go straight to bed?'

He thought for a second. 'A smaller glass of whisky, and straight to bed.'

She smiled. 'It's already waiting on the bedside table. You go up, have your shower, and I'll lock up. And do me a favour, don't mention Oliver Hardwick again tonight.'

***

Will Brent stared at the emailed list. Six addresses, different areas of the city – where to start? He didn't have enough manpower to have one search team per property, so he needed to prioritise, and go for the most likely, first.

He had organised search warrants for all the properties already, and had contacted every member of his team to tell them it would be an early start; he wanted everyone there by 5.30am. Nobody groaned, nobody queried it, they all said *yes, sir*, and he knew they would be there even earlier. This case had touched everyone's heart; it felt as though it was coming to an end, and it would be a good result.

He printed off the email, closed his computer and left the building. It had been a long day, and his hopes for the morning were high.

Sleep was intermittent for all the team; adrenalin was coursing through them when they assembled by five at the station. DI Brent gave them a briefing on the work that had been done at Banton and Hardwick the previous evening, and then he hand out photocopies of the lists.

'I've split us into three teams, so each team will have two properties to search. Tanya has photocopies of who you're with. Team 1 will take properties 1a and 1b, team 2 will take 2a and 2b, team 3 will take 3a and 3b. We have three minibuses outside. If you receive opposition from whoever is living in it, don't mess about, bring them in. A few hours in a cell should sort them out. However, I don't really expect Philip Latimer and Jacob Chambers to be held in an occupied property. I think it will be an empty one. If they are in an occupied one, it would suggest Oliver Hardwick was paying his tenant to take care of his prisoners. If that were to be the case, our victims could be in considerable danger, so anybody kicking up a stink, arrest them. Any questions?'

He glanced around the room, and was impressed by the quiet determination present on all their faces. Tanya handed out the team listings, and they left the room, heading for their designated minibuses.

Ten minutes later, the station car park was back to normal, not a minibus in sight.

Brent had four people with him. He had included Lynda in his unit, aware that she hadn't been on an operation like this before. He had also included Steve Peters; he liked the lad, and, as with Lynda, could see him climbing the ladder before much longer. Once this case was put to bed, he would have a chat with them both.

Their first address was at High Green. He had checked on Google Earth during the long sleepless hours of the previous night, and it appeared to be a detached property. He could find no evidence that anyone lived there, and he was hopeful that this first address would be the right one.

The minibus pulled up a short walk away from the house, and even in the dark of the winter's morning they could see it was empty. The windows were boarded, and the grey stone walls seemed to be blackened by soot.

'Looks like a fire-damaged property,' Lynda whispered. 'We need to be really careful in case floors are damaged.'

Brent nodded. 'Hold back, everybody. Let me see if I can get any information on this before we go in. If it is fire-damaged too badly, we may need the fire service here to get us in safely.'

He thought for a moment. 'Let's go to our second property. Everybody back on the bus.'

Two minutes later, they were heading for a small village on the outskirts of Rotherham. Thorpe Hesley boasted a mix of old and new properties, and it was one of the older ones they were heading towards. Brent spent the journey on the phone to the fire service, who confirmed it had been badly damaged some eight months earlier. They arranged to send out a team of firefighters, who would lead the way if it was deemed to be safe to venture inside it.

Brent felt frustrated by the situation, but knew he couldn't take risks; if the two missing persons were there, the fire service would soon find them, and much more efficiently than his own team.

They reached Thorpe Hesley, and the sky was beginning to lighten. The house was set back from the road, and appeared to be empty. It had a sold sign in the garden, leaning precariously against a privet hedge, obviously forgotten by the estate agents. The five officers approached with caution, and then spread out as they looked through ground floor windows. There were no signs of life, so after two banging rattles on the door, and shouts of *open up, police,* Brent ordered that the door be opened.

The team poured through the door, and began the search. Every room was empty, not even carpets were in existence. They clattered around, shouting Phil's name, but there was no reaction.

Eventually, Brent called a halt. 'Okay, everyone, there's nothing here. Let's go back to the first one, the fire service people are at the scene.' Two maintenance men were already outside the door, summoned by Brent, and they were boarding up the door by the time everyone was back on the minibus.

They returned to Thorpe Hesley, and en route Brent took messages from the other two teams that their first properties were checked and clear. They were down to three possibilities only.

They could enter the property at High Green, but only accompanied by fire officers. The cellar was reasonably untouched, and they searched it thoroughly before progressing to the other two levels. Nothing.

Brent felt frustrated, and when the other two teams reported they had drawn blanks at their second properties, he ordered them all back to the station.

They sent out for bacon sandwiches, and everyone had breakfast in the briefing room. Will took them through all the details of the morning, confirming that there had been no signs of occupation at five of the properties, with the second house allocated to team 3 the only one to have a tenant.

Tanya filled them in on this residence, said the tenant was happy to cooperate, handing them keys to three outbuildings as well as a key to the cellar. They had found nothing, except a bit of a mini-brewery in one of the outbuildings. It was clearly for personal use, and they had thanked the man and his partner for his good humour so early in the morning, before leaving.

Bacon sandwiches finished, they looked to Brent for instructions. He had none to give them.

'Okay,' he said. 'Thank you, everybody, for your work this morning. While it may not have proved to be the answer, at least it's ruled Hardwick's properties out. Steve, how did you go on with tracking the brother down? And that construction company in Chesterfield. Did that throw anything up?'

'Yes, sir, it threw up a lady owner, a Patricia Hardwick. And that's as much as I know about her, but now this morning's exercise is over, I'm back on to it. Update as soon as I know anything further.'

Brent nodded. 'Thank you. Thoughts, anyone?'

It seemed the team were devoid of ideas. The adrenalin rush of maybe finding Latimer and the baby had seemingly dissipated, and the air of gloom felt all-pervading.

'Okay. Every witness statement, every report, in fact any damn thing, I want re-checking. Even the tiniest snippet may give us the answer we're looking for. Come on, team, we're so close to cracking this, I can almost taste it. Further briefing with any thoughts at 4.30, then if there's nothing to chase up, we can have an early night.'

They drifted away to their desks, and Brent knew he could do no more to lift them. It would simply take a comment by one of them to lead them in a different direction; they would bounce back.

50

Jake had been crying constantly for a long time. Phil knew what was wrong, and the baby couldn't be distracted. He was hungry. Not even Peppa and George could help with that; it would take more than two little pigs to comfort Jake.

Phil had tried giving him a bottle of warm milk, and that had appeased him for a while, but the cries were becoming frenetic.

Finally, he gave in. He handed one of the dessert pouches to his son, and watched as he gulped it down.

When it was empty, fully drained of the sweet tasting pear, apple and banana, Jake threw it to one side. 'Da,' he said.

Phil had no idea what da meant, but Jake seemed to say it a lot. He changed his nappy and put him down to sleep. The crying had tired him, and Phil guessed this was his night time sleep, a little earlier than normal, but Jake was ready.

He was worried. His plans for making the baby food last for both of them, had survived one day. He couldn't expect Jake to live on one pouch a day, it simply wasn't enough.

Phil had had his pouch, some revolting stuff that said it was Shepherd's pie, and he vowed that if he ever got out of that place, he would ring up the manufacturers and tell them they had branded it incorrectly. His stomach was rumbling, and he nibbled on a small square of chocolate. There were only three pieces left. He had a tiny sip of milk, and then climbed into bed. Jake was asleep, and even Phil felt more comfortable, warmer. He wondered if the weather outside was turning milder, heralding the return of spring. He hoped to God they would both see summer.

51

Julia arrived at Liz's home unannounced. Liz didn't feel particularly warm towards her, and simply wanted the visit to end. With the funeral the next day, she could have done without having to be polite and welcoming to visitors. Especially Julia.

'I had to come,' Julia tried to explain.

'Why? Because the man you married killed the man I'm burying tomorrow?'

Liz knew she sounded harsh; she watched as Julia's face crumpled.

'I'm so so sorry,' she sobbed. 'I'd do anything to change things…'

'Get me my son back home,' Liz snapped. 'Think, Julia. You must know somewhere else that Oliver could have hidden them. Surely he didn't keep everything from you.'

'I've told Brent everything I know, which, believe me, is very little. I certainly didn't know about these six properties I apparently own, unless he's left them to some bloody dog's home, or something.' Her voice became more strident. 'I knew nothing, Liz, nothing. And I certainly didn't know he was a murderer.'

'Julia, go. I really don't want to know how hard it is for you. And don't come anywhere near the funeral service tomorrow.'

Liz looked at her one-time friend, unable to say anything further. Julia turned and left, and Liz watched as she drove away. There was a squeal of brakes, a strident honking of at least two car horns, and Liz knew Julia was probably trying to drive through her tears. Liz turned away from the window, and felt a surge of anger towards Oliver Hardwick, it almost blotted out every other emotion in her.

'Bit harsh, weren't you?' Dan was standing in the doorway watching her.

'Harsh? She's lucky I didn't stab her.'

'Mum, come on, this isn't you.' He moved into the room, and put his arms around her. 'You're not nasty, never have been.'

'And I've never had my baby stolen before, either.'

They stood for a while, holding on to each other, lost in their own individual thoughts.

'I'll be so glad when tomorrow is over,' she eventually said.

'Me too.'

There was a knock at the door, and she spun around, expecting to see Julia once again.

It wasn't. DI Brent was there, on his own.

Dan went to let him in, and whispered, 'Don't upset her. She'll bite your head off.'

DI Brent smiled. 'She usually does. I'll let you into a little secret – I don't think she likes me much.'

'You want a drink?'

'I'll have a water, Dan, thanks. I'm only here because I was passing, and I thought I'd see how you're both doing. Tomorrow will be hard.'

'Mum's in the lounge. I'll bring your water through.'

Liz didn't say anything, just waited for him to speak.

'We had six properties to check, Liz. Six damned properties, and I felt sure we would find them, but nothing. A complete waste of time.'

She sighed. 'No, it wasn't. You ruled them out. And I am really grateful for everything you and your team are doing. I know I can be a bit of a cow, but it's only when I get defensive where my family are concerned.'

'He never mentioned a holiday home, or anything like that? I asked Mrs Hardwick, but she looks blank. I think he kept her in the dark about everything, but you were in a unique position at work. He never asked you to do any work on another home, might not even be in this country?'

She shook her head. 'Nothing. He really was a private man, spoke only about work. Totally different to Tom, and yet I liked him. It's why I'm having such a problem coming to terms with what he did. And it's why I didn't recognise him on that CCTV footage. He would never dress like that, for a start. And yet the figure was him, I see it now. Right size, right way of walking. It was the hoodie that threw me. If only I'd seen it at the time…'

'None of us saw it, and yet we'd all met Oliver Hardwick by then, so don't beat yourself up about it. His wife even went so far as to say we'd got the wrong man, he would never have worn leisure wear, and definitely not a hoodie.'

Dan brought in the glass of water for Brent. 'Mum? Drink?'

'No, I'm fine, thank you, sweetheart.'

She watched as Brent took a strip of tablets from his pocket, and popped two into his hand. 'Not well?' she asked.

'Stinking headache. I can't remember the last time I slept all night, and the last three nights have been virtually sleepless, hence the headache. It'll soon go.'

'You'll be there, tomorrow?'

'I will. Lynda and Tanya are both going to be there, as well. Can I suggest you take it easy, today? Spend time with Dan, make it the two of you. It's going to be hard tomorrow, you'll be leaning on each other.'

'Do you know, DI Brent, you can be quite nice when you're not shouting at me,' she smiled.

'And I could say the same about you,' he responded, with an answering smile. He finished the glass of water and left.

'Dan,' she called. 'Don't make anything for tonight's meal, we'll go out to eat.'

'Yeah!' she heard, from somewhere distant. *Right answer, Dan,* she thought, *right answer. Just don't suggest KFC.*

52

The sun had no warmth in it, but it was a bright, spring-like morning. Liz and Dan sat either side of the back seat of the car following the hearse, both of them feeling as though the gap between them was a million miles. In the end, Liz reached across and clasped her son's hand.

'Be brave, Dan,' she said. 'There'll probably be the press there, and it's okay. It's their job. If they get too much in your face, I'll step in. I'm used to their invasive tactics.'

Liz saw his nod, telling her that he understood, but he didn't say anything. She accepted that he didn't want to speak, simply wanted his dad back again, not lying in that box in the hearse.

The cars pulled up at the crematorium, and they were both helped out. There were cameras clicking, but they ignored them, and went to take their places behind the coffin, as it rested on the shoulders of the smartly dressed men from the funeral directors.

Liz was quite shocked by how many people turned up – they had little family, and yet she recognised several people that she wouldn't have thought to invite. They had simply come to say goodbye to Gareth, and to show support for her and Dan.

It was a beautiful, deeply moving service, and as they congregated outside after it was over, she felt a touch on her arm. It was Tom.

'I can't stay, Liz, I'm due in court later, but you know, don't you? Anything you want…'

She nodded. 'I know, Tom. And thank you.'

She watched as he went to retrieve Chloe from a lady with blue rinsed hair who she didn't recognise, and then it was over. They were driven back to the local pub, where Liz had arranged for food to be served to anyone who returned with them, and many did. Gareth had clearly known lots of people, and they all wanted to talk about him.

Tom arrived at court with three minutes to spare, planned that way to stop anyone talking about Oliver. Word was out, but details were sparse, and Tom realised everyone would be curious. The case didn't last long, once the prisoner changed his plea to guilty, and Tom arrived back at the office by three, intending to show his face, then depart for home. It had been a difficult day.

He went into Karen's office, and she looked up, startled. 'Goodness, I didn't expect to see you back.'

He waved a file at her. 'Can you put this for archiving, please. I think Liz uses the bottom drawer of the filing cabinet, then when she's built up a fair number, she does them all at once.'

Karen took the file from him, and crossed the room. She opened the bottom drawer and slid it in. Then stopped.

Deeds. She'd seen enough deeds to last her a lifetime, during the long night of searching through them, and this bundle definitely looked as though it contained deeds. She pulled them out, and carried them to her desk. Tom paused in the doorway.

'What's that?'

'Deeds. For a place at Mosborough. Oh, not to worry, it's the new offices you're going to be opening, isn't it? I'd forgotten.'

It was as if a light bulb had exploded in Tom's brain. He walked slowly towards her, his face set in a hard mask of rage. He was mortified when he realised he had scared Karen; his next words told her that he wasn't directing the temper at her, but at his dead partner.

'The bastard,' Tom growled. 'No wonder he said he'd take on the building work, see to everything. Get me DI Brent, quick as you can.'

***

Brent lay back in his swivel chair, thinking about the morning. As funerals went, it had been a good one. Not too mushy, like a funeral should be. He briefly closed his eyes, and tried to think about what to do next. They could end up going around in circles, looking for Latimer and Jake. It needed one small break, somebody to hear a child crying in an empty house, somebody to hear shouts for help…

His phone rang.

He reached out without opening his eyes. 'Brent.'

'We've found another property.'

His eyes flew open, and he brought the chair up to its vertical position.

'Where?'

'Mosborough. It's the new house we've bought to expand our business. It's been Oliver's baby from the start. I saw it once, gave him the go ahead, and let him get on with it. I've got keys…'

'Meet me there. Text me the address, I can be there in five minutes.'

'Then don't wait for me. I'll still come out, but get in any way you can. I'll see that it's made secure afterwards.'

The address came through while he was putting on his coat, and he dashed into the briefing room. 'Right, we've another property to search. Tanya, Lynda, Steve, and Dave, come with me please. Steve we'll need the Enforcer. We've got permission to get in any way we can.'

They were on their way two minutes later, heading down Moss Way at considerably more than the permitted forty miles an hour.

'Where are we going?' Lynda's voice came from the back seat. Steve was driving, with Will Brent beside him. Tanya and PC Dave Harmer were following in a second car.

'It's a house owned by Banton and Hardwick as a company. It's why it wasn't found when they went through all their deeds. The deeds to this place were still in the office, not archived, because it's an ongoing project. It seems Hardwick had full responsibility for it, once they had bought it, and nobody else has been near it.'

Just

The trees flashed by, and then Steve slowed for the bad bend at the end of the road, before cruising down to the road junction.

'Turn left,' instructed Brent, 'then left again at the roundabout. If you take your first left after that, we're on the right road.'

Steve nodded without speaking, and drove at speed.

They pulled up at the bottom of a drive, and Brent got out to open the gates. They were padlocked, and he looked around for something big enough to use to smash the lock.

Steve jumped out. 'Hang on, sir, there'll be something in the car.'

He opened the boot and removed a small lump hammer. One blow and the padlock fell to the floor.

They were soon outside the house, with the second car following them up the short drive.

'Right, before we go damaging the property, let's separate and go right round the house. We're looking for the easiest way to get in.' The house was large, and had several outbuildings. They ignored them, choosing, for the moment, to concentrate on the house.

No windows were open, and all doors were locked. They met up again at the front door, a solid-looking piece of wood that could be difficult to breach.

'Right, I think we should probably go through the back door. It's not flimsy, but it doesn't look as hefty as this brute does. Yes?'

They were all in agreement, and Steve carried the Enforcer round to the back door.

'Right, go for it Steve. Let's get in here.'

It took two massive swings to get the door to burst open, and bang into whatever was behind it. They looked at each other, and Brent stepped through the doorway. 'Let's see what we have, then,' he growled.

***

Jake was asleep, and Phil was thankful. He felt drowsy; he knew he was ill, and had collapsed on to his own bed to try and clear his head. He realised it was lack of nourishment, but he would have to hope his body could get used to it. He daren't increase his own consumption of the baby pouches, he needed them for his little boy. And while Jake was sleeping, the baby wasn't feeling hunger pangs.

He closed his eyes and drifted into a deeper sleep. He didn't fight it, had nothing in him left to fight anything. From a distance he heard a bang, and he stirred. He drifted off again, unable to stay awake.

Jake mumbled in his sleep, and his daddy didn't hear him. Too many months of deprivation of everything had finally taken its toll on his body, and he lapsed into unconsciousness. His carefully worked out plan hadn't considered his own weakness.

***

Brent stared around the kitchen, just looking. Oliver had proved to be a devious calculating man, and he didn't want any surprises for his team. Brent led the way cautiously into the hall. It was dark, the only daylight coming from a small sunlight set above the front door. There were three doors leading off the right-hand wall, as far as he could see, and two doors leading off from the left. He held up a hand, and the team behind him stopped.

'Just listen,' he whispered. They all stood for a few seconds, and then he opened the first door on the left. It was small room, measuring no more than ten feet by ten feet, but it was lined with screens. There was other technical stuff, and Brent cautiously entered. He leaned forward to one of the monitors and clicked it on.

They sprang to life and they stared in horror at the pictures on the brightly illuminated screens. Phil Latimer was lying, unmoving, on a bed, and Jake Chambers was in a travelling cot, asleep. His arm moved, and there was a collective exhalation of breath.

'Lynda, get me an ambulance.'

She took out her phone, and could be heard giving instructions to the operator. Lynda stressed the urgency, explaining who the victims were, and repeated the address twice.

There was a sound from the back door, and all five of them jumped, so intent were they on watching the screens.

'DI Brent!' Tom called, not wanting to go over the threshold without somebody saying it was okay.

'Tom,' Brent called. 'Get Liz here, can you? We've found them. She should be at home now; the wake will be over.'

Tom backed outside and dialled Liz's number. She answered immediately, and he quickly explained that Jake and Phil had been found. He told her where he was, and disconnected.

He re-entered the kitchen, and followed the sound of the team's voices. They had stepped back out into the hall, and realised that the next door along was made entirely of metal.

It was locked, and had additional security of two bolts. They had already slid the bolts back, but had no way of opening the door.

'Did you bring the keys?' Brent asked, and Tom nodded.

'I did, but there's only a front and a back-door key on them. Nothing that will open that.' He moved forward and unlocked the front door, ready for the arrival of the emergency services.

'It must be somewhere. There were no keys with him when we found his body, so they must be here. Lynda, Tanya, can you check through that room with the monitors? Dave and Steve, can you go through the kitchen? It's bound to be a fair size key, this is a hefty lock. I'll head upstairs. Tom, can I ask you to go outside and look for the ambulance, and Liz.'

Tom nodded again. He walked out of the front door and continued down the drive. He heard the approach of the ambulance, and waved as it drew close. The driver stopped.

'Front door, mate?'

'Yes. Go straight in, but they've not managed to get to the prisoners yet.'

'Prisoners?' he looked shocked.

'Sorry, they've been imprisoned. The missing man and the baby? They've been found, but the door is still locked. You'll see when you get inside.'

The driver nodded, and drove to the front door. A second ambulance pulled up and Tom gave the driver the same details, watching as they moved things into the house, ready for ministering to their patients.

Tom stayed at the bottom of the drive, and less than a minute later, Liz and Dan arrived. He pointed to the side of the gravelled area.

'Park over there,' he said, through her window. 'There's half a chance we may have to send for the fire people to get through a metal door.'

She nodded, couldn't speak.

Dan grabbed hold of the hand nearest to him. 'Come on, Mum, we can do this. Jake's going to need us.'

She turned and flashed a brief smile, then drove the car to where Tom had directed.

He waited for Liz and Dan to reach him, then took them through the front door.

'We can see Jake and Phil,' he explained, 'but can't get to them unless we can find the key. They're searching for it now.'

Liz saw Brent as she walked through the door. 'You've found the key? And Oliver was definitely here. I can smell his aftershave, Creed.'

'No, not found it yet. I've already called the fire service in, I think they'll have to cut through it. Come here, Liz.' He took hold of her hand, drawing her gently into the room with the monitors.

She watched her son, still sleeping, for the first time in what seemed an eternity. 'Jake,' she breathed his name.

As if in response to her voice, the baby moved his arm. Liz's smile lit up the room.

'And Phil? He's not woken?' She could see him lying on the bed, unmoving.

'No. The ambulance men are waiting to get to him, but we can't do anything without that damn door opening.'

Her heart lurched. She couldn't lose him, not again. This man who had been keeping their child alive, he had to get through this.

'This is the dumb waiter,' Brent said. 'This is how he managed to keep Phil and Jake alive without Phil knowing who he was. Clever little contraption, could only be operated from up here, not down in the cellar.'

He led Liz to what appeared to be a small cupboard in the corner of the room. 'I know this is a Victorian house,' he said, 'but this looks like a new construction. I don't think for one minute it's an original feature. He certainly planned this well.'

'I'm still struggling to believe it. This isn't the Oliver I've known for all these years.' She turned to look at Tom. 'Tom?'

'I agree. And the worst part is, I didn't notice any changes in him, not even these last few days when he clearly knew he would be dead shortly. I can't begin to imagine what must have been going through his mind, because nothing showed outwardly. He said no goodbyes, not even in his letter – what caused such a massive personality change? I know he blamed you, Liz, but really you did nothing.'

Tanya appeared in the doorway. 'Can I have another recce in here, please? We can't find a key anywhere else, but logically it should be here in this room. One last look and then we'll have to admit defeat and assume he threw it away.'

They all moved out, allowing Tanya and Lynda to double-check places they had already searched.

Five minutes later, with the fire brigade one minute away, Liz could see that Phil still hadn't moved, but she could also see that Jake was standing in his cot, and leaning over the side looking at Phil.

'Oh, God,' she said, 'look at him. Look at my boy. I was starting to think I'd lost him for good, and he looks so well. It won't be long now, and I'll have him back.'

'He'll be going straight to hospital,' Brent said. 'Let Dan go in the ambulance with him, and you follow in your car. That way, he'll have a familiar face for the journey, and you'll be able to get back from the hospital easier. They may want to keep Jake for a couple of days. He's possibly dehydrated and under-nourished, so let them take care of him.'

'And Phil? Have you notified Rosie?'

'Not yet.' He didn't expand.

Liz stared at him. So, he did have a heart. He was allowing her to see Phil first, before telling Rosie that Phil was on his way to hospital.

'Thank you,' she said quietly. 'Thank you.'

Seconds later, the fire engine arrived. They had come fully prepared for cutting through a door, and it took them little time to get the equipment off the vehicle and inside the house. They did a full inspection of the door, then cut around the lock area.

It was noisy; sparks were cascading around, and Liz moved out of the way, standing inside the monitor room. Jake was crying, and looking over his shoulder, presumably towards the door area. The noise would be frightening him. Phil still hadn't moved, and Liz felt sick.

Life couldn't be this cruel, surely Phil wouldn't be snatched away from her at the last minute. As if sensing what she was thinking, Dan put his arms around her.

'Chin up, Mum. You'll be with them in a couple of minutes. It may not be as bad as it looks.'

The four paramedics picked up their gear and moved closer, sensing the door was almost open. It finally went with a bang, and they trod down the stairs with caution. They too wanted no boobytrap surprises.

'Wait here, Liz,' Brent said. 'I'll call you when I'm sure it's okay. Let us do our job, please.'

He turned to the firemen and thanked them. 'We'll pack our stuff away, but we'll hang on for a bit, in case there's anything else. We'd like to see the little lad, as well.'

Brent smiled. 'Thanks. That's fine.'

He went down the stairs into the cellar, and across to where the paramedics were already working on Phil Latimer. There was no movement from him, and no colour in his face.

Jane, the one who seemed to have taken charge, had her fingers on his neck for what seemed an eternity. The other paramedic was fitting an oxygen mask over his face. Jane gave an almost imperceptible shake of her head, and muttered 'very weak'.

She put in an intravenous drip of saline, and then checked his blood pressure. Again, she checked his pulse; again, the small shake of her head.

'He's not...' Brent asked in a low voice.

'Very close,' Jane answered.

Brent went back to the bottom of the stairs and called Liz's name. The word was hardly out of his mouth before she was standing in the doorway. 'Come down,' he said.

He held her hand as she reached the bottom of the stairs. 'Go to Phil. The paramedics are looking after Jake, and he's doing fine.'

She stared at Brent, allowing what he was saying without speaking the words, to sink into her brain. 'No,' she whispered, and moved across to Phil. Everything about him seemed sunken, the muscly toned man she loved had all but disappeared. He was clearly non-receptive to anything happening around him, and she reached for his hand.

'I love you,' she whispered. 'Phil, don't give up, you're my life.'

She watched as Jane felt at his neck once more, and then saw her look at her partner. 'Let's go. We're losing him.'

Liz stepped back with a small cry, and Brent moved to her side. 'Come on. Jake needs you. Let them do their job and get him to the hospital. Northern General?'

Jane said yes, and within a minute they had taken him up the stairs and out to the waiting ambulance.

Liz pushed thoughts of Phil aside, and turned to her son. He too had a drip attached, and was staring at it in fascination.

'Jake.' He turned to her, and lifted his arms.

***

She parked her car in the multi-storey at the Children's Hospital, and ran across the road to the entrance.

'My son's been admitted by ambulance,' she said breathlessly to the receptionist. She was given directions to the appropriate department, and spotted Dan in a corridor, looking for her. 'Is he okay?' she asked.

Dan's smile was infectious. 'He seems fine. A doctor is with him. He's quite the little celebrity, loads of nurses have popped in to see him, now that word's got out that he's been found. He was fine in the ambulance, I chatted to him all the way here, and he made brave attempts at chatting back to me. Seems to say "da" a lot.'

Liz stood in the corridor and let the tears finally fall. They rolled down her cheeks and dripped off her chin. She didn't care. Weeks of worry had ended, and Jake was safe.

Dan, being fifteen, didn't really know what to do with her. He held her and let her cry, not speaking, knowing he wouldn't have the right words.

'Mrs Chambers? Your son needs you,' the doctor smiled. 'You want some tissues?'

He disappeared to return a few moments later with a box of tissues, and handed it to her. 'Take your time. He's not going anywhere for a couple of days, so you've many hours in which to get to know each other again.'

Jake was sitting up in a cot, only wearing a nappy.

'We're not putting any clothes on,' the nurse explained. 'He's got a bit of a temperature, so we don't want him getting any warmer. He's on antibiotics, because the temperature is probably due to a small infection. He'll be feeling much livelier tomorrow. All in all, he's doing extremely well, considering what he's been through. Thank goodness you've got him back, Mrs Chambers. We've all been following this story, as you can imagine, and I feel honoured to be his designated nurse. Now, go and give him a cuddle.'

And, finally, he was in her arms. The little boy she had ached for, over so many long nights, was back in her arms, and snuggling up to her.

'You want a cup of tea?' the nurse asked.

'No, thank you,' Liz smiled. 'I've got everything I need.'

***

Rosie looked down at her husband. She wouldn't have recognised him; his appearance had changed completely. He had aged; he was so pale as to appear dead, and she knew without having to be told that he was near death.

She leaned forward and kissed his head. He felt cold.

In her head, she had already given him to Liz, but Rosie was beginning to realise that he would be always hers. *Till death do us part,* she thought.

The doctor finished writing his notes and checked Phil's pulse and blood pressure. The doctor initially made no comment, until Rosie said, 'Well?'

He removed his glasses and looked at her. 'Are you planning on going home?'

'Yes, I have a young daughter...'

'Where is she now?'

'With my mother.'

'Then I suggest you ring your mother and ask if she can keep her overnight.'

The implication was clear.

'We'll provide you with a chair bed so that you can rest, but I do have to tell you that your husband is extremely weak. If he makes it through the night, then there will be some hope. However...'

'I understand, doctor. I have a however, too. However, I don't think I'm the one my husband would want by his side. I will be going home. I need to explain to Melissa that her daddy has been found, but he is poorly. She has to come first, now.'

She touched Phil's hand. 'Bye, my love. You're in my prayers.'

The doctor watched her leave the room; his mind was reeling. He had never had such a reaction before, when he had been forced to deliver news of the worst kind.

He didn't expect this man to still be here in the morning, and the only thing he could do for him was make sure he wasn't alone. He left Phil's room and headed for the nursing station, to give instructions that he wanted someone with Mr Latimer at all times.

53

Sadie Fremantle's funeral went off without a hitch. There weren't many people there, and her few close relatives went for a meal afterwards. The circumstances surrounding her death were known to all of them, and it made talking about it difficult. Christian talked about the life he had shared with his mother before his departure to Solent, and eventually everyone joined in, remembering the good times they had experienced with her.

DI Brent had been there, and Christian was grateful. He could so easily have cancelled; the case was over. He had shaken Christian's hand, and wished him well. 'Don't let this stop you aiming high. Good luck with everything you do.'

Christian thanked him, and watched as he walked away.

He had decided to go back to the south coast, and his bags were already stored in his Nan's car, ready for the journey. The next time he would visit Sheffield would be to make the house tidy for selling.

Christian knew of the rescue of baby Jake, and had left a message on Liz's answerphone, saying how pleased he was. She hadn't responded, so he guessed she would be at the hospital. That was his last tie severed. He climbed into the car, and they left.

54

Tom went in to work the following morning, and finally told all the staff the full story. He recognised that they would probably have press hounding them for details of Oliver's background, so he thought it best they knew the truth.

Except Tom didn't really know why it had happened, why Oliver had suddenly changed. He had hoped the autopsy on his friend would reveal something medical like a brain tumour, but it hadn't. It seemed he had suddenly become paranoid about different things, and the end result had been two murders, and two kidnappings – possibly three murders if Phil Latimer didn't make it.

He knew they would never open a second branch now, acknowledging that it had all been Oliver's baby anyway; he hoped the house had been bought for the right reasons, to increase their business, and not for the sole intention of kidnap.

He would wait a year and then put it back on the market. In the meantime, he would work with the existing staff to hold tight to the business, and trust that their previously excellent reputation would see them through. He would clear out Oliver's office and leave it empty; maybe one day a new partner would be brought in, but that was a long time in the future.

At the moment, though, the future looked pretty damn bleak.

Epilogue

It had been hot for most of July. The garden looked well, now that Liz had the time to spend on it. Her decision to leave Banton and Hardwick hadn't been easy, but it had been right. Karen, who had taken on Liz's job officially, spoke to her on a regular basis, but she knew that would fade, as Karen became more confident.

Tom still contacted her, but she almost thought that was out of guilt. His partner had caused her so many problems, and Tom was still hurting. She knew that, too, would disappear, and then she would really feel that she could get on with her life.

Julia had rung once, to say she was glad she had Jake back. Most of Oliver's money had gone to various charities, and he had left instructions that the properties he owned were to be sold, and the proceeds given to the Salvation Army. Julia was left with the house she lived in, and she had decided to simply cut her losses and not contest the will. She was going to sell up and move to London.

Liz put the bed linen into the washing machine, and switched it on. It was the first load, and on such a lovely day it wouldn't take long to dry. Through the open door she could hear the sounds of Jake's laughter, as Dan pushed him on the swing. Jake's giggles always made her heart rate accelerate, and he was a proper little toddler. She remembered how shocked she had been in the hospital when she had sat him on the ward floor to play with some toys, and he had stood up and walked. He hadn't been walking when Oliver had taken him from her.

Sitting quietly on a lounger, and smiling at the antics of his new family, Phil was a picture of contentment. He would have liked to stand and get out the lawnmower, to try and help Liz with the more strenuous of the garden chores, but he knew he couldn't. He looked up and smiled, as she came down to sit with him, carrying a tray of drinks. He took the small pot of pills from her, followed by a glass of water.

'Here, time for tablets,' and she gave him a kiss.

'The nurses never used to kiss me at tablet time,' he remarked, thoughtfully.

She smiled at him. 'They'd better not – you're mine now.'

Despite the diagnosis from Phil's consultant. She couldn't help but feel he was getting better. Thanks to the sunshine and the warmth, his skin had lost the pallor, and he was finally starting to put on a little weight, although his frame was still skeletal.

The consultant had explained that they'd barely got Phil through that first night. His organs were closing down, and he was in advanced heart failure. They had discussed the possibility of a heart bypass, but Mr Enwright had been quite adamant that Phil would die during the operation. They could give him tablets to help prolong his life, maybe give him six months of a reasonably comfortable time with his family, but the failing organs wouldn't stand up to a six-hour operation.

Liz knew that Phil was in acceptance. He took the medication, saw Melissa and Rosie at least twice a week when they came to Liz's for a meal, and spent every night holding Liz tightly, never wanting the morning to come, forcing himself to let her go to start the new day.

She handed him eight or nine pills, and he waited until she sat in the lounger placed at the side of him, before reaching for her hand.

'All of that, those bloody awful months, it's all been worth it, to be here with you, Jake and Dan. And I know I'm leaving you in safe hands with Dan.'

'You're going nowhere, Phil Latimer. You're starting to improve, looking a whole lot better. Let's not talk about the future, it's what's happening right now that's important.'

He simply nodded, and they sat in silence for a while.

'Can I ask you a question?' Liz said. 'It's the one thing that's bugged me about everything that happened. I mean, I understand what drove Oliver, and really that was down to a mental problem that he managed to hide from everybody, even his wife. And I understand Rosie not reporting you as missing, because she genuinely was trying to come to terms with you having left her, or so she thought. But what I don't understand is why you didn't pay a cheque in for nearly £100,000.'

He gave a small laugh. 'I didn't want to pay it in. At the time I was hurting so bad from losing you, knowing you were going through a pregnancy without me by your side, and holding on to that cheque was kind of keeping you with me. I did intend paying it in, but wanted to hang on to it for a bit longer. And besides, I thought you might one day contact me, to find out why it hadn't been paid in. It seemed that if that money was in the bank, it would be the final thing between us, put to bed. That cheque was in my wallet when I was taken.'

'Was it? Oliver must have destroyed it, because it wasn't there when they found your wallet. That's cleared that little mystery for me. When you really stop and think about it, it's a good job you didn't pay it in. If you had, Rosie would have continued believing you'd left her, and I wouldn't have had a reason to contact her and discover you were missing.' She squeezed his hand. 'Thank God we found you both.'

Dan lifted Jake out of the baby swing, and set him down on the grass. He hauled himself up and headed for his parents.

'Da.' he said.

'Da,' his father responded.

Liz watched her son as he giggled. 'They had no idea what da meant, but Phil had explained it had been their form of communication while they were locked away. An assumption that it meant *dad* had proved to be wrong; Jake said da to everything. He had six teeth, combined with an awesomely cheeky grin, and Liz was slowly finding the courage to let him out of her sight occasionally.

Dan followed him up the garden. 'We've got steak for tea – are Rosie and Melissa coming?'

Liz nodded. 'Yes, they are. They'll be here about three. Shall we barbecue?'

'You mean, will you barbecue, please, Dan?'

'Whatever.'

'And, Phil, the rest of us will be having salad, you'll be having chips with yours.'

'Am I complaining?' Phil smiled. He knew Dan had every intention of turning him into Billy Bunter; he had seen the horror on the young man's face the first time they had met. It seemed it was the chef's mission in life to build him up. But Phil knew it was pointless. It would only make the coffin so much heavier to carry.

'I'm going across to the shop, Mum, get some fresh salad. We don't have enough in to feed all of us. I'll pop Jake in his pram and take him with me, it's easier for carrying the shopping. Is that okay?'

There was a brief moment of hesitation and Liz squashed it. 'Yes, of course. Take care crossing the road.' A mum's automatic response.

'Mum, I'm sixteen.'

She threw a peg at him. 'Go,' she said.

Phil leaned back in his chair and smiled. He felt a couple of pains in his chest, and took out his GTN spray. The pains had been there since before the rescue, and were a direct result of the rapid starvation diet he had endured while imprisoned.

'Okay?' Liz asked.

'Just the usual twinges,' he said. 'Don't worry.'

They sat quietly, happy in each other's company. Liz's phone pinged, and she picked it up.

'Text from Rosie,' she said.

She opened it. **Melissa wants to come over early to play with Jake. Think she's also got a crush on Dan. Will that be okay?**

She immediately messaged her back. **That's fine. We're in garden, so text when you get here, and I'll come to the front door. Dan will be impressed that anybody could have a crush on him.**

Dan and Jake returned, and she could hear them in the kitchen, Dan explaining to Jake that he had to put all the salad stuff in the fridge, and then they could have their lollipops.

Phil was holding her hand, and she felt him squeeze it. 'Did we know they were going for lollipops? We could have had one.'

Her eyes remained closed. 'Not sure I've got the energy to eat one.'

'Maybe, you're right.' He glanced at her and before his courage failed him, he continued. 'God, I love you, Liz Chambers. Shall we get married?'

Her eyes were wide open. 'What?'

'I've probably got two, maybe three months at the most. Let me make you Liz Latimer while I still can.'

'You've only been divorced three days.'

'So? Your point is?'

'I don't know.' She gave a slight laugh, a nervous laugh. 'Yes, yes, I will marry you. But what about Rosie...?'

'I've already told her. Texted her last night, told her what I wanted, and she's happy with it. She's over me, Liz. In fact, I half think there's someone in her life.'

'You don't hang about, do you?'

'We'll tell them when everybody's here, then?'

'My only worry is Dan...'

'I've already asked his permission.' Phil smiled at her. 'I've covered all the bases. Oh, and I had to choose this online and send Dan to get it, but I hope you like it.' He took a ring box from the pocket of his joggers, and handed it to her. 'Marry me, Liz.'

The solitaire diamond sparkled in the sunlight. It sparkled even more through her tears. 'Yes, yes, of course I will.'

He took the ring out of the box and slipped it on her finger. 'One week, you have one week to arrange everything. We'll organise a special licence, then you go to Meadowhall and get everything we need. Dan and I will take care of Jake.'

'You've thought everything through! I love you, special man.'

He smiled, and held her hand again. 'Now can I go back to sleep?'

Five minutes later Liz's phone pinged again. **Just parked. I've brought a friend as well. X**

'Looks like you might be right about Rosie. She's brought a friend, as well as Melissa.'

Phil smiled, his eyes still closed. 'Told you so.'

'Just going to let them in.'

He nodded. 'Don't be long, wife-to-be.'

She kissed him, and walked up the garden. She threw a glance at the mess created by a sixteen-year-old and a baby eating lollipops at the kitchen table, and continued past them to the front door. Rosie and Melissa, accompanied by a tall brown-haired man, were walking down the drive.

She welcomed them, and Rosie introduced Carl. 'We met at the book club, she explained. 'We're kind of seeing each other.'

'Melissa,' Liz said, 'go to Dan and Jake, they're in the kitchen eating ice lollies. I'm sure they'll be able to find you one, as well.'

She led Rosie and Carl through to the back garden. They walked down the path, and everything felt strangely silent and serene. No sounds from the kitchen, no words from her guests. Liz crossed the lawn and bent down to kiss Phil.

He didn't move, didn't respond in any way. Oliver had claimed his third victim.

'No,' she whispered. 'No.'

The End

Acknowledgements

I am eternally grateful for several individuals who have seen me battle my way through this book; for the initial idea, my daughter, Kirsty Waller – thank you. I know you didn't foresee all this murder and mayhem, but you started it all!

Secondly, I have to thank Barry Manilow, whose songs have carried me through the darkest parts of the story, and have lit up the good parts. Ah, Barry, you know I can't smile without you… and another lady I have to thank is Alexa, my trusty Echo Dot, for the brilliant way she plays whatever I want her to play.

There are a few people I need to thank for allowing me to use their names; Karen Lee, my designated number one fangirl, Lynda Checkley for being the competition winner for naming the café in the prologue, and Rick Naylor, my decorator guru, who cried at Strategy. Thank you to all three of you; I didn't turn any of you into a corpse.

My biggest thanks go to Fred and Betsy Freeman, at Bloodhound Books, along with Alexina Golding, Sumaira Wilson and Sarah Hardy. Without the three of you being there day and night for Bloodhound authors, life would be a lot more difficult. Huge thanks also go to Morgen Bailey, my editor – I promise never to use the word 'now' again.

And last, but by no means least, I thank my writing buddy, Donna Maria McCarthy. We praise each other when it is merited, and bully each other when it is necessary. I salute you, Donna with the long name, and thank you. You're my rock.

70307886R00153

Made in the USA
San Bernardino, CA
27 February 2018